LOST LITTLE
ANGELS

BOOKS BY HOLLY S. ROBERTS

Detective Eve Bennet series

Only Girl Alive

LOST LITTLE
ANGELS

HOLLY S. ROBERTS

bookouture

Published by Bookouture in 2023

An imprint of Storyfire Ltd.
Carmelite House
50 Victoria Embankment
London EC4Y 0DZ

www.bookouture.com

ISBN: 978-1-83790-105-0
eBook ISBN: 978-1-83790-104-3

For Tammy Poe—readers know her as Tamm—the police secretary extraordinaire who should have been a detective. In real life, Tammy slapped me down a peg by finding a stolen horse saddle in a fake wall and did her best not to rub it in. She's one of the nicest people I know and she's a lifelong friend. If I make her out to be unbelievably amazing, it's because she is. Thank you, Tammy, for your compassion in police work.

PROLOGUE

Her eyes opened to a faint stream of light entering the room from the slight opening between the curtains. Her hand went to her lower belly. She'd given birth five days ago. For the first time since her daughter was born, she hadn't been woken during the night for feeding. Her sisters were a godsend to allow her this sleep.

She had been honored with a child and chosen to bear this miracle. The eight months the baby grew inside her were partly terrifying and partly filled with grace. It wasn't always easy to obey the rules she'd been taught since she was a little girl. Now she had a baby, a living miracle who gave her joy.

Could it be the hormones that instigated a lack of commitment to her husband, causing her to place the baby first in their marriage? She had no one to ask and the consequences were too frightening if she did.

After climbing from the bed, her arms went above her head and she stretched to her toes. The top of her garment pulled up. Once her heels were touching the floor again, she tugged it back into place, aware of the slight pooch since her daughter's birth that she never wanted to disappear. This was wrong of her. She needed to remember her teaching and her purpose, but could it hurt to dwell in the rapture of motherhood for a bit longer?

Pressure built in her breasts as she hurriedly took the day's clothing from the closet. The hallway was clear and there were no sounds on the upper floor. It was Saturday and the only day of the week her husband and the older boys could sleep for an extra hour. Her sisters were most likely downstairs preparing breakfast. She walked by the baby's room. The door was closed and it was possible one of the women was inside rocking her. The ache in her breasts grew and she hoped the baby hadn't yet eaten this morning. Bonding with her child was not seen as important but she couldn't help herself. She felt self-righteous in her need to safeguard her daughter. She wasn't warned about these strange feelings and knew she had to keep it to herself.

She washed quickly and put on her long dress. She hadn't arranged her light brown hair since the baby's birth, but today she used a hot iron to straighten the front into a high sweep and secured it in place with hairspray and a clip. She re-braided the back and flipped the long uncut tail over her shoulder.

She left the bathroom and crossed the hall to the baby's room. The nursery hadn't been used in years and now it held their miracle. She turned the cool metal knob and walked inside.

The white walls were bare of ornaments, the room holding only a rocking chair and crib. The baby items were kept in the closet. There weren't many and she would need to do laundry today. It surprised her that the rocking chair was empty. The curtains were closed and the entire room was shadowed.

She stepped closer to peer inside the crib that had been taken out of storage before the birth. It too was white with straight slats of wood that needed repainting. This was unimportant but she wanted so many things for her tiny daughter that would never be. She needed to curtail unnecessary thoughts of grandeur.

A smile was on her face when she looked inside the crib. Then her lips curved downward. The baby was not there.

A slice of dread entered her stomach. She walked to each door in the hallway and peered inside. Her sisters and their sons were sleeping. At the end of the hall was her husband's room. She quietly opened the door. He would be angry if she woke him. The bed was empty and unmade. He wasn't there.

Blood pounded in her temples. Her hands, damp with sweat, came together in front of her. She could not panic. There was an explanation and she would be holding her daughter soon.

A door closed downstairs and relief swept through her. She quickly turned and ran to the lower floor, unable to hold back her smile. She stopped at the foot of the stairs and faced his empty arms.

"Where is the baby?" she asked, trying not to show emotion.

His expression was stricken, his eyes red with tears.

"She is gone. It is for the best."

She shook her head, her body beginning to tremble. The knot in her stomach went ice cold, twisting tighter, making her short of breath.

"No," she gasped. "What have you done?" She grew weak and fell to her knees in front of him. The front of her dress slowly grew wet with breast milk. She lifted her arms in front of her. They ached for her baby as did her heart.

What had she done wrong?

How could loving her child be so bad?

She fell forward and covered her face with her hands, unable to contain her emotions. Her head came up and she looked at the man she'd married. His eyes were filled with disgust.

Her screams began and they didn't stop.

ONE

Eve woke to the sound of her ringing phone. It was the middle of the night. She scrambled to grab her cell off the nightstand and shake off the sleepy fog clouding her mind.

"Hello," she said groggily.

There was breathing, followed by a soft click, then an infant crying. The line went silent.

Eve turned on the bedside light and waited for her eyes to adjust to the brightness. She checked her phone. The screen read NO CALLER ID. There had been two previous calls over the past few weeks. Each had lasted a total of eight seconds.

The calls were psychological games meant to intimidate her.

Her stepsiblings, Charlie and Becky, were born with genetic disorders common to the small rural community of Hildale, Utah. The prophet believed inbreeding was essential to keep the polygamist bloodline pure and children suffered because of it.

Charlie was born with a genetic disorder and taken away by the midwife when he was six months old. No one questioned his removal or the fact he never returned. The midwife came for

Becky, who had a cleft palate, when she was only a few days old and history repeated itself.

Her stepbrother, Aaron, the county attorney in the center of the polygamist community, had no problem using their baby brother and sister to scare her away from doing her job which was law enforcement oversight of Hildale, Utah. He followed the commands of the prophet too and had six wives on last count. Months before, in their worst confrontation, she'd accused him of lusting after her since they were children. In the same volatile conversation, she'd given him ammunition against her by mentioning their baby siblings who'd disappeared. Eve had shown him she cared and it had been a crucial mistake.

Aaron knew a crying baby would torture her.

Her anger helped displace the ache caused by her sister and brother's loss. She was not one of Aaron's wives and his only way to control her was to destroy the foundation she'd spent years building. Mind games were all he had.

She turned off the light and settled beneath the covers. Daisy, her cat, snuggled against her back.

Aaron and his cult would not stop her from finding justice for those without a voice.

TWO

Eve activated her blinker and turned right at the traffic signal. She was several miles from her apartment. She'd spent the evening with her boyfriend, Clyde; she would soon be thirty-six years old and it felt strange to think of him as a boyfriend.

Clyde was a Black man in law enforcement in a state that had little ethnic diversity. They'd been good friends for years, but their relationship had changed a few months ago after she'd survived the most horrifying case in her career.

Dating Clyde was a huge step and she smiled over how great it was to have him in her life as more than a friend. She didn't feel any man would want to tackle the challenges of her past. In Clyde's case, she was wrong. He saw her as a woman who could stand on her own, fight her demons, and win.

To swallow pride, swallow emotions, and suffer silently – all known as keeping sweet – had been ground into her psyche from the ages of four to twelve. Showing emotion was a huge sin for women. Having a boyfriend was unheard of. The prophet arranged all marriages and every girl was prepared to turn herself in to the prophet at the first sign of womanhood. This was the same prophet who now sat in a Texas prison for savaging children.

Clyde didn't blink when she cried, or raged, or laughed in joy. All three had been missing from her life until recently. He allowed her to be human, though she was still learning. Thankfully, he was a very patient man.

It was dark on the quiet street and there was only one car in the area, a few car lengths behind her. It made the same turn after Eve. The vehicle suddenly sped up, pulling within feet of her bumper. Her brain was slow on the uptake until the driver activated their brights which momentarily blinded her. She pushed the rearview mirror up so she could see.

Eve had not worked in this district in her early years as a highway patrol officer, but it was possible someone recognized her. Even though the state of Utah had lower than normal crime rates, police officers made enemies.

The vehicle didn't back off when she tapped her brake. Eve picked up her cell and hit speed dial for dispatch.

"This is Eve Bennet, badge DS851," she said as soon as the call was answered. "I'm traveling northbound on 3640 West and Cannery. There is a vehicle following close behind mine with its brights activated. Please send a squad car to this area for backup."

She ended the call and retrieved her duty weapon from the secured holster beneath the driver's seat. She glanced around carefully, keeping one eye on the vehicle. She was looking for a cop patrol car approaching or even another vehicle that might inadvertently scare the one behind her away.

Eve exhaled slowly and tightened her grip on the steering wheel. There was a small niggle inside her head that said this was intimidation brought on by her work in the polygamy sect. As she was considered an apostate, the fundamentalist community believed she'd abandoned God and walked beside Satan. She was dangerous to their way of life. Five of her stepbrothers, all of them but Aaron, had assaulted her a few months before because of this thinking. Their faces were hidden and she'd been unable to legally identify them, but she knew who they were. The church, however, gladly supplied an alibi which didn't help either.

The vehicle behind her backed off slightly, giving her a little time to relax her tightened muscles. For a moment Eve wondered if it was a drunk driver. A screech of tires was all her mind registered before the car picked up speed and rammed the back of hers with a solid crunch.

THREE

The jolt swung Eve's head forward then sharply back against the headrest. Thankfully, it didn't activate her airbag. Her training came into play and she prepared to pull over and take cover. The vehicle backed off. She was ready for it to ram her again.

Eve breathed a sigh of relief when the car performed a U-turn and sped away. There was no license plate light, so she was unable to catch the numbers. She continued straight, hoping a squad car would intercept quickly.

She peered down the dark side streets while keeping an eye on the rearview mirror. A moment later, a marked patrol unit turned onto the road in front of her. She called dispatch and told them she was pulling over and to have the officer stop. She got out of her car without her gun and felt naked. She raised her right hand with her badge and credentials carrying her driver's license and registration in the other and waited for the officer to approach.

"They rammed the back of my vehicle. I'll need pictures and a full report ASAP," she told him, after they'd made introductions.

He was a city police officer, dressed in a blue uniform with his shiny badge prominent on his chest. He had a regulation haircut with no beard or mustache. His expression was standard cop, all business and ready for any situation. She was nervous over what happened yet still wanted to tell him to relax. She wouldn't because it would make no difference. This was the contrast between detectives and street cops. Detectives needed vital information and tried to put people at ease. Street cops saw weapons around every corner. It kept them alive; she remembered those days on patrol when backup was rarely available.

She dreaded seeing the damage to her vehicle but walked around to the back with the officer. The dent was large and the entire panel would need to be replaced.

"Left some black rubber on your bumper," the officer said while shining his flashlight over the damage. "I don't see paint. Do you know what color the vehicle was?"

"Black. It may have been an older model Buick. Car identification was never my strong suit so it's a guess."

"An older vehicle like that would explain the rubber. They have large bumpers. I'll call in another unit in case they return."

"Thank you." She put away her badge but couldn't relax with her hands empty. "My gun is in the car and I'm going to holster it on my hip. I don't like being unarmed after what happened."

"Yes, ma'am. If you want to sit in your vehicle, that's okay too."

"No, I have too much adrenaline running through me. I'll stand out here and call a member of my taskforce team to give him a heads up."

She moved closer to her car door and peered around the dimly lit area before grabbing her gun along with the paddle holster she carried in her glove compartment. After she had the weapon secured, she took a relieved breath then pulled her phone from her back pocket. She hit Clyde's number while she peered around the dark area.

"Did you forget something?" he asked cheerfully.

She hated to ruin a great evening with her bad news but had no choice. "I'm on 3640 West and Cannery. Wait..." She turned and looked at the street that intersected where she was now. "Zenu, not Cannery," she continued. "Someone rammed my car from behind and left without pulling over. I'm unhurt and there is an officer on scene." She spoke quickly. "I don't need you coming out here, I just wanted you to have a heads up. This might have been someone who recognized me from my earlier career as an officer, but I don't want to take chances."

Before Clyde became a homicide detective, he'd commanded a state SWAT unit. His voice changed to police mode. "I'm heading to your location."

She inhaled deeply. "I wish you wouldn't."

"Too damn bad."

"Okay," she said, giving in but a little annoyed at his insistence. "I'll let you know if they clear me to leave before you get here."

"Traffic reports take forever," he huffed. "I'll be there before they're done."

She took another calming breath and walked closer to the officer while he was taking pictures. Her eyes continued darting around the area. This was too coincidental not to be someone from her past. Another squad car pulled up. The second officer quickly introduced himself before he went to help with the report.

The next vehicle that arrived was Clyde's. He immediately shut off his headlights so she could identify that it was him and he didn't get shot.

"He's my second in command," she told the officers who had placed their hands on their holsters. Clyde's six-feet-two height, bald head, and large build—thanks to a rigorous workout schedule—could be intimidating and she didn't want the officers any more on edge.

"Are you okay?" he asked while looking her over from head to toe, assuring himself she was.

"Yes, not a scratch. Angry more than anything."

He didn't hug her, but she could see he wanted to. She also noticed the tightness of his shoulders and if there had been enough light, she knew she would see the lines of anger creasing his forehead. He watched the area, looking for threats. She remained piqued that he was at the scene and had disregarded her request that he stay home. This was not the time or place to change his attitude, but she had a feeling the time was coming.

It took the officers another ten minutes to finish the report. The first officer walked over with the paperwork.

"If you can sign here, you can be on your way. Sorry this happened," he said.

Eve signed her name where he pointed and handed the clipboard back.

"Please send a copy of the report to my office," she told him, and handed him her card.

"Yes, ma'am." He walked over to the other officer and they chatted for a few minutes. They wouldn't leave until she and Clyde cleared the scene.

Clyde walked with her to the back of her vehicle so she could show him the damage.

"You know this is meant to intimidate you," he said.

"That was my thought too."

"I'm following you home," he told her.

She was ten minutes from her apartment, but she didn't argue. The crying-baby phone calls had her more on edge than usual.

They pulled into her complex. It had adequate lighting but also plenty of shadows. She was trained to handle these situations and her irritation with Clyde grew a tad higher.

He walked her to the front of her apartment and stopped on her doorstep.

"Are you sure you're okay?" he asked, pulling her against his chest. "Neck, shoulders, head?"

"It was a solid jolt, but I don't feel a thing." She pulled away slightly and looked into his concerned eyes.

"I'm worried about you," he said, allowing anger to fill his voice. "Tonight crossed the line."

This was difficult, but it was time he backed off his high-handedness.

"I can't dress in bubble wrap," she stated firmly, reminding him she was a police officer just like he was.

If she had to point to something negative about Clyde, it would be his protectiveness since their relationship changed from friends to lovers.

Clyde frowned, getting the message. He'd been navigating their relationship carefully but sometimes, like tonight, he forgot she was able to take care of herself.

"You aren't sleeping because of the damned phone calls and I'm on edge. When I see the dark circles beneath your eyes, it's worse," he said honestly.

Detective Bina Blau, the team's electronics guru, had traced the last two calls. They came from trac phones that could be purchased cheaply and discarded. Eve's stress level rose with each call and her nightmares had also returned. When she looked in the mirror, she could see the strain this was having on her. Of course, Clyde would notice and it would affect him.

"We're both upset," she replied. "The caller is getting exactly what he wants and it makes me angrier. This type of warfare is impossible to fight." She shrugged. "I'm frustrated more than anything. They have no power over me and they can't stand it. This is simply one more game they play."

His hand smoothed over her back.

"Come back to my place?" he asked huskily. He had never

pushed before and it irritated her that he'd do it when she was feeling vulnerable.

"You can even bring the devil cat," he added, which took some of the annoyance away.

Advancing their relationship was an aspect of her life she had to work at. This was all new to her. Clyde had befriended her even though she'd tried hard to push him away.

He was divorced because he was married to his job and his wife had wanted more from him. She'd had an affair which was mentally devastating. After the divorce, he carried most of the blame on his shoulders. She'd remarried and Clyde was happy for her. It didn't mean there weren't scars. He openly shared these aspects of his past and Eve still hesitated to discuss hers. When she did, it was a robotic recitation without emotion like someone looking down on what happened without being part of it.

She tempered these feelings of inadequacy by concentrating on what they had in common. Their combined dedication to the law enforcement oversight taskforce was one of the reasons their relationship worked. They understood long workdays and all-consuming cases. When it came down to it, Clyde was the only person she was comfortable with. He'd become an important part of her personal life. Small actions like he'd displayed tonight interfered with their work and private relationship.

Being a couple brought conflicting thoughts. They slept together, but Eve always went home afterward. It saddened her that she couldn't take the next step and stay the night. To others it might be an easy progression, but to her, it was tied somewhere to her puritanical past. She tried not to judge herself and hoped, when the time was right to advance in their intimate dynamic, she would feel more comfortable about it.

Expressing her worries to Clyde was much more difficult than hiding them. When she thought of her failings, it ignited an endless circle of self-doubt which inevitably turned to anger. She had a long way to go. She was on an emotional tightrope of damned if she did and damned if she didn't.

Keep sweet rang through her head. This happened whenever she was emotional. The police academy and years on the street as an officer further enhanced her inability to express her feelings. She wanted to be free of her doubts and to do that she had to overcome the past.

Then there was the squad.

To lead a taskforce filled with type-A personalities, she had to be tough and decisive even though the team was more like a family now. They hadn't started that way. It took their last devastating case for her to understand she didn't need to be an emotionless robot to lead them. Understanding and accomplishment were two different things and she was searching for the balance.

Showing her human side would help in her leadership role and make the team more comfortable coming to her with their problems so it was worth the effort.

"I'm okay," she told him. "Text me when you get home." She gave him a quick kiss and entered her apartment. Eve didn't look back. She couldn't take the hurt she knew would be in his eyes. She locked the door behind her. Clyde rattled it, making sure she was safe, which added to her guilt. He cared about her. She loved him. And she still wasn't sure if their relationship was what either of them needed.

Daisy circled her legs as though Eve had been gone for days and not a few hours. Taking a treat from the cupboard to settle her down, Eve gave her a quick pat on the back and headed to her bedroom.

As soon as Daisy finished eating, she sat on the bed and watched Eve perform her nightly rituals. Completely unimpressed, she licked her paw then used it to wash her face, waiting patiently for Eve to join her in the bed. As soon as Eve climbed in, Daisy made herself comfortable. All was right in the spoiled cat's world.

Eve's phone buzzed a short while later.

Home and safe. I'll call tomorrow.

He would call and never mention that she'd upset him. *If* she'd upset him. That was Clyde. He accepted her shortcomings. It was why she'd allowed their friendship to grow in the beginning. So why was she struggling with this aspect of their personal relationship?

FOUR

Eve had just managed to nod off after hours spent tossing and turning when her phone rang. She checked the caller ID, ready to throw her cell into the closest wall if it was another harassment call. There was a number on the screen, but it was one she didn't recognize.

"Hello," she said.

"Detective Bennet?"

"Yes." Eve sat up and turned on her bedside light.

"This is Linda Wall."

Linda was Hannah Tanner's aunt. The Tanner homicide case had left lasting scars on Eve and her team. The family was discovered murdered in their beds. Hannah was the only one who survived. The Walls had disappeared with Hannah before Eve had a chance to interview her about the homicides. Eve and her team hadn't known at the time that Hannah, the victim of unconscionable abuse, had committed the murders.

Toward the end of the investigation, Linda dropped Hannah off at the Tanners' home and Eve found the child upstairs in the attic. Hannah tried to kill her with the same knife she'd used to murder her family after drugging their food.

Eve was faced with the idea of defending herself by killing a child. It hadn't happened, but she'd had her gun pointed at Hannah and it had been close. One of her recurring nightmares was the scenario with a different ending.

Linda had not come to Hannah's judicial hearings, which broke Eve's heart. Even after all that transpired, Eve didn't blame Hannah, she blamed the adults who didn't protect her. The two women had never met. Linda Wall was low on Eve's list of people she wanted to speak with late at night.

"Why are you calling?" she asked with none of the animosity in her voice that she felt, though the question was direct.

"I need your help."

Eve heard Linda sniff and her voice grew shaky. This was strange coming from a married woman of the polygamist community. Keep sweet. Women were trained to never show emotion and Linda was crying.

"My newborn baby is missing and she's in danger."

FIVE

"Aunt Linda brought me here. She didn't want me to hurt the baby in her belly," were Hannah's exact words before she'd lifted the knife and tried to stab Eve.

Eve's brain had replayed that scene in the attic so many times.

"Have you made a police report?" she asked Linda.

"I can't. My husband says we must forget about Allison and not mention her again."

This was eerily close to what Eve was told when the midwife took her little brother Charlie.

"Where are you calling from?" Eve asked, reaching into her nightstand for a pen and notebook she kept there.

"I'm outside our home in my husband's truck. I'm using his phone."

"Are you still in Hildale?"

Eve had never discovered where the Walls went after they left their home with Hannah.

"Yes, we are back in our house, by my sister's home." Her sister was Marcella Tanner, one of the family members Hannah murdered.

"Do you know who took your baby?" Eve asked next.

"No, she was missing when I woke up yesterday morning." Linda sniffed.

A full day, almost two. The baby could be out of state or the country by now.

"Did someone from the church have reason to remove her from your home?"

Women and children were often reassigned to other men. One day a woman was married to one man and the next to another. If her husband failed to provide enough money to the prophet, or went against his dictates, he could lose his standing in the community along with the number of wives he had. Wives were a man's symbol of his righteousness and success. Women and girls were the cult's biggest commodities.

Eve hadn't heard of a young baby being reassigned from its mother or father, but it was possible and she had to ask.

"Was the child reassigned?" Eve repeated when Linda didn't immediately answer.

"You don't understand," Hannah's aunt said softly.

"I need to, so please explain. It will take me and my team a minimum of four hours to get there and time is of the essence right now. The police in town will start an investigation imme-diately."

"I'm worried they will kill her." Linda started crying again. Women in the community rarely showed emotion, which was why the tears surprised Eve so much. No matter what tragedy happened, fundamentalist women were programmed to suffer in silence.

"I'm trying to help you," Eve said. "Please tell me what is going on."

"I am sorry, I cannot say any more." The line went dead.

"Damn," she muttered.

Eve rarely swore aloud and usually it was her stepbrother Aaron who caused it. She checked the time. It was a little after midnight. She tried to call Linda back, but the phone rang without being answered. There wasn't even a recording to leave a message.

She hit Clyde's name on speed dial.

"Is everything okay?" he immediately asked.

"With me, yes, but I just received a very strange phone call." She explained the situation.

"What do you want to do?"

"Alert the team and drive to the community," she told him. "I'll call Tamm and I need you to send an emergency text to the others.

Tamm was their secretary and she would have their van and SUV ready for them when they arrived at the office.

"Okay, but I'm picking you up," Clyde told her. "I'll be there in thirty minutes."

"I'm more than capable of driving myself," she said testily. She was tired and his overprotectiveness from earlier was still fresh in her mind.

He took a moment to reply.

"If it were Ray or Collin who were purposely rear-ended and the perpetrator was still at large, would you want them driving almost that same route within hours of it happening?"

She didn't need a moment. "Point taken," she agreed. "Pick me up."

Eve sent a text message to Katie, her pet sitter, and another to her mom who she also referred to as Maggie. In fundamentalist polygamy households, mothers were known as "Mother" followed by their first names to stop confusion for children. Neither messaged back, but it was late and Katie knew to notify Maggie if she couldn't look after Daisy.

Daisy watched, while Eve quickly checked her travel bag which was always packed and ready. She took a quick shower, dressed, and waited for Clyde after filling Daisy's bowls with enough food and water to last several days, just in case.

The cat was aware something was up and stayed close by. Eve bent over and smoothed her hand over her back.

"I'll be home as soon as I can," Eve assured her. "You'll be spoiled so don't give me the cold shoulder." Katie made home-made treats for the animals she watched and if Maggie came to the apartment, Daisy would be showered with affection so in either case, the cat would be pampered.

Clyde knocked on the door, putting an end to the one-sided conversation. Daisy took off down the hallway. Eve didn't need to see where she went to know Daisy had scurried under the bed. At least Eve was saved from the "sorrowful eyes" routine.

She grabbed her bag and gun, checked the peephole, and opened the door. Clyde wore what had become the team's unofficial uniform: black tactical pants and boots. The red clay in the Hildale community left stains on lighter clothing when they needed to kneel outside. He'd added a burgundy short-sleeved polo that hugged his muscled chest and displayed his powerful arms.

He waited patiently while she checked the sliding glass door off the living room to be sure it was locked.

"Do you think this is connected to the phone calls and what happened tonight?" he asked once they pulled out of her apartment complex.

"I have no idea." She rested back against the seat and wished she could relax enough for a short nap.

"Do you think someone would harm the baby?" he asked next.

Eve could tell he was alarmed over the possibility of a missing child. She was too, but until they had more information, she would stay positive. The reassignment of wives and children was still poking her subconscious, but then maybe she wanted it to. The possibility of a child abduction and the amount of time that had passed was too disturbing to contemplate right now.

"If a baby has some sort of medical problem that requires a lot of money, it's possible," she said, answering Clyde's question. "I keep replaying the call. She didn't give us much to go on. I'll admit I'm worried, but for now, I need to focus on the facts and not the inside knowledge from my past."

Clyde took her hand, his warmth settling her racing thoughts. The team knew about Charlie and Becky. They were horrified to think anyone would neglect or kill a child because money was more important than surgery, as in Becky's case, or more important than taking Charlie to the hospital.

Eve still had trouble mentally dealing with Babyland, the graveyard that was the final resting place for many babies under a year old in the Hildale community. Lack of prenatal and infant care were two factors. Forced inbreeding also caused a high rate of physical and mental abnormalities. These issues tragically led to a higher-than-normal infant mortality rate.

"Have you informed the county attorney?" Clyde asked.

He refused to refer to Aaron as her stepbrother. He disliked Aaron almost as much as she did. Aaron's fundamentalist, racist teachings caused even more friction. Aaron treated Clyde like he didn't exist, along with Bina due to her Indigenous heritage, and Ray Gonzales, one of Eve's other investigators, because of his Hispanic roots. The only person on her squad Aaron acknowledged was Collin. Aaron's position as the county attorney, and the necessity of dealing with him, made the situation volatile at best. She knew he was behind the harassment calls to her cell phone. Proving it was another matter entirely.

"No. I didn't call him," she said. "If the prophet had the baby removed from the home, Aaron should know about it. If I decide he needs to know about Linda, I'll meet him face to face to see his expression. He wouldn't have a problem lying, but fortunately, he's not particularly good at hiding his lies."

Interference in their cases didn't stop at Aaron. His dislike was shared by the members of the fundamentalist community in general. Eve, as an apostate, was the last person they wanted responsible for law enforcement oversight. They'd tried and failed several times to get the federal judge to rescind his order for oversight. Eve's job included the entire county's justice system. The community had a history of demanding its members follow the laws of the prophet and not the laws of Utah or the US. For a year and a half now, Eve's team had thwarted the idealism that the prophet was their law. If she was around for the entire ten-year sanction, she doubted this would change, but she was determined to win justice for all the children and women who needed it.

SIX

It took them twenty minutes to get to their office parking garage. Tamm Mackity stood in front of the SUV and an oversized evidence van. She wore a purple skirt and bright orange gauzy top, her frizzy red hair unbound.

Tamm was a miracle worker. Eve had stolen her from another department and never regretted it. The woman was fifty years young and tough enough to leave department heads shaking in their boots. If the team needed something, Tamm would find a way to get it. Her smile reminded you of every child's dream grandmother, but at heart, she was a shark and her teeth bit deep. As a civilian employee it wasn't easy to hold your own with police officers, but Tamm had no problem. She was the team's backbone and Eve didn't know how they would survive without her.

Another vehicle pulled up and Bina Blau stepped out.

"Clyde mentioned the hit and run," Bina said when she was close enough. "Are you okay?" She was dressed in all black from her boots and tactical pants to a short-sleeved polo shirt that revealed the beautiful bronze skin of her arms. Her toned body was that of a runner. She was striking with dark eyes and black hair which was secured in a single braid down her back.

Eve couldn't help but feel a touch envious over the near perfect beauty that Bina never seemed to work at.

"Yes. I'm good," Eve told her. "Like everyone else, lack of sleep leaves me feeling grouchy and you are now forewarned. Did you manage any rest?"

"Three hours," she said, but didn't add anything more.

Bina's usual good disposition was lacking. Eve saw strain in her expression and wondered if she had something personal going on.

Tamm walked over and handed Bina the keys to the SUV.

Bina, at five feet nine inches tall, towered over Tamm's five-three height.

"Is our coffee packed?" Bina asked.

"What do you think?" Tamm chided. She looked Bina over and probably noticed the same thing Eve had. "I wouldn't send my favorite people in the world out of town without a decent cup of coffee." She spoiled them and purchased expensive coffee out of her paycheck and refused to take money for it. She was a caffeine connoisseur and never drank anything cheap.

"Just making sure." Bina stepped back, but Tamm followed her and wrapped her in a big hug. Bina closed her eyes and sank into it a bit before she pulled away.

The secretary turned to Eve and gave her a questioning look. Eve replied with a small shrug. No one on the squad was really the touchy-feely type, but Tamm had quasi-adopted Bina and the two women usually hugged when greeting one another. Maybe Bina would talk about whatever it was during the drive.

"Do you want me to contact your insurance and take care of your POV?" Tamm asked. POV meant "personally owned vehicle" and Eve had been worried about finding time to notify her insurance.

"What would I do without you?" she asked Tamm. It was a

relief to know she wouldn't need to worry about the dent in her car.

"Drink bad coffee and worry about other issues when you need your full attention on a case," Tamm replied with a smile.

Another vehicle pulled into the underground garage. It was Collin's car and he had Ray with him. They both looked tired when they walked over. Clyde put his hand out to Tamm.

"Keys," he said. "Neither of them is capable of driving." Clyde usually rode with Eve and Bina.

Ray smiled and winked. "My hot date was cut short."

Ray Gonzales was single, good-looking, and still lived at home with his mother and siblings. He and Collin were best friends who'd met at the police academy. Ray had an analytical mind that even rivaled Bina's technical brain. He wrote solid search warrants, and he kept Collin's wild ideas in check.

As the only Mormon on the squad, Collin Smith was sometimes able to open firmly shut doors within the fundamentalist community. He did not condone or practice polygamy. Even if it weren't a felony in the state, his wife, Laura, would strangle him if he mentioned marrying another woman. They had four children and when not working, he was running his kids around to one of their sporting or school events.

Ray, Collin, Clyde, Bina, and Tamm were Eve's family. She'd brought the squad together because of their qualifications and history of success as solid investigators. The taskforce worked hours from the city. Each squad member had multiple specialties that included forensics so they didn't need to delay a case waiting for crime scene investigators to arrive from out of town. They were their own CSI team.

After eighteen months they'd become a tightly knit unit and were united against the corruption they faced.

"Clyde gave you the rudiments of Linda's call. Are there any questions?" Eve asked before they split into different vehicles.

All but Bina shook their heads. She stared toward the east side of the garage which was nothing but lined-up government vehicles at this time of night.

"The clock is ticking. We need to be on the road." They all knew Eve was speaking about the possible child abduction without her saying the words.

They had little to go on and from experience, it would be worse once they arrived in town. Unethical men would stop at nothing to keep their power structure intact. Her team gave Eve hope. They were as tenacious as she was and if the child could be found, they would find her.

Bina was mostly quiet during the drive. She usually talked about random things if she needed to stay awake. Eve put it down to tiredness, which she felt too.

SEVEN

They arrived in town three hours after leaving the city and filled the gas tanks at the minimart before they went to the hotel and checked in. It was early enough that they weren't followed, but they knew cameras monitored the main streets and their arrival had most likely been noted. They needed a few hours of sleep before the day started and went straight to their rooms.

The alarm sounded at 7 a.m. and Eve rolled over to shut it off. Bina was already in the shower and walked out of the bathroom a few minutes later.

"Your turn," she said. Her hair was wrapped in a towel and she was carrying a large Micky Mouse coffee mug curtesy of Tamm. The smell was almost enough to make Eve take a mug of coffee in with her but decided against it. She was out and dressed in fifteen minutes, ready for the coffee she'd passed on.

Carrying the steaming mugs with them, they went to the lobby for the newly advertised continental breakfast. Clyde and Collin were already there.

"Where's Ray?" Eve asked.

"He needed extra beauty sleep so I'm picking up his food," Collin said with a grin. "I spoil him."

It was nice to smile in the face of the coming investigation that was weighing heavily on her. Bina's lips didn't move with the usual grin she would have given to Collin's jibe at Ray. Eve had missed the opportunity earlier when they were alone to ask Bina what was bothering her.

They took their plates to Eve's room and Collin sent their missing squad mate a text. Ray knocked on the door a minute later. His brown hair was wet so they knew he had just gotten out of the shower. Collin liked to tease him about his perfectly groomed hair because Ray's mother cut it every three weeks to keep him looking handsome. Those were her words. She wanted him to meet a nice girl and settle down to raise more grandbabies for her to spoil. Ray's mother had no problem throwing Collin's wife and four children into conversations and mentioning what a good son Collin's mother had. Ray was good-natured about it and as far as Eve knew, he had no intention of marrying anytime soon.

Today, Collin pointedly looked down at Ray's socks and mocked him with an eye roll for coming to the meeting shoeless. Collin was a stickler for these things.

"If you were married, your wife would fix these obnoxious habits," he teased.

It was Ray's turn to roll his eyes.

"Exactly why I'm not married," he quipped back.

They were seated around the small table using extra chairs Clyde had brought from his room. Ray, as the last one to arrive, sat on the bed.

Ray put on his boots. After they were laced, he stood and adjusted his gun holster followed by his badge which was clipped to his belt. He did a slow circle for Collin's benefit.

"Am I missing anything?" he asked.

"You have a nose hair out of place," Collin replied with a straight face.

"Meeting in session," Eve told them. She enjoyed Ray and

Collin's banter, but they had to focus. Both men turned instantly serious. "We need to speak with Linda Wall. The God squad will follow us and it will cause trouble for her."

God squad was a term used by the community for those who patrolled the streets and provided security. These were coveted roles, and younger men were assigned only if they were in good standing with the prophet—in other words, if they or their families provided money to line the prophet's pockets even though he sat in prison. The God squad also acted as the town's enforcers, with two primary goals. One was to make sure women abided by the religious laws of subservience, modesty, and strict separation from non-household members. Gossip was a woman's sin so friendships outside their immediate family were not allowed. The second reason the God squad existed was to follow and harass outsiders so that they would leave town quickly and wouldn't return. Legal oversight had added a third purpose. They followed Eve and the team everywhere to report their movements to the church hierarchy.

"I may visit Aaron after speaking with Linda," she told them. Aaron, as the county attorney, ought to be informed of all investigations, but she didn't trust him and it was becoming harder to play by the rules that worked in most places.

She addressed Clyde. "The best way to lessen the ramifications for Linda is to confuse those tailing us. Go with Collin and Ray and make bogus stops such as the post office and minimart to keep them guessing. I'll use Hannah's case as an excuse to see Linda. I'm unsure if it will work, but it might buy us some extra time before the interference starts."

"It's worth a try," he said. "I'm sure we can find some trouble if we look hard enough."

"I'm good with that," said Ray. "I need excitement to keep me awake. What about you, Collin?"

"I'm good at stirring up trouble," he replied.

"If you visit the county attorney's office, will you take Bina inside with you?" Clyde asked Eve.

She and Clyde had discussed this months before, and he was reminding her of their conversation. She hadn't forgotten and she had been the one to originally bring it up. Lack of sleep was making her irritable and she bit back the retort she wanted to give.

Was her annoyance caused from the night before when Clyde had shown up at the scene though she'd specifically asked him not to? Or was it her lack of sleep? Perhaps both? Worry about Linda's baby was another factor.

"Yes," she responded. "Aaron needs to become accustomed to dealing with all of us, not just me," she said for the benefit of the entire team. "He might as well make all of us miserable." She glanced at Bina. "Are you ready?"

Bina lifted the keys without saying anything.

Her sullen mood was not improving. Hopefully she would talk during the car ride to the Wall residence. Digging into Bina's personal business made Eve uncomfortable and she was worried she would step on her toes. But Eve was learning to share her own pain and as Bina's supervisor and friend she needed to make sure she was okay. Their job took a toll. If Bina told her to back off, Eve would respect her wishes.

"We'll use one of our stops to pick up sandwich supplies and snacks before we come back to the hotel," Clyde told her. "Call if you need us to head your way." They kept lunch meat, bread rolls, and other items in the small room refrigerators in case they didn't have time to stop for food, which often happened during their cases.

They threw their trash away, tidied the room, and headed to their separate vehicles. Collin, driving the van, turned in the opposite direction from Eve and Bina. Two God squad trucks were waiting and one pulled in behind the SUV. It was easy to identify the black lifted trucks that were big enough to roll over a small building. The church owned them and their size was just another intimidation technique in their bag of tricks.

Bina remained quiet.

"Anything we need to talk about?" Eve asked.

"No. I'm tired, that's all."

Eve realized she'd made a poor attempt at gaining insight into whatever was bothering Bina. She was at a loss. Facing emotional conflict head on was something Eve was still working on. She couldn't tackle this using her detective training. While Bina drove, Eve gazed out the SUV's window and tried to come up with another approach. She was uncomfortable with this type of personal interaction. As she watched the buildings go by, her thoughts rambled.

She had lived in this town as a child and it had seen very few changes. The large multi-level homes were essentially prisons for girls and women. The tall block fences surrounding each home kept curious eyes from seeing the antiquated clothing and plural wife ideology. The prophet insisted women wear long dresses in solid colors that made them look like their clothes came out of a nineteenth-century dress catalog. Women could not question their husbands and their husbands didn't question the prophet. There was no middle ground and they would be punished harshly for not wearing the appropriate clothing.

The entire lifestyle here was backward. Things like television and the internet were not allowed. These were the tools of Satan. The fundamentalist community was told the outside world was evil. The worst thing someone could do was disavow the prophet's word and become an apostate. Eve faced their condemnation for choosing to be more than an article traded by sexual deviants.

The outside world did not understand the generations of indoctrination that ran the community. Eve did. This town represented the evil of her past. After eighteen months, the team had more insight on the uphill battle they faced. She'd known it from the beginning, but until you saw it for yourself, the totality of brainwashing was hard to grasp.

Her attention focused on the landscape again when they passed the large Fundamentalist Mormon Church. It consisted of a long gray rectangle building, the front half one story and the backside, two. She'd learned as a detective that the far-right side housed the town's security center. Pole cameras were located throughout the community and took over where the God squad left off.

The security cameras could have been helpful for some of her team's investigations, but mysteriously, they malfunctioned whenever they requested footage via a warrant. She'd almost become accustomed to the interference they encountered. Almost.

Next, they drove past several of the largest homes. The area wasn't what you would call pretty. The houses were well-maintained inside and out, because a house full of women and girls labored every hour of the day. Idle hands were hands reaching toward Satan, or so Eve had been taught as a child.

Utah juniper and serviceberry trees dotted the high desert yards and roadside. They only grew to about fifteen feet and needed little water to survive. As much money as possible went to the prophet and was not used for things like watering trees or grass. She noticed a few desert willows that were just regrowing their leaves after the long winter. She'd always thought they would be fun to climb because unlike other children, Eve had vague memories of playing outside. Play was a sin to the fundamentalists. There were no parks or playgrounds. The prophet had outlawed toys.

In contrast with the homes, businesses showed little maintenance. They were all in need of fresh paint or a new roof. If the walls stayed upright, they were operational enough to make money for the prophet. Aesthetics was unimportant.

The heaviness in Eve's gut grew the closer they got to the Wall home. From experience, she doubted they would uncover the secrets that would find the missing baby. Bina remained quiet, which also didn't help Eve's outlook.

On a rise in the road, she could see inside the high fence surrounding the Tanners' home where the family was murdered. It stood dark and silent in the distance. Eve was relieved. It wouldn't have surprised her if another family had moved in. The house had held an evil secret, hard even now to contemplate, and no matter how ridiculous it seemed, she felt it was better off empty.

They passed the house, turned onto the next road, and then made a left. The God squad vehicle drove past them to the end of the street and pulled over. The Wall home had a high cinderblock fence around it. The wrought iron gate was unlocked and they walked through.

The toyless yards always bothered Eve. Toddlers followed their mothers around and learned to strip beds, empty trash-cans, and other small tasks tiny hands could do.

Eve had learned to hang up clothes outside on the line as soon as she and her mother moved in with their new family. She'd been four years old and had to stand on a wooden crate to reach. Her childhood memories were filled with subservience and punishment. It was those memories that gave Eve the forti-tude to do her job.

She knocked on the front door several times before a blonde-haired woman in her early twenties answered. She wore a royal-blue prairie dress which was starched and pressed. Her hair swooped high in the front.

"I'm Detective Sergeant Bennet," Eve said. "This is my partner Detective Blau. We need to speak with Linda about her niece, Hannah Tanner."

The woman shook her head slightly. "Sister Linda is not here," she said in a deep, slightly slurred voice, nervously checking over her shoulder. Talking to outsiders was forbidden.

Linda had called Eve eight hours ago.

"I need to speak with the senior wife," Eve said firmly.

The woman leaned out the door closer to Eve.

"Sister Linda," she whispered, and then stopped talking. Again, she looked over her shoulder. "One moment." The door closed and Eve heard the lock engage.

Like Eve, Bina had a stubborn set to her jaw at the abrupt action. The woman wanted to say something about Linda but had changed her mind. Eve knew there were times the women wanted to speak out but the endless indoctrination stopped them.

An older woman walked outside and closed the door behind her. The dress she wore was identical to the younger woman's and she had the same hair swoop but with a touch of gray at her temples. The wife with the most authority was usually the oldest.

This applied to Aaron's mother who had overseen the women and children in Eve's polygamist family. This gave Aaron more standing with his father. He was raised to take his father's place in town and he'd done it.

Favored wives tended to be bullies and this woman played the part. Her gaze was pure condemnation and censured everything from their appearance to their audacity. Her body language made it clear she did not appreciate that Eve and Bina were standing at her door.

"Why do you wish to speak with Sister Linda?" she snapped. Her lips were tightly pursed, her hands fisted at her sides. She was not happy with the visit, but Eve hadn't expected her to be.

"We're here to discuss Hannah Tanner. We were hoping Linda could offer advice on a court matter."

The woman stiffly folded her hands in front of her, gazed

quickly at Bina, and met Eve's eyes again. "Sister Linda no longer resides in this household. I have no information on her whereabouts."

"Hannah mentioned Linda's pregnancy, did she have the baby?" Eve smiled even knowing it would do no good.

The older woman's expression changed from irritation to anger. She placed her hand on the doorknob.

"There is no baby in this home and Sister Linda did not give birth. You must leave."

The woman walked inside and shut the door.

Eve and Bina stood for a moment looking at each other in confusion.

"We need to go see Aaron," Eve said.

On their way to the SUV, a noise came from above them. Eve looked up at the home's second story. The young woman who first answered the door had opened a window. She tossed an object out. It landed in front of Bina and the window immediately closed. Bina picked it up and tightened her fingers around it. She handed it to Eve as soon as they were inside the vehicle.

It was a rolled-up white sock. There was a piece of paper inside. Hand-printed with large letters, the note looked like it was written by a child in primary school.

Linda left early this morning.
  She's being punished for her child of sin.
  Please find the baby, before she is no more.

EIGHT

"What do you think a child of sin means?" Bina asked Eve as they drove to the county attorney's office. Eve's concern for Linda and the baby was even greater now that the senior wife had denied the child's existence.

"I'm unsure. Hopefully Aaron will fill us in." The term "child of sin" was as new to Eve as it was to Bina.

They drove past the small postal center, turned the corner, and pulled up to the office parking area. The white stucco building was nicer than local businesses because government money maintained it. Gravel lined the sidewalk leading to the entry.

"Are you ready for this?" Eve asked Bina.

She nodded, her silence saying more than words.

"I'm not impressed," Bina said into the quiet room after they entered the building.

The waiting area was a square room with a desk behind a four-by-four glass window positioned opposite the front door. There were ugly, vinyl office chairs against the sidewalls, ten chairs total. As often as Eve had been here, she had never seen anyone waiting. The wall's paint was crisp white, almost too bright with the overhead inset florescent lighting. There were no plants, fake or otherwise, nor were there pictures. Simple bare white walls were the town's theme.

She gave Bina a quick glance before she walked up to the glass window. The last time Eve was here, she'd been surprised to find a woman at the desk. When Eve voiced her amazement to Aaron about employing a female receptionist, he'd told her they were married and working in the office took Denise's mind off her inability to have a child.

The prophet only allowed children using a seed bearer. These were men, selected by the prophet for their pure blood-lines to impregnate other men's wives. It was also possible Aaron was one of his chosen. The thought was horrifying. When the secret about seed bearers came out during an interview with an abused woman in one of Eve's first cases as the head of the oversight squad, she was horrified. Husbands held their wives down while another man sexually assaulted them. What made it worse was the women were programmed to take the forced sexual abuse as their duty to the prophet.

Outside of using a seed bearer, sexual relations between husbands and their plural wives were forbidden. The prophet said it was a revelation from God, but in Eve's opinion, he was in prison and couldn't take advantage of his eighty-plus wives so no other man would either. Why the people in town didn't see through his wall of immoral revelations could only be explained by understanding the level of complete mind control he held over his worshippers.

"May I help you?" the man behind the glass asked without meeting their gaze. He wore long, white shirtsleeves. A dark blue jacket rested on the chair's back. He had light brown hair and blue eyes. Eve noticed a resemblance to one of the families from the area but couldn't place which one. He was likely a close relation to several. His age, somewhere in his forties, told Eve he could be one of the attorneys filling in while Denise was away from the desk.

"We're here to speak with County Attorney Owens," she said. "Please tell him Detective Sergeant Bennet requests to see him." She'd thought about calling and decided against it. The more off guard Aaron was, the better chance they had of gaining information.

The man examined Eve from neck to knee and still didn't look in her eyes. His perusal was meant to intimidate. Eve stood her ground. Her clothes, gun, and badge went against his idea of a woman's place in life. After a long moment, he lifted the receiver and buzzed Aaron's office.

"The Bennet woman is here to see you," he said, making his contempt more obvious in case Eve or Bina misunderstood his revulsion.

Bina kept her eyes on him but remained silent. If they showed hostility, things would get worse. The oversight squad had become good at hiding their annoyance when faced with racism and misogyny. It was rampant here and hadn't changed in over... well, ever. They fought the battles they could win and had to let the others go or anger would keep them from doing their job.

"I'll bring them back," the man said, then paused a moment without hanging up the phone. "Yes, she has another..." He hesitated and looked at Bina, giving her the same neck to knee inspection. "Another woman with her."

Eve was an apostate and, in his mind, she deserved complete derision. Both women deserved his contempt and he let them know it. He not so gently put the receiver down and pressed the button that unlocked the door to the offices.

"Follow me." His movements were stiff and it surprised Eve that they couldn't see the large stick up his butt.

Hold it together, she told herself. Bina nudged her gently with an elbow. Whatever had bothered Bina earlier was not at the forefront now. She was helping Eve retain her cool demeanor and she appreciated it.

They followed the man down the narrow hallway that Eve knew well. There were three office doors on each side of the hall and only two attorneys inside their offices. Each small room held a desk with a family photo facing the door. Otherwise, there were no further decorations except law books located on a case behind the desk chair. Pride and success were obtained by the number of wives a man possessed. As a polygamist husband, he had to be sure his wives were on display, so others understood his exalted position in his narrow-minded society.

Aaron's office was at the end of the hallway and twice the size of the others. As usual, he sat behind his desk and didn't bother standing when Eve and Bina entered. Two chairs were in front of the desk, Eve took the one closest to the wall and Bina sat in the one by the door.

Aaron didn't look up from the file he was reading and made them wait. His bloodless lips and extremely pale features caused her insides to clench. Not even a gallon of sunscreen and a month on the beach could take away his seemingly bleached skin. He looked like walking death. Sadly, as a child Eve had longed for the Owen family coloring. She had hated that she stood out as an outsider. Eve's olive-toned complexion, with brown hair and eyes, came from her Italian father. He was the man who'd beat her mother and the reason they'd landed in the arms of the polygamist sect.

Aaron finally looked up from the paperwork and glanced at Bina before turning his gaze to Eve. His face grew paler and the term "bug eyes" came to Eve's mind. She allowed herself an internal grin when she realized why he was having such a strong reaction. It was the first time he'd seen her since she'd chopped off her hair. His creepy fascination with her dark tresses had started when they were children. He liked to push her down and kick her when they were alone, but pulling her hair was something he could get away with when others were around.

The squad had noticed his disturbing interest even though she'd kept it in a tight bun at the nape of her neck when it was long. Today, his face went through a myriad of emotions. Anger, sadness, resignation. As a man of his church, he had complete control over women... and then he ran up against Eve. She had cut her hair to let go of the past and Aaron's reaction was a bonus.

She lifted her hand and flipped the short strands over her shoulder. He swallowed making his large Adam's apple more prevalent. Bina cleared her throat. Aaron's entire display bothered them both. His eyes finally met hers.

"You wanted to see me?"

"We have a report that Linda Wall's baby is missing."

He couldn't hide his startled look or the tightening of his fingers which were threaded together on the folder placed in front of him. This was what she called his self-righteous pose.

"You have been misinformed." He looked away before meeting her gaze again. "I would have heard if Sister Linda had a child."

He was a horrible liar, and that was why she'd wanted to have their conversation face to face.

"Her pregnancy is in my report from Hannah's case. Did you read it?"

His blue irises turned into pinpoints of animosity. Women did not stand up to Aaron and no matter how often she confronted him, he expected her to bow down to the superiority he'd been told he possessed since birth.

"You believed the words of a child who slaughtered her family?" Aaron asked. His question was meant to make her angry. Eve had threatened him with going public with the inside details of the case if he tried to have Hannah locked up in a prison facility. He ended up working with the defense attorney and the judge to get her placed in a psychiatric hospital.

"Unlike you," Eve said. "Why would she lie?"

NINE

As county attorney, Aaron had been the highest law enforcement authority in the area. At least until the prophet went to prison and a federal judge ruled that law enforcement in the county needed oversight. This included Aaron's office and no matter how much he resented it, he answered to Eve.

"Will I need to have you removed from my office?" he asked, his jaw clenched, his eyes furious.

He didn't like being called a liar.

"Go ahead," she told him. "I have a report of an endangered child. I'll have the judge on the phone so fast your head spins. Judge Remki will take this case seriously." Remki was Eve's liaison with the federal judge and oversaw most problems Eve ran into. "The question right now is, will you help or hinder my investigation?"

The pink that had slowly been creeping into his neck and face turned red. He leaned back in his chair and took a moment to gain control of himself. He knew the judge would be on Eve's side.

"Sister Linda cannot have a child. If she did, it would go

against the dictates of the prophet and be considered a child of sin. I would be aware if that were the case."

He'd answered the question the note inside the sock generated without Eve needing to ask him about it. This might be the only thing they learned from this visit, but it was worth it.

"Did you just call an innocent baby a child of sin?" she asked, astounded, anger coming through in the question. Her reaction was foolish because nothing that came from his indoctrinated brain should have surprised her.

"That is what the child would be."

Bina's leg was jumping, and Eve knew Aaron's statements were provoking them both. It was her turn to take a moment. She had to stay calm to find out where Linda and the baby were.

"What about the fathers of one of these innocent children?" she asked, and managed to keep her tone level.

"What about them? Men are tempted by the unholiness of women. Seduction is a woman's sin. Do you know that Sister Linda had a child? If that is the case, I need to notify the high council."

He knew about the baby and was throwing it back in her face. She had no idea what his reasoning was, but it would never be to help her.

"I want to clarify," she said. "A child of sin is a child created without using a seed bearer assigned by the prophet?" Eve needed to be absolutely clear that she understood. Aaron hadn't liked it when she brought up seed bearers at the end of the Tanner case.

"I am not at liberty to discuss this with you." His eyes cut like a knife.

No, he didn't like it that she'd brought it up this time either.

"What happens to the women and babies if a child is born under these circumstances?"

"They leave the community. What do you think happens to them? Do you think we bury them in Babyland?"

It was nearly impossible to stay in her chair. She wanted to reach across the desk for his throat. If she'd had any doubt about his involvement in the crying baby phone calls, they were now put to rest. Any mention of Babyland hurt her emotionally so he'd used it. She also couldn't help wondering if Linda's call was a setup. Women would do whatever their husbands told them. The young wife who threw the sock could also be part of it. Eve was borrowing trouble by having these thoughts, but it was too risky not to consider the possibility.

"Set up an interview with Howard Wall," Eve said. "If Linda and her baby are safe, I'll be out of town quickly."

"Do you have evidence that a crime has been committed?" Aaron asked casually because he'd seen the fury in her eyes over the Babyland comment and he was once again basking in his power. He, however, did not argue about the baby, which told her something.

She couldn't tell him about the note thrown in the sock. If Eve's only lead wasn't part of a giant conspiracy, she didn't want the wife who helped them to disappear as Linda seemed to have.

She'd come here knowing she wouldn't get direct answers but sometimes Aaron slipped up.

"Arrange the interview with Howard Wall. If he gives satisfactory answers, I won't have a case."

He smiled, but it was filled with contempt and didn't meet his eyes.

She stood and Bina did the same.

"Your hair is prettier long," Aaron said right before she walked out.

Eve didn't have an immediate comeback. He hadn't seen her hair down since they were children.

TEN

"Is he always that disgusting?" Bina asked after they were inside the SUV. She was fighting her anger and gripped the steering wheel so tightly her fingers had white splotches.

"He wouldn't be if I brought Collin, Ray, or Clyde. He holds women in contempt. It's part of his indoctrination. You did an excellent job with the secretary and with Aaron. Take a breath."

Bina did exactly that and her fingers loosened, the color returning slowly.

"From the picture of his family on the desk, his wives look similar to him," Bina said. "Is he related to them in any way besides marriage?" Bina didn't usually ask these types of questions.

"The chances are good Aaron's related to all his wives," Eve responded. "I try not to look at the picture. I'm always worried I'll recognize any of them as one of his half-sisters."

"I wish you hadn't said that."

"We're in danger here," Eve said, changing the subject. "Clyde, Collin, and Ray have a degree of safety because they are men. I learned the hard way that they will attack us alone.

I'm ordering you to stay with me or one of the guys when we're here."

"It's an order I have no problem following. I've just had an oversized dose of reality." It was a relief when Bina started the engine. "Where to next?" she asked.

"The Wall residence. We're interviewing every adult inside. Aaron slipped up—he knows about the baby."

"I realized that too." Bina turned in the direction of the Wall home while Eve sent Clyde a text.

Just left Aaron's office. Going back to Wall home to interview everyone.

His reply came in seconds.

Need help?

No, keep the God squad on their toes for now.

Will do.

When they arrived, there was a white heavy-duty pickup truck in the courtyard along with a large eleven-passenger van. It looked like the family was leaving. Eve knew she shouldn't be surprised. The town had a way of hiding members when she needed answers.

"I believe Howard Wall is home," she told Bina.

Bina's facial muscles tightened. Nothing about today was getting easier.

Eve knocked on the door and less than a minute later, Howard Wall jerked it open. He was exactly as Eve remembered—tall and gaunt, in his late forties, with acne scars covering his face. He didn't say anything. He simply looked at Eve with condemnation. Over his shoulder stood a man she'd run into before—and it hadn't been a pleasant meeting. Brother Hammon was somewhere in the prophet's command structure, but Eve had no idea how high up.

They could no longer claim they were there on Hannah's behalf. Aaron would have immediately made phone calls. She suspected Hammon held enough religious authority to call the shots on interfering with any case. She made a mental note to have Tamm look into him.

"Mr. Wall," she said, ignoring the other man. "I have a report that your child was taken and I need to speak with you."

"You are mistaken. My wife was traumatized by her niece's actions and has not been herself for months. She is delusional and under the care of a doctor."

"The person I spoke with felt the baby was in danger. I want to help."

"I am aware my wife called you. I drove her to the hospital early this morning. She is under a doctor's care," Howard repeated. "This is very upsetting for my wives and we are having a family prayer session." He briefly looked in Hammon's direction before turning back to Eve. Hammon said nothing and simply watched the interaction.

Howard Wall was nervous. Hammon had the same effect on Aaron. If Eve had to describe him, "weasel" would be the word that came to mind. Hammon wore a dark suit that hung on his thin frame. He was somewhere in his sixties. He gave off a vibe that left a tingling sensation on the back of her neck. He was the more dangerous man of the two in front of her.

"I need the name of the medical facility Linda was taken to," Eve insisted.

It came to Eve what bothered her about Hammon. She had met the current prophet, who now resided in prison, as a child. He'd visited her home with his father. The prophet possessed the same strange vibes as Hammon. He was not someone you wanted to meet alone in a dark alley and neither was Hammon. Eve decided Hammon needed added attention.

"Mr. Hammon, if I remember your name correctly," she said. "Why are you here?"

"That is not your concern." He looked at Howard Wall and nodded.

Wall slammed the door in their face.

"What now?" asked Bina.

"We're not leaving, but we're sitting in the SUV while we wait for backup. I don't want the Walls disappearing again. If that happens, our only witness besides Linda will vanish too. I'm calling Judge Nelson's office to let him know the warrant is pending."

Judge Nelson was a local and non-fundamentalist. He had helped during Hannah's case. Tamm had discovered him when Eve was desperate. Judges were elected officials. The women in town didn't vote and the men voted only for church members. Eve was still unsure how Nelson had achieved his office. She needed a miracle right now and sent out a silent plea to the universe that she would get one.

She messaged Clyde, requesting that he, Ray, and Collin drive immediately to their location. She then called the judge.

"It's your lucky day," he said after his clerk got him on the phone.

Eve had yet to meet him in person, but it was a relief simply to hear his voice. She was feeling increasingly anxious over Linda and the baby's disappearance.

"Why is it my lucky day?" she asked.

"My vacation starts tomorrow. How may I help you?"

The stars had aligned. She gave him a brief rundown of what she had.

"This doesn't sound like their family reassignment practice. How old is the baby?"

"Allison is a newborn." She used the baby's name on purpose.

"Get the warrant here as soon as you can," he told her.

"Thank you, Your Honor," she replied. Eve had no idea how long he could hold his position as judge, but she was thankful he had it for now. "Can you seal the probable cause statement so I can keep the wife who corroborated the missing baby out of this?"

"I'll speak to my clerk and have her seal the file while I'm on vacation. It will keep the county attorney from obtaining a copy until after my return. I heard a rumor that he's your brother?"

"Stepbrother."

"My deepest sympathies. He's become a thorn in my side."

"He's a dagger in mine, so I understand. Have a good vacation and thank you."

"No promises until I read the warrant."

"Understood." This was how a judge should behave. The system in town had been corrupt for far too long. Judge Nelson was a breath of fresh air in this polluted area. Eve relaxed internally.

Less than a minute later, an unknown SUV pulled next to them, a God squad truck following. Two men inside the dark SUV gave her and Bina hard looks. Hammon walked through the gate and climbed into the backseat.

"Are we letting him go?" asked Bina.

"We don't have enough information to hold him for questioning." Eve watched the vehicle turn the corner through the side mirror at the same time the van with Clyde, Collin, and Ray turned onto the street. A different God squad truck was following them. It drove past and stopped behind the one that had tailed her and Bina.

She lifted the radio mic. They had them set to car-to-car transmission only.

"Stay put," she said. "We'll do this in the van."

"Copy," said Collin.

"I need your warrant skills," she told Ray once they joined the men. "I'll type the probable cause while you do the rest. Bina, explain to Collin and Clyde what we have." Ray would learn the details when he read over the probable cause statement before it was sent to the judge.

"I have the previous one for this house on my computer," Ray said. "Start typing. My end will take five minutes." He handed over her computer case.

"The Wall family is not leaving," Eve told Clyde. "If they try, place them in temporary custody. One of the women in the home has information and I need to speak with her without Howard knowing about it. It will take added time, but I'm interviewing them all."

Clyde nodded. He, Bina, and Collin went to the SUV while Eve and Ray typed.

It took about thirty minutes before she emailed the warrant to the judge. She called his clerk to give him a heads up.

Eve watched another God squad truck pull up next to the other two. She didn't recognize the driver as the one who came with the vehicle that picked up Hammon. She wouldn't be surprised if Aaron came to the scene too.

The judge called after ten minutes of intense waiting.

"Just signed it and emailed back. Good luck."

The van was set up with everything they needed for this kind of work including a solar power supply and portable printer. Ray had two copies of the warrant ready minutes later.

Eve rolled down the van's passenger window and called out to Clyde who was standing at the gate now. He waved to Collin who was at the end of the street. Collin brought Bina who had been watching the Wall home from around the corner.

"We're looking for anything that shows proof a baby was here recently. A crib, bottle, diapers, anything," Eve said when they were all back inside the van. "After the home is secure, I will interview the women one at a time. Questions?" They shook their heads. "Clyde, take over from here," she said.

Clyde had served more warrants in SWAT than the entire team combined. Warrants were dangerous situations and required expert safety measures. Adding to the risk was the team's distance from backup officers they could trust. Clyde took his job seriously and had them train defensive tactics, high-risk vehicle stops, and building clearance on a regular basis. Eve trusted each member on her team enough to hand over command when their specialty came into play, and this was Clyde's.

He'd grabbed a bag from one of the bins. It held radios and he handed them out while speaking. They each had an outer Kevlar vest which also had added pockets for extra gear such as their Tasers. They prepared while Clyde relayed assignments.

"We know the layout of the house," he said. He looked at Eve when she made a small noise. "Okay, everyone but Eve knows."

Due to a concussion caused by her stepbrothers' assault during the Tanner case, Eve had had no choice but to stay in the SUV when the team had gone into the Wall home looking for the murder weapon and any other evidence they could find. The only part of the home Eve had seen was the garage, which was filled with hunting supplies and a dead, smelly deer carcass.

"Ray and Bina, you're taking the back," Clyde continued. "I'll carry the Betty."

The Betty was their door ram. Eve was unsure who'd come up with the nickname, but it had stuck.

"Collin knocks, I'm second, and Eve third," Clyde said. "Collin, you have the children. Everyone will be moved to the front room. There were no guns found in the home during the last warrant, but there were very sharp knives in the garage. If anyone has that twinge telling them something doesn't feel right, call it out immediately. Eve will search the women and girls, I will handle Howard Wall and older juvenile boys."

"Questions?"

They shook their heads.

Clyde looked at Eve to see if she wanted to add anything. She didn't. With only five of them, they were spread thin for these large home warrants. The state had first agreed to fund a four-person oversight team plus a secretary. Eve had fought for the fifth position with Tamm's help. Tamm had gone through state police case files and pulled numerous search warrants and homicide investigations listing the number of people needed to conclude the case with a guilty verdict. They couldn't argue with Tamm's analysis and Eve got the extra funding. When they ran into dangerous situations, Eve could use twice as many detectives on the team, but they made it work because they were highly trained and among the best investigators in the state.

"Spread out as soon as we clear the van for a fast radio check. It's time," Clyde said after the okay from Eve.

They jumped from the van and fanned out, each holding up a hand when Clyde's transmission came through.

"Here we go," he said.

ELEVEN

They moved quickly through the gate and to the front door. Bina and Ray went to the back and would be called around after the team were inside if no one tried to leave.

Howard Wall answered as soon as Collin knocked. He quickly pulled a copy of the warrant from the back of his belt and handed it over.

"Search warrant," he said, and pushed past Howard, who didn't appear surprised.

"Everyone downstairs including the children," Clyde told Howard in his deep authoritative voice. He had Howard lift his arms and began patting him down, telling him what they would be doing.

The older woman Eve had spoken with earlier was at the bottom of the stairway.

"You're coming with me to gather the women and children and bring them down here," Eve told her. "Is there anyone else on the bottom floor?" she asked.

The woman shook her head then looked at her husband. Eve's team didn't have their guns drawn and things would run smoothly if everyone cooperated. Clyde told Howard Wall exactly that.

The older woman preceded Eve up a few steps just as a young man tried to walk inside the front door. Collin stopped him.

"Three men in the courtyard," he told Clyde, and blocked the younger man's body with his arm on the doorframe.

Someone must have ordered them to approach the house and cause trouble. Hammon was most likely behind it.

Clyde keyed his radio.

"855, 854, to the front."

"Step away from the door," Ray called from outside the home a moment later.

Eve ran downstairs when Collin was pushed back against the wall. He lunged forward and made it outside before she did. Bina had her Taser pulled on a third young man while Collin and Ray subdued the first two and cuffed them.

The man Bina guarded raised his hands.

"I'll go back out to my vehicle," he said.

"You'll go to jail if you enter the courtyard again," Eve told him. She turned to Collin and Ray. "Bring the other two inside. They can sit with the children since that's what they are acting like."

Maybe she should have held Hammon as an investigative lead. Detaining people was a fine line and sometimes seen as harassment. He had every right to visit the home, but Eve knew he was more involved than she could prove right now.

The men, their expressions sullen, were led to the door with a steady hand on their forearms. The one who pushed Collin tried to jerk away before he went inside. Collin's thumb and knuckle dug into a nerve behind the young man's ear and he cried out. As soon as Collin let up, he struggled again.

"Calm down or you'll be kissing cement until we're finished," Collin told him sternly.

They were placed on their butts against the wall in the gathering room, one looking down, the other staring defiantly at Collin. The gathering room was what most US families referred to as the living room. The fundamentalists used it for family prayer gatherings.

Eve didn't want to book them into jail, but it might happen. She realized they were little more than boys. To be on the God squad they had to be eighteen, but they looked younger.

Eve's attention returned to the senior wife who remained on the stairs. For the first time she appeared nervous. Eve waved her forward and followed her to the second floor.

"Are there any weapons in the house?" Eve asked.

"No."

The women and children, all at least eight and older, stood in the hallway. The senior wife told Eve they were all accounted for when she asked. She had them remain in the hallway while she checked each room.

In all, there were seven wives and fifteen children. Two of the boys were teens. Everyone followed directions and didn't panic when she checked the women and children for weapons. They didn't speak or cry, not even the youngest ones.

During the first months in the community, the team had been surprised at the lack of emotion, especially in the young children. They were taught to keep sweet, even the boys, until they were old enough to work outside the home. Emotion was seen as a weakness before God. Tears were punished. Still, she knew the youngest were frightened even if they didn't show it. She tried to reassure them. They wouldn't look at her. Children never went anywhere alone and did not speak to strangers. This went far beyond Stranger Danger taught in schools around the US. Polygamists lived in secrecy because their way of life was a crime. Children were trained to never jeopardize the family. Satan, his helpers, and the fires of hell were a potent deterrent.

The two teenage boys wore pants and shirtsleeves and she

didn't see bulging pockets or anything that would identify a weapon. Clyde could search them. When possible, Eve and her team followed the community's religious protocol that said older boys and girls never touched the opposite sex, unless married. So far, they'd been able to do it without compromising safety.

"Downstairs," Eve told them when her search concluded. "We'll get this done as quickly as possible." She smiled and softened her voice for the benefit of the young ones.

They walked down the stairs in single file, the teen boys in front, Eve behind the group. She directed them to the gathering room. This was where they held daily prayer. Her gaze turned briefly to the teenagers in handcuffs. They were both looking at the floor now.

"I've searched the women and children," she told Clyde, and nodded to the two older boys. "They're yours." She turned away.

"Sister Wall," Eve told the senior wife, "I'll interview you first and then you can stay with the women and children while I interview the other adults."

"I will not speak with you," she said bluntly.

"That works. I'll escort you to our vehicle and put handcuffs on you out there so the children don't need to watch me do it in front of them. When I'm done speaking with the adults in the home, I will bring you back inside."

Eve couldn't make her talk, but by separating her from the others, she could make sure the woman couldn't give them cues on how to act or what to say. Eve used authoritative tactics because it was the only way to gain cooperation. Women and children were accustomed to taking orders. Maybe someday this would change, but for now, it was the fastest way to help Linda and her newborn.

The woman looked at her husband. He gave Eve a look of death and then a slight nod to his wife. Her gaze met Eve's.

"I will speak with you," she said.

"Where can we talk that we won't be disturbed?"

"Use my office," Howard said.

Eve followed senior Mrs. Wall to the office. Once a husband capitulated, things usually went smoothly. It was why Eve gave her instructions in front of him. The interviews had to be completed as swiftly as possible. The longer it took, the higher the chance of additional interference. She also expected Aaron on scene any moment.

She'd heard Clyde order Bina and Ray to remain out front to keep everyone from entering. Hopefully Aaron would give Bina a reason to tase him. The God squad idiots had slowed the warrant, but they wouldn't stop it. The team worked cohesively and they'd learned to improvise when needed.

She entered Howard's office. It was sparse with a wooden desk, a nearly empty bookcase, and one extra chair other than his. There was an old family portrait on the wall behind his desk. He'd had three wives and six children at the time the picture was taken. She recognized his senior wife though she was younger in the photo. Linda Wall wasn't in the picture and Eve wondered how long they had been married and if Howard was her first husband.

The office reminded Eve of her stepfather's. It was where he handed out discipline. She had hated the sound of the door closing. One of his favorite tactics was starvation and Eve had gone to bed many nights without dinner. She shook off the memories and pulled the desk chair around so the two seats were about two feet apart and faced each other. She then took a small notebook from her pocket along with a pen. Her recorder was running but it was easier to remember the wives' names if she kept a written list.

"I need your name and date of birth," Eve said.

"Barbara Wall, July 15, 1975," she answered.

She was in her early forties.

"Where is Linda?" Eve asked bluntly. There was a reason for the direct question. Eve wanted her off balance. She would fight Eve on even the smallest bit of information.

Barbara's lips compressed and she remained silent.

"I can't make you speak with me, but the sooner you do then the sooner we're out of here and your life can go back to normal."

"I do not know where Linda is. Husband took her to the hospital this morning."

Eve knew this was a lie. Fundamentalist families did not pay for medical treatment unless they were forced to. A mental health facility was outside their Band-Aid and Neosporin budget.

"You saw Linda before she left?"

"Yes."

"What was she wearing?"

"A dress like mine."

"Did she appear distraught?"

Barbara looked around for a moment, her expression anxious.

"This is a felony investigation," Eve said, "which makes it a crime to lie." She repeated the question. She was also studying Barbara's movements. In a perfect scenario, this interview would be recorded with audio and video and another detective would watch to pick up on behavioral clues. This was another example of how the team adapted to the difficult circumstances that arose within the fundamentalist community. Eve had grown accustomed to doing the interviews on her own.

"No, she was not distraught," Barbara finally uttered stiffly. Her fingers were joined in her lap and they started tightening and loosening subtly. Her shoulders were lowering the more disconcerted she became and there was a minuscule drop of her chin, but Eve noticed.

Howard had told Barbara and the other wives what to say but hadn't thought about Linda's mental condition. Barbara was realizing how their lies would not match. He'd probably told the wives what to say as soon as he'd closed the door in her and Bina's faces, realizing they wouldn't be able to escape. This was customary. Eve was groomed as a child to lie to the authorities if she were ever questioned. Child services were a threat to their family and lifestyle. The days and nights with no food would have had Eve quickly removed from her home, but she never would have told the truth. No one ever questioned her and the abuse she suffered was never reported. She and her siblings had all taken their punishments in silence. Eve had lived with so much guilt over the disappearance of Charlie and Becky. She'd asked herself a million times why she hadn't gone to the police. Now she knew they wouldn't have helped, but at least she would have tried.

"What day was the baby born?" she asked next, shaking off the thoughts that shadowed her adult life. She'd been a child and she needed to forgive herself.

Barbara looked confused over Eve's question. She'd expected Eve to ask if there was a baby.

"Umm." She hesitated. "Sister Linda did not have a child," she finally recited stubbornly.

"Will we find baby items in the house? We'll also search the outside garbage."

"I do not know what you will find."

It wasn't a no which meant it was likely a yes. Eve let it go. The search would give them clues. They needed solid evidence. The next interview would be with the wife who tossed the note which would help build the case.

"If I ask the children, will they mention the baby?"

"No."

Again, she didn't reiterate that there was no child. Barbara was fidgeting in the chair now. The longer she was in the office, the more obvious her lies became and she had no idea how to save herself.

Howard would have told the children the baby didn't exist and that was what they would say. Eve had no intention of interviewing them and making them lie. She wanted it known in town that her team didn't pursue anyone underage if it were at all possible. It was time to let Barbara off the hook. If something bad happened to the baby, this interview would come back to haunt her, Eve would see to it.

"I'll follow you downstairs and you can stand with the others. If the children need anything, let Detective Smith know. He will have introduced himself as Collin. He's Mormon and has four children of his own. He will help you if you need it."

Eve followed Barbara back into the front of the house and asked the younger wife who had thrown the sock to follow her.

"I'll be quick so no one suspects you have given me information," Eve told her after she closed the door to Howard's office.

The woman's hands shook nervously. When she sat in the chair, she folded them on her lap to keep them still. Eve handed her a business card. It had her cell number on it.

"Call me if there is trouble."

"Thank you." The woman placed the card in her pocket. Her cheeks were slightly pink, her blue eyes were jumping around nervously, but she hadn't hesitated in taking the card.

Eve knew from her experience as a child inside the community that girls, though forbidden, hid notes from young men. She would hide the card somewhere it wouldn't be discovered.

"What is your name and date of birth?" Eve asked.

"Danielle Wall, March 3, 1996."

Danielle was too young to marry a man of Howard Wall's age, but this was typical in the community and she was of legal age.

"I appreciate how you've tried to help. I need to know what happened to Linda and her child."

Danielle's hands stopped moving and she slowly inhaled.

"Someone took Allison, but I do not know who." Her words were slow and steady. "Husband was upset for a few hours but then became angry over Sister Linda's refusal to keep sweet. She would not stop crying about the baby and she was finally sent to her room as punishment. We were told not to speak of the child again."

"Linda told me her baby was in danger. Is that true?"

"Yes, she is in danger too. You spoke with Sister Linda?"

"Early this morning before she disappeared. Linda called and asked me to help find Allison," Eve replied. "Could you tell me what condition the baby was in the last time you saw her?" There were multiple reasons for this question. With Eve's baby sister and brother's unsolved disappearances, she wanted to establish if Allison suffered from any visible genetic problems. Eve was determined that one day, she would find a judge who saw Babyland as the horror it was and help her find conclusive answers. Eve also needed to establish the overall health of the child before she'd disappeared for prosecutorial reasons.

"Allison was tiny, but she nursed well. She did not often cry. I only saw her twice, but she appeared in good health."

"How was Linda's labor?" Eve asked next.

"I only know she delivered early. Allison cried right away and I was relieved."

"Thank you. Is there anything else you know that would help me locate Allison and Linda?"

"My birth sister, umm, biological sister, Adella, also had a child of sin. He was taken away the day after his birth. Adella does not know what became of him. When she refused to remain silent, she was placed in isolation for six months. I think that is possibly where Sister Linda is now."

"Isolation? Please explain," Eve asked. The ease with which Danielle had called the baby a child of sin made the hairs on the back of Eve's neck stand up. She'd said it in the note too. It was hard to hear a baby described this way. Aaron had used the same words. It wasn't Danielle's fault. She referred to the child as it was taught to her. It was so incredibly sad.

The other reason Eve felt disturbed was far more personal. For now, she needed to stay on track to help Linda and her baby. Eve would delve into her personal thoughts when she had time.

"Isolation is cruel," Danielle said, and crossed her arms, her fingers rubbing the sleeves of her dress. "I fear it as punishment above all others." She stared around the office, her anxiety almost tangible in the air. Her gaze finally came back to Eve's. "Adella told me she was kept in a trailer with little food or water. The conditions were horrible and she is terrified she will be sent back. Adella changed after her return. She is no longer the light-hearted sister I grew up with. She lives in fear and I worry for her."

The next questions would be difficult, but Eve needed both the location of the trailer and to speak with Adella.

"Do you know where this trailer is?"

"No." She shook her head. "I do not."

"Even a general location would help."

"My sister never told me. I tried to get her to talk more about her time in isolation because I thought it would help her, but she cried whenever I asked. I had never known her to shed tears. She is truly terrified."

"What would be the best way to speak with her?"

"At her home but they would know I told you. Please do not do this to me or my sister. They might send us both to isolation." Her eyes had grown larger in panic but her voice firmer. She wanted Eve to understand how dangerous this was for her.

"I don't want to cause trouble for either of you. Could you give her my phone number and ask her to call me?"

"I can, but she will be upset. I do not know if she will call you. Since her return, she has had nightmares and does not sleep well. Her husband forbids his wives from using his phone, but she calls me sometimes when he sleeps. I try to calm her and sometimes sing while she cries. She is so afraid she will be sent back."

Songs were one of the few joys women had. They revolved around God and the prophet, many made up in homes like this one and shared at assembly. The prophet made recordings of his songs and wives often listened to him sing while they worked.

"It's vital for Linda and her baby that I speak with your sister. I will try to respect her decision if she does not contact me." Eve switched gears, needing to take Danielle's thoughts away from her sister's fear. Eve would not make promises she couldn't keep. She couldn't press any harder for Adella's help. Danielle would do what she could. "Have you heard anything, even a rumor, about Adella's baby once it was taken away?" she asked. Eve refused to call them children of sin.

Danielle's eyes teared up and she lowered her head.

"Adella was told her son was given back to God. He was her only child. She thinks he is dead."

TWELVE

After the prophet's arrest, a judge decreed that all births within the fundamentalist community had to be recorded. Jail sentences and fines were stiff if families were caught hiding a baby's delivery. Eve now had a frightening suspicion that children born outside the prophet's laws were possibly murdered. It was a horrible realization that could only be carried out if there were no birth certificates.

Girls as young as eleven were turned over to the prophet so he could assign them in marriage. Depending on their age, they were often sent to other states or countries and passed off as the husband's daughter. It was one of the horrors uncovered during the federal investigation. The community didn't see this as wrong. Once again, females were a commodity. Birth certificates weren't much but offered one way to help protect these girls.

Like Hannah's case, this one was uncovering dangerous secrets. It was hard to comprehend "children of sin", the reason they were called this, and isolation for mothers who objected to their newborn babies being stolen. Eve's mind was trying to wrap what she'd learned from Danielle into a neat package because the ramifications of this information were beyond horrifying. The biggest question in her head was, how many children did this involve?

"Thank you for your help," she told Danielle, doing her best to suppress her troubled thoughts. "I won't keep you any longer or the others will be suspicious."

"Please find Linda and baby Allison." Her eyes were now dry. She held her head high and met Eve's gaze. Danielle was an extraordinarily strong woman.

"I will do everything I can," Eve promised.

When Eve followed her back to the front, Clyde and Bina were searching room by room downstairs. The children were on the floor or the couch beside their mothers. The two young men in handcuffs sat quietly, their heads still down. It was a calmer atmosphere. Howard stood by one of the couches, Collin by the other.

"Ray is outside guarding the front," Collin said, nodding toward the door. "The county attorney is out there and he isn't happy that he can't come in."

Aaron was here to hinder the investigation and his interference could wait.

By now the entire town would be aware that something big had happened involving Eve's team. She remembered her stepfather coming home from work early a few times when she was young. He reminded their family that strangers were not to be invited inside the home and reiterated they were never to talk to non-members. All the lights in the house would be turned off and the children sent to their rooms where they were to remain quiet. Sometimes this went on for days. Eve would hear her stepmothers talking about the evils of the state police and child services after the danger passed. Secrets and hiding were a way of life. The oversight team was now the community's biggest threat.

Eve checked the time. She was exhausted, but the day

wasn't close to being over. Nothing new was learned from the five remaining wives. They reacted as Barbara had. Eve made them aware they would be subject to prosecution if she discovered they lied. It didn't change their story.

Howard Wall was the last interview.

"I can't force you to speak to me," Eve told him after she sat in one of his office chairs. "If I catch you lying, you will be charged with felony interference. My only goal is to find your baby." She didn't mention Linda because Howard *was* responsible for her disappearance. Eve hoped he had a small bit of compassion for his child, but she knew it was doubtful and the chances were good, he knew exactly who had the baby. She was not a fan of Howard Wall. He had done everything he could including disappearing with Hannah to keep Eve from discovering the truth about the Tanner murders. Maintaining an even tone in the face of his failure to keep his baby and Hannah safe, wasn't easy. "Please state your name and date of birth."

"Howard Wall, June 16, 1972."

"Tell me about Allison's birth," she said.

Howard's lips tightened into a firm line. He held eye contact and remained silent.

"Don't you want to find your child?" she tried.

Silence.

"You can be prosecuted if anything happens to the baby."

Howard's chin lifted higher and his shoulders went back. His eyes drilled hers with contempt.

"There is no baby. I refuse to speak to Satan's daughter. You were raised properly and know you are damned to hell. I will spit upon your grave."

He'd lost his cool. That wasn't a bad thing.

"We need your help. You're aware Linda called me. She was distraught. She said you were upset too. We need to make sure Allison is safe." Eve hoped using the baby's name would touch some part of his cold heart.

"You and your people will burn in the fires of hell. I refuse to answer your unholy questions."

The interview was over.

Clyde and Bina had finished the lower floor and gone upstairs to search before she'd interviewed the last two wives and Howard Wall. They were waiting by the front door when she returned to the gathering room with Howard.

"Detective Blau," she said to Bina. "Please go upstairs with the women and children until we clear the house." Clyde had a plain paper bag at his feet. It would contain evidence and she wanted to know what he and Bina had found.

Eve lifted her chin to Collin and he returned a small nod. He would watch Howard closely.

"There was a broken-down crib in the corner of the garage that wasn't there during our last warrant. It's in the van. We found dirty diapers in a bag in the garage." Clyde spoke softly so they weren't overheard. "They're tiny and look like preemie diapers." His jaw was locked, showing his anger. A premature baby was an added danger. They had to find her.

"We're taking him into custody," she told him.

Eve walked to Howard and Clyde stepped behind him.

"Howard Wall. You are under arrest for child endangerment and lying during a felony investigation." Eve took a card from her pocket and read him his rights. Even though she knew them by heart, a Miranda card was critical in these situations. If she was asked about Miranda on the witness stand, it kept her from stumbling if she had to recite the rights to the jury. She would take the card out and read from it exactly as she did now with Howard.

He looked down on her with all his superiority wrapped tightly around him and remained silent.

"Do you understand these rights?" Eve asked from the last line on the card.

"You will burn for eternity," he said.

Eve ignored him. His prophesies needed an update. He hadn't asked for an attorney and she could still question him. She radioed Bina and Ray while Clyde held on to Howard Wall's upper arm.

"We're clearing out. Three in custody."

Bina came down the stairs quickly and Barbara followed her halfway. Eve could arrest six out of seven wives for lying, but Eve didn't want to give Danielle away for helping them and it would only hurt any headway she'd made at all within the community. If the baby or Linda were harmed, she would change her current position.

"Detective Blau, we're escorting the two men." Eve was purposely shaming them by having her and Bina as escorts. She wanted them to think about interfering in the future even knowing her thoughts were futile. They would always follow commands.

Barbara stayed where she was and watched them open the front door and walk out. Clyde led her husband outside, through the courtyard, and to the SUV. The two men were next with Bina and Eve holding each by an arm so they didn't trip with the handcuffs on.

Aaron waited outside the gate. Collin had understated his anger. He was furious and his body language and expression showed it. His face was so red he might have a coronary.

"I'm unhandcuffing you both. You will go to your vehicles and leave or you will go to jail," she told the two young men without looking at Aaron. "I don't want to see you again today. Do you understand?"

They remained silent.

"The cuffs are not coming off until you answer me. Do you understand?" she repeated.

One added "ma'am" to his "yes" and the other grunted a "yes." Eve released them.

Bina had the bag of evidence beneath her arm and took it to the van.

"I want to speak with you immediately," Aaron demanded. She watched the two men walk to their trucks and get inside. She held up her palm toward Aaron while she made sure they drove away. When they were off the street, she didn't bother looking at her stepbrother and headed to the van. He tried to follow.

"Call my office and make an appointment," she told him. "This is a felony investigation and Howard Wall is under arrest."

"What for?" Aaron practically spit the two words at her.

"It will be in the booking paperwork."

Clyde sat in the driver's seat of the SUV.

"Go with Clyde," she told Bina who had walked up beside her. Eve continued ignoring Aaron. "I want to look at what you found before I speak with Howard again at the jail. Turn on your recorder in case he makes voluntary statements, but don't ask questions."

Her stepbrother listened, but there was nothing he could do. She hoped he would try to give Howard a heads up to keep his mouth shut. It would make her day because she would give the recording to Judge Remki.

"Got it," Bina said.

Eve climbed into the van, Ray behind her with Collin at the wheel.

"We're going to the jail," she told them.

Aaron stood alone, watching the team drive away. One God squad truck remained with the third young man she hadn't handcuffed. He followed behind them.

Eve put on gloves then lifted the brown paper bag and placed it in her lap. She opened it where it folded at the top. The first thing she pulled out was a small pink baby blanket. It smelled like a baby and she hesitated before she placed it back inside and removed another smaller bag. It held three soiled diapers. She lifted one out. It was much too small and looked as if it would fit a baby doll. The ball in Eve's stomach tightened and grew colder. She looked around the van to keep her tears at bay. Her gaze landed on the pieces of a white crib stowed behind the bench seat in front of her.

Linda would have breastfed. When Eve grew up, she'd never known one of her moms not to. Allison had been away from her mother more than two days now. Eve had to find them both and it had to happen quickly. She couldn't allow the weight of the case to bury her and she began counting backward by three to gain control and not give in to the emotions that were closing in.

THIRTEEN

The jail had a small interview room that Eve had used before. It was most likely wired for video and audio but getting her hands on it could be a problem. She kept her recorder running. She'd brought Collin inside with her in case Howard was more receptive to him.

"We found evidence of a young baby at your home," she told Howard. "Would you care to explain?"

"I will speak to an attorney, not to you," he said with finality.

There was nothing more Eve could ask him and she couldn't give Collin a shot now that Howard asked for an attorney. If there were a can close by, she would have kicked it. She reminded herself that Howard believed children belonged to God and not to the parents. He didn't care what happened to Allison.

She filled out the booking paperwork and walked out of the jail with her mind on a million different things. Collin followed her back to the van. He was deep in thought too. They still had no idea where the baby was and time was running out.

"I'm going to ride with Clyde and Bina. You and Ray take the warrant return to the courthouse," she told him.

"We'll pick up lunch on our way back if that works for you?" Collin asked.

Eve was upset and she wasn't hungry. Lack of sleep was giving her a headache. If she didn't eat and rest, she would crash and burn.

"That sounds good. See you at the room." She walked to the back door of the SUV and looked at the two black trucks. God squad security had expanded by one while she was inside the jail. One followed the van as Collin and Ray drove away and the other stuck with the SUV. She didn't notice either of the two men she'd warned. Lucky for them because Eve would have made another arrest and been angry over the wasted time.

A text came in on Eve's cell.

I'm feeding Daisy and I've let your mom know. I'm free for the next six weeks and then go on vacation.

Eve was a horrible cat mother. With everything going on, she had forgotten to check in with Katie. Eve typed back.

Thank you.

The parking lot was almost empty when they arrived at the hotel. It catered to truckers who parked their big rigs in the lot next door where the God squad usually waited. The owner of the hotel had placed Eve and the team's rooms on the opposite side so they didn't need to listen to truck engines warming up in the morning. The drivers arrived in the late afternoon and usually left before 5 a.m.

Clyde went to his room and said he would meet up with the team when Ray and Collin arrived with lunch. Eve was sure he wanted to lie down and grab a quick nap. She had the same idea. Bina looked no worse for her lack of sleep, but the expression Eve had noticed earlier was back with added ferocity.

Eve pulled out her keycard, slid it through the scanner, and stepped inside when the small light turned green. She almost tripped when she noticed a square folded paper under her foot.

"Stay back," she told Bina, and pointed to the notebook paper.

"Could it be from the hotel?"

"I doubt it. Their bills are printed on computer paper. Grab my camera from the SUV."

Bina returned with the camera a moment later. She also carried plastic gloves and a manila envelope which Eve placed on the table next to where she stood. The note looked as if it had been pushed under the door, but Eve couldn't see that there was enough space between the door and carpet to slide it between the two. The door had to be gently shoved to open it all the way because it grabbed the carpet.

The note was everyday school-notebook paper, folded several times.

"Did you check the bathroom or behind the beds?" Bina asked.

"No, I haven't entered farther into the room."

Bina drew her gun and slowly walked through the room.

"Clear," she said a moment later, and her gun went back into its holster.

Eve snapped two photos, put the gloves on, and picked up the note. She slowly unfolded it.

I have information about the missing baby.

   Meet me behind the abandoned tire shop two blocks from the hotel 8 p.m. tomorrow night.

It wasn't signed.

"It's easy to guess which room we stayed in," Bina said,

peering over Eve's shoulder. "But I don't see how it could be pushed beneath the door."

"We're in agreement. I'll speak with the hotel's owner. I've seen her and one other woman, cleaning the rooms. Someone with a key card left this here." Eve and Bina made their beds each morning they stayed at the hotel because they used the room for their meetings. She couldn't tell if it had been cleaned.

Eve snapped a photo of the note first with her camera, then her cell phone so she could show it to the guys. She placed the note in the manila envelope, sealed it, and marked the date and time on the outside. She gazed around the room and decided to keep it in the side pocket of her suitcase so it wasn't left out in plain sight. She would enter it into evidence and store it in the van's locker after Ray and Collin returned.

Bina followed her to the front office. The owner sat behind the counter, working on a computer. She looked up and smiled when they approached.

"Hi," Eve said, and handed her a business card.

"My name is Harina. How may I help you?" the woman asked with a smile. Her perfect English was slightly accented. It was the first time she'd offered her name. She wore a beautiful blue saree, with a lighter blue design dyed into the material. She was somewhere between forty and fifty years old. Eve had seen her wearing jeans and a T-shirt or dressed as she was now. She didn't appear intimidated by the closed-minded people in town and Eve had liked her from the first time they'd checked into this newer hotel.

"There was a note under my door and I wonder if you know who left it there?" Eve asked.

The woman's expression turned guarded and the smile disappeared. Her eyes jumped to Bina and back to Eve's.

"Please don't be alarmed," Eve reassured her. "I was simply surprised to find a note inside my room and it wasn't signed."

"I placed the note in your room. I did not read it," she assured Eve.

Eve smiled and Harina's shoulders relaxed.

"Who asked you to deliver it?"

The woman nodded and her smile returned.

"He is a kind man. He works at the deli inside the market. I saw him this morning and he asked about the woman officer who stays at my hotel. He said to give you the note, but you were not there after I returned from the market. I opened the door and placed it directly inside."

Part of the mystery was solved even though Eve still had no idea who the man was. People in this area were not friendly to outsiders or anyone different from them. His kindness to Harina struck Eve as odd.

"Do you know his name?" she asked.

"The badge he wears says Eric."

"What about his last name?"

"I am sorry, only Eric."

"You have been very helpful," Eve told her. "Thank you."

A last name would be better, but she would take what she could get.

"Thank you for being our guest."

Eve went out with Bina slightly behind her. They were halfway back to the room when Bina nudged her side.

"Three o'clock," she said.

Across the parking lot, approximately twenty-five feet away, there were two large white trucks. The tinted windows did not obscure the faces of the four men sitting inside watching them.

Eve stopped walking and Bina stayed beside her. The truck doors opened and the men stepped out. Eve recognized them, but she could only put the correct names to two.

"My stepbrothers have come for a visit," she said. "Goon one on the driver's side of the vehicle on the right is Mark and goon two from the left driver's side is Patrick. The younger ones are up for grabs because they were babies when I last saw them. One is missing."

"Oh goody, a family reunion." Bina didn't sound the least bit happy.

The Owen family genes were impossible to miss. Their sickly pale skin was a dead giveaway. Her heart rate had accelerated. The last time she'd faced them, they tried to kill her by stoning her to death with rocks. She'd ended up in the emergency room.

"A definite resemblance to Aaron," Bina said. "It's not a compliment."

Eve almost smiled.

"What do you think they want?" Bina asked, her hand resting on the gun in her holster.

"They're cowards," Eve said in a low voice. "They're here to intimidate. We won't escalate the situation if we can help it." They were both armed and her stepbrothers didn't appear to have weapons although Eve knew they could carry at their backs. She wasn't taking her eyes off them. The SUV was parked feet away and they could take cover behind it if they needed to.

The men had moved to the front of the trucks and stood shoulder to shoulder.

"Is that all they have?" Bina asked. She sounded as if she were ready for a physical fight.

"This was the same greeting they gave me outside Aaron's office during the Tanner case," she replied. "We may be blessed with the word 'abomination' if they're using the same playbook."

"He who holds eye contact longest wins." Bina let out a long breath, her right hand not moving from the butt of her gun.

"We'll win," Eve replied.

FOURTEEN

It took Eve a moment to calm herself and regain control of her heart rate. She didn't fidget or take her eyes away from them. Bina's confidence and willingness to take them on helped.

Eve remembered the prophet's trial transcript that she'd read after his sentencing.

During the closing statements, the prophet stood and faced the judge. He let his eyes do the talking and his mouth didn't move. His silence lasted forty-five minutes. He then held each juror's eyes for two minutes. The jurors held their ground the same as the judge. This man had committed unimaginable crimes against children. Before he took his seat, his gaze returned to the judge and he said, "I'm at peace."

The standoff between Eve and her brothers continued. She estimated it had gone on for five minutes. Her phone rang and she lifted it so she could see the caller ID without dropping her gaze. It was Aaron. She placed the phone to her ear.

"Convenient timing," she said while staring at the goons.

"What is that supposed to mean?" He didn't sound happy, but neither did she.

"Your brothers are attempting to intimidate me and my

detective at the hotel. It's like a western duel. Neither side has drawn their weapons."

"What are you talking about?" he demanded, his voice rising an octave.

"They are across the parking lot standing in front of their vehicles," she simplified. "Did you put them up to this?"

"I'll call you back." The call disconnected.

Seconds later, Mark, a step down in age from Aaron but the oldest of the group in front of her, took his phone from his pocket and placed it to his ear. He listened for a moment and then said something Eve couldn't hear. He appeared angry. He put the phone back in his pocket and spoke to the other men. With a last look of contempt, they got inside the trucks, revved the engines, and made sure they burned rubber on their way out of the parking lot.

"That's a win," said Bina without smiling. "It's also bullshit."

"They're thugs."

They had just walked inside the room and closed the door when her phone rang.

"Yes?" she answered.

"I did not tell them to pull that stunt. I need you to come to my office," Aaron said.

"Your needs are not high on my priority list. A baby's life is in danger."

"You have no idea what you're messing with," he told her stubbornly.

It sounded like the threat it was.

"By now, I would think you would come up with a better warning. My job description is *messing* with the corrupt law enforcement in this town and that includes you. I don't care if I've angered the men you answer to. My only concern is a baby small enough to need preemie diapers." Her voice rose. "They were three inches across, made for a tiny defenseless infant.

This threat is one you need to take seriously. Stay out of my way." Each word was precise and perfectly clear.

Eve hung up the phone wishing it were the one in her office and she could slam the receiver down. She looked at Bina.

"Danielle, the woman who threw the sock, told me her birth sister's baby was taken for being a child of sin. Her name is Adella. She thinks her child is dead and the case is very similar to this one. Too similar. I have no way of getting in touch with her without causing trouble for her and Danielle. I'm not sure why I even care at this point. Babies' lives hang in the balance."

Bina's expression changed to the one Eve had noticed earlier. It was somewhere between sad and furious.

"There's more," Eve said. She told Bina about the isolation trailer and Adella's fear.

When she finished speaking, Bina got up and went into the bathroom. She needed time and maybe she was upset that Eve didn't want to approach Adella. Guilt ate at her and still she couldn't stop thinking about the years her mother was missing and the isolation trailer Adella was placed in. Looking back, Eve remembered Maggie's terror for years after Eve was rescued from the cult. When Eve was older, she thought it was worry that Eve would be kidnapped and returned to the cult. Maybe the fear went beyond that. Maybe her mother had been kept someplace where she was isolated with little food or water.

A lack of sleep was making Eve's anger worse and she felt like throwing something. At least there was a trash can in the room if the desire to kick a can returned. She sat on the bed and lay back against the pillows, staring up at the ceiling.

Bina came out and sat on her own bed.

"We have a baby reported missing, and we have corroboration that there is a baby," Eve said, holding up one finger. "Now the mother is missing." The second finger came up. "We're getting no cooperation from the family." Three. She held up the fourth finger. "We have a note with limited information from a man named Eric. That's it. There's got to be someone who will help."

Eve rolled slightly so she faced Bina who was looking at her. The sadness was gone, replaced by evident fury.

"Something's bothering you," Eve said the obvious. "If you want to tell me to mind my own business, go for it."

Bina exhaled slowly. It looked to Eve like she was searching for words. Eve gave her time.

"It's this town, this cult, this secrecy," she said at last. "Any other place and the entire community would be out searching for a missing baby. Grid lines, media attention, posters. We're lucky we even received a phone call from the mother. They don't care about children. They don't care about women. Howard Wall should have human decency, but he does not. The other women in his home covered for him." Bina's voice cracked. As she looked away, she wiped the side of her eye.

Bina had as much trouble showing strong emotion as Eve did and she was at a breaking point. Eve gave her a moment. Bina's gaze came back to hers.

"Do you need to return to the office?" Eve asked. Bina was vital but her sanity was more important. They had worked on one horrible case after another, then had to investigate the Tanner murders. Now this.

"I want it to stop," Bina said. "I want the people here to care." She didn't speak for a moment.

Eve gave her time to put her feelings into words. She felt more than anything that Bina needed to talk and get this out. But who was Eve to understand someone's emotional turmoil when she faced so many demons herself? It was frustrating that she didn't have the perfect words to help her friend.

"In our cases we see babies and toddlers," Bina said. "It always reminds me that their mothers were subjected to forced breeding. There is no possible way men with so many wives will not have sex with them. It goes against human nature.

Without birth control, babies are the consequence. How many newborns have been taken from their mothers or worse?"

Eve had wondered the same thing.

"I was raised on the Navajo reservation here in Utah," Bina continued. "My family lived in a hogan until I was thirteen. We had no running water or electricity and the floor was dirt."

Bina had never mentioned this before. Eve only knew she'd grown up on the Navajo reservation. Eve had seen hogans at a distance along the highway but knew little about them.

"My grandparents lived with us," she added. "We didn't have much." Her lips formed a soft smile. "We didn't know that." Her eyes traveled to the window with its closed curtains, but Eve knew she wasn't seeing it. "It didn't matter how little we had. My parents loved us. They would die for our family. In this town they have these big houses with numerous women and children, but they don't see love. How do the women live like this? I've tried to understand the generational brainwashing and separate the crimes we solve from their beliefs and not judge. I've failed. I'm angry. I don't understand why they continue this way. Their prophet is in prison. He's a monster and still they follow him."

Eve should have seen this coming. It was hard enough for her and she had grown up here. The team accepted her explanations about the cult's beliefs and rarely questioned her unless it was for clarity. Both Collin and Ray were more vocal about some of the irrational things they uncovered during cases. Bina had always seemed to take it in stride. When they discovered Hannah murdered her family, Bina had accepted it more easily than the rest of them or so it seemed.

"I don't want to make this about me," Eve told her honestly, "but I can only explain the indoctrination through the eyes of my childhood. You know some of it."

Bina nodded and lowered her gaze to her hands. "I don't wish this to be painful for you," she said. "I want to do my job.

My anger is interfering. It started before Hannah. It was even worse after your stepbrothers assaulted you. I sense this evil here and it won't let me go. The story of your baby brother and sister haunts me. These people killed babies even if it hasn't been proved. You and I both know it. No"—she shook her head and amended—"that's not right. The entire team knows it and we continue doing this job. Are we making a difference?"

Eve sat up and faced her. She'd had the same thoughts but refused to dwell on them and tried to separate the cases from her past. The team was trained in child abduction. After one hour, the chances of finding a child alive dropped and each hour after that, were worse. The clock was ticking and Bina heard the silent minute hand in her heart just as Eve did. This time it might have stopped before they even arrived in town. She was also concerned that the harassment phone calls she'd received were a prelude to Linda's missing child. There were so many what-ifs. Those calls lasted eight seconds. It would take less time to kill a baby.

"Yes, we are helping," Eve said emphatically. "There are women in this community who want to escape the indoctrination," she stated. "Danielle is one of them. She was more concerned for Linda and the baby than she was for herself or she wouldn't have thrown the sock from the window. The same dogma programmed into her was indoctrinated into me too. Women are breaking the cycle and we need to hold on to hope. My stepsister Sheila helped us during the Tanner case. There is a bright light in this town buried beneath the evil you're talking about. The man who gave the note to Harina was kind to her. These are small wins. Not everyone here is bad, but dealing with felony cases, it seems that way. I believe we're making a difference."

The pep talk was meant for Bina, but it helped Eve too.

"If you need time off, take it," Eve told her. "We'll all reach a point where we'll need a break from this place. It shows our humanity and we must keep that no matter what we face."

"I can't leave," Bina said sadly. "I don't want off the squad or to take a leave of absence. I want to be effective and you've reminded me that we are."

Eve still felt inadequate. Bina's doubts matched hers. They needed to discuss their feelings before they were this bad. Eve needed to share more. Even her anger stayed hidden whenever she could manage it. Saying she was angry and showing it were two different things. Maybe she needed to kick the can when she felt like it.

"We will find Linda's baby alive," Eve said with conviction. "We'll both feel better with a good night's sleep, but for now, we have work to do."

"Thank you for listening. I feel better," Bina told her. She got up and went to her suitcase. She grabbed a bag of gummy bears from the side pocket and tossed it to Eve. "The cure-all for everything."

Eve opened the bag and took one out and popped it into her mouth. "This only works for you, but I'll try again." Eve realized Bina hadn't taken them out on the drive to town when she usually munched on them constantly. She needed to be more aware of the team's emotional stability. She needed to speak with Tamm about finding a police therapist.

"I'm texting Clyde to let him know about the note and my stepbrothers," she told Bina. She picked up her phone and jumped slightly when it rang in her hand. It was the same number Linda called from.

"Hello?" Her eyes went to Bina.

"This is Danielle." It was obvious she was crying. Eve couldn't help thinking there was something bad going on in the Wall home. Maybe not the Tanner level of bad but close.

"Are you in trouble?" she asked.

"I am so sorry. I need your help. I should have said something when you were here, but I was frightened."

"It's okay. I'll do whatever I can."

Danielle breathed heavily into the phone and sniffed twice before she finally said why she called.

"I am pregnant. It will be a child of sin. I do not know what to do and I know they will take the baby away. I cannot allow that to happen."

This was tragic. Eve thought for a moment, putting a plan together.

"Where are you now?" she asked.

"I am in my room. Husband did not take his phone. I grabbed it and carried it up here in my pocket. It must be returned. I did not know what else to do."

"Do not pack or show any sign you are leaving. I will come to the front door and knock," Eve said. "Don't bring anything with you, just walk straight out when it's answered. If someone tries to stop you, we will intervene." Eve's mind raced. "Your husband will likely make bond soon. I'll try to get there before that happens, but even if he is home, we'll take you out. You have rights and you're an adult. Legally, they cannot stop you. Do you understand?"

"Yes."

"We'll be there within thirty minutes." Something occurred to Eve that she should have thought of before. "If you can, keep the phone and bring it with you. It may have answers about Linda and the baby."

"Thank you." The call disconnected.

Eve quickly told Bina what Danielle said. Then she did something she'd never done before. She took Bina's hand.

"We are making a difference, I promise."

Bina's fingers tightened before they released each other and went into work mode.

"Call Tamm and get her in touch with the New Life Shelter," Eve said. "Have her speak to highway patrol to provide an escort. I'll call Clyde and get the guys rolling."

Clyde sounded tired when he answered. Eve's adrenaline was running high and the last thing she was thinking about was sleep. She quickly told him what Danielle had said. "Call Ray and Collin and have them return to the hotel immediately. We'll fill the cooler and take it with us."

"I'm heading to your room," Clyde said.

He knocked minutes later; he was talking on his cell and relaying what was going on to the guys.

"What's their ETA?" Eve asked after he disconnected.

"They were waiting to order and left the line. They should be here in a few minutes."

The three of them discussed plans while Bina packed the cooler. If Howard was still in jail, they shouldn't have too much trouble taking Danielle away. Eve had no one to call but the detention officers to check on his release and she couldn't trust them. He could be on his way home.

There was a knock on the door.

"Bina, you go with Ray and Collin and explain everything that's happened. We'll use the same approach to the house that worked during the Tanner case. We don't want the God squad knowing where we're headed until the last minute."

Bina opened the door and stopped the guys from walking inside. She took the cooler off the table and left with them.

"I'm with you, we'll talk in the van," Eve heard her say.

Clyde and Eve were right behind them. Clyde had the keys to the SUV. They were on the street a few minutes later. The van pulled out and traveled in the opposite direction.

She told him about the visit from her stepbrothers when they were a few blocks away.

"Your stepbrothers worry me," Clyde said. "They are acting outside what the county attorney is aware of. I don't see them thinking for themselves. Did it occur to you that it could have been them in the vehicle that rammed yours?"

"I thought about it and you're quite possibly right. I spoke to Bina about not going anywhere alone. I won't either. They have no fear of women, not even with us armed."

"Thank you," he said, and took her hand. "We'll find the baby."

"I'm beginning to think it's all connected: the phone calls, the hit and run on my vehicle, and now the missing baby. I feel like a wild conspiracy theorist."

"I think you're right though. There are too many coincidences." His fingers squeezed a bit firmer.

"I agree. With the prophet in prison, someone else is orchestrating what's been happening and that person has a lot of power. That reminds me," Eve said.

She pressed Tamm's name on speed dial.

"I'm waiting for a call back from highway patrol." Tamm said immediately.

"I need you to run a check on a man, last name Hammon." She spelled it. "He's known as Brother Hammon, unknown first name," Eve told her. When Eve first met Hammon, he had been with another man who was introduced as Brother Bockstater. Eve thought it was strange that both men were referred to using only their family names. "I have a description. I'm looking for anything connected to this community or others where the prophet owns property." Eve gave her the description and added Bockstater to the search.

After the call ended, she leaned against the seat.

"I feel so inadequate," Eve said honestly. She should have had the men checked out before.

"You aren't responsible for everything," Clyde reminded her. "We're good at this, but things slip past all the time. We'll solve this case just like we do the others. We're a team, remember?"

"Yes," she said. "We're a team."

Clyde made a right. Once they reached the hill, Eve could see the evidence van on a street below them. The street the Wall home was on had a dead end, but the street before that could be reached from two different directions. That's where the two vehicles would converge. Hopefully they would have Danielle out the door before others were called in to interfere. Eve and her team would not be stopped but others might persuade Danielle not to go with them.

Eve called Ray and told him to put the call on speakerphone. Eve did the same so Clyde could hear.

"Ray, you cover the gate," she said. "Bina and Collin stay to the sides of the front door. I will knock. Clyde has our back which includes holding off the God squad. When we see Danielle, she's coming out with us and we're hustling her inside the SUV and driving away quickly. Keep the van close on our tail."

Eve was determined they would save Danielle and her baby before it was too late.

FIFTEEN

Clyde slammed on the breaks and Eve climbed out and ran through the courtyard to the front door. Ray was right behind her. He stopped inside the gate. Clyde remained at the vehicles.

Eve pounded on the door.

Barbara opened it; she appeared angrier than she had earlier. Her emotions were slipping through. Eve saw Danielle running down the stairs and stepped inside slightly. Collin's arm came up and he pushed the door all the way open, above Eve's head.

"What are you doing, sister?" Barbara demanded when she realized Danielle was heading in Eve's direction.

Danielle didn't say anything. Barbara blocked her and grabbed her arm.

"Satan sends them. You know this. They have tempted you. Don't go with them. I only care about your salvation," Barbara pleaded.

Danielle looked at Eve. She was wavering. Eve could not plead or it would look like coercion if Howard filed charges. This was a decision Danielle had to make on her own. More women came down the stairs behind her.

Dannielle started shaking.

"Sister, think of what you are doing." Barbara knew she was getting through. It was incredibly sad because Eve couldn't imagine one of the wives running away when she'd lived in the community.

Danielle gazed at Barbara; her eyes filled with fear. Eve almost backed away. Danielle jerked her arm from Barbara's grip and pushed forward. One of the women on the stairs cried out, but Danielle didn't turn around. Bina closed in behind Danielle while Collin blocked the door so the women couldn't follow.

"Never come to this house again," Barbara shouted.

Eve wasn't sure if she was yelling at her or Danielle, or both. It didn't matter. Danielle had made her decision.

Collin followed as soon as the group reached the gate.

"You're in the SUV with me," Eve told Danielle.

She opened the back door and ushered the shaking woman inside, closed the door, and climbed into the front passenger seat. Clyde took the wheel and pulled out with the van right behind them. It took under five minutes.

"Put your seatbelt on," Eve told her as she adjusted her own. "Two women from a shelter will meet us on the highway. They will take you to the city and keep you safe. They will also have a police escort so no one interferes. Are you okay?"

"Yes, I am good." Danielle's voice trembled. Her hand went to her stomach. "Thank you."

"Try to relax. We have at least an hour's drive before we meet the ladies from the shelter." Eve looked into the side mirror. Collin was only one car length behind their bumper. She could see the tail end of the black truck behind him and the other truck behind that one. Eve hoped they would turn around at the county line.

"Are you hungry?" Eve asked her.

"A little."

"After we're out of the county, we should be able to pull over and grab food from the van. Was your husband back at the house?"

"No. We did not hear from him. I was afraid he would know I spoke with you. He did not protect Sister Linda and I knew he would not protect me or my baby. I'm sorry, I almost turned back." She covered her eyes.

"This is a huge step. You are placing your child first. I believe that's how it should be no matter how we were raised."

Eve believed it was instinct for a mother to protect her child and provide unconditional love. The cult did everything they could to take away those instincts. It was wrong and it was sick. She was so grateful they hadn't had to leave Danielle behind.

"I am sorry," Danielle said. "I cannot call Adella or her husband will answer. I usually see her at the assembly—the next one is tomorrow—and pass her a note."

"Is there a chance Adella would leave her husband?" Eve was willing to go in just like they had with Danielle. She was sick of the men in town getting away with what amounted to slavery. Children in danger was where she drew the line. She'd had enough.

"I do not know. She has two sons. They are four and six. I do not think she would leave them."

That made it harder. Getting children out of the community was difficult. Even women who managed to leave and were awarded visitation rarely saw their children again. Kids were quickly reassigned and moved outside the community. The church had years of practice and they were good at evading judicial orders. The only way for a mother to reunite with her children was to rescue them like Maggie had done with Eve. It had taken Maggie four years. She'd had to use force and outside help. It didn't matter that Maggie was Eve's biological mother and her stepfather had no legal rights over her. Her mother didn't trust law enforcement or the courts back then. Even now, judges still awarded fathers visitation rights with their biological children. Even though the children disappeared regularly, the courts still prioritized a father's parental rights.

Eve handed Danielle her notebook and pen.

"Write down Adella's address and I will see what we can do. No promises unless we can talk to her first."

"I do not know the address, but I have been to the home and can draw a map."

"Thank you."

Danielle's hand came between the seats holding a cell phone.

"I hope this helps," she said.

Eve took it and placed it in the center console until it could be checked into evidence. She called Ray.

"I have Howard Wall's cell phone. I needed a warrant as soon as possible."

"I'll have it done by the time we intercept the women picking up Danielle," he said.

"Sign it and send straight to Judge Remki. With Nelson leaving on vacation tomorrow, we may need Remki. It will help if he has a heads up. Add a little extra to the probable cause if you can."

Eve wasn't ready to talk to the judge, but she would if they had a lead on Linda's baby and he could help.

They hit the city limits and Clyde picked up speed. Collin backed the van off a few additional car lengths. The God squad trucks stayed behind them. Her phone rang and she looked at the screen. It was Aaron. She ignored the call. He called back twice more over the next five minutes. She finally placed it in silent mode.

Clyde gazed at her with a question in his eyes then quickly turned back to the road.

"Aaron," she told him. "I'll speak to him when I have time."

She didn't miss the slight upturn of Clyde's lips.

They reached the county line twenty minutes later and the God squad turned around. She waited a few minutes before she called Ray.

"Have Collin pull over so we can grab food from the cooler. We need to do it quickly."

Eve jumped from the SUV and Ray met her with the cooler.

"Is she okay?" he asked.

"Yes."

He gave her a relieved smile and they returned to their respective vehicles. Eve placed the ice chest on the passenger seat next to Danielle.

"Do you mind distributing food?" Eve asked her.

Danielle smiled. "I want to be useful."

"Clyde, our driver, eats the disgusting protein bars and fruit if it's in there," Eve said when Danielle looked stricken and announced there were only two sandwiches.

A bar was hurriedly passed up front along with an apple, chips for Eve, and two bottled waters. Clyde began driving again and when he finished his bar, Eve handed him an apple.

When they finished eating, she asked Danielle additional questions about the case.

"Did anyone come to the house in the days prior to Linda's baby disappearing?"

"Only the midwife."

A knot formed in Eve's gut. Aunt Bertha, the midwife, had picked up Little Charlie after he became ill. That was the last time Eve saw him.

Aunt Bertha's husband, Uncle Todd, ran Babyland. At the back of the cemetery, there was a long row of unmarked graves. This was where Eve suspected Charlie and her sister Becky were buried. She had tried to get a court order to exhume the graves and discover how the babies died, but Judge Remki had denied her request. Uncle Todd had died years before and Aunt Bertha was now in her nineties.

"Let it rest," the judge told her.

Eve didn't think that would ever happen.

"Who is the midwife now?" she asked.

"Sister Bonnie assisted with the birth," Danielle whispered, and looked out the window.

"What is Sister Bonnie's last name?" Eve asked, trying to take Danielle's mind off the vehicle behind them.

"Keb."

The vehicle's radio interrupted her thoughts.

"9420 to DS851, copy?"

Eve lifted the mic.

"Go for DS851," she replied. DS851 was her badge number.

"10-17 to Cedar City ETA fourteen minutes."

"10-4," Eve answered. "ETA is twenty. 10-25 at the Pit Stop."

The Pit Stop was a small convenience store with two gas pumps, a restroom, and a minuscule selection of snacks. Her team stopped there for bathroom breaks and to stretch their legs when driving to and from town.

She called Ray to make sure the others had heard the transmission.

"Got it," said Ray.

When they arrived at the Pit Stop twenty-four minutes later, two women stepped from an older blue van. They were middle-aged and dressed in jeans and T-shirts. One wore her brown hair in a short bob, longer in the front than in back and the other had light brown streaked with gray hair, pulled back from her face with a barrette. They both had light complexions and blue eyes.

A highway patrol officer waited in the lot. Clyde went to speak with him.

The women introduced themselves and smiled at Danielle.

"They'll give you a phone after you're settled," Eve assured her. "Do you still have my card?"

Danielle nodded and patted her pocket. She looked scared but kept her back straight and her chin up.

"Send me a text message so I have your number," Eve told her. "I'll do everything I can for your sister and her children."

It surprised Eve when Danielle hugged her.

"Thank you," Danielle said after releasing her. She turned and walked with the women to their vehicle.

After the women from the shelter and the officer drove away, the team went inside the Pit Stop. They grabbed coffees and Collin bought an energy drink. They were back on the road within minutes, heading toward town.

Aaron's name flashed up on Eve's phone and she decided to answer.

"What do you think you're doing?" he yelled.

"Saving women from men like you," she said. She'd planned to speak with him for longer, but his attitude told her the conversation would go downhill quickly. She had no time for one of his tantrums and disconnected.

SIXTEEN

Her phone was still in silent mode, but the screen lit up when Aaron called once again. Her finger hovered over the answer button.

"You shouldn't answer," said Clyde. "He's a sniveling worm who will not help us under any circumstances."

He was right, but Eve was the one who dealt with the judge. She needed to act professionally and to be able to say she tried. Eve scrutinized her phone as it continued ringing and finally placed the call on speakerphone so Clyde could listen.

"Come to my office when you are back in town," Aaron demanded as soon as she answered. "It's important and your childish games are not helping your case."

"I want answers, Aaron. I've learned they will not come from you."

"Eve." A loud huff came over the line before his tone turned cajoling. "We need to speak."

"How late will you be there?" He didn't know they had help transporting Danielle into the city and Eve wouldn't volunteer the information. The less he knew, the better.

"Just come to my office when you are back."

Eve had no intention of following Aaron's directive. They went by the hotel room first. Everyone gathered in her room. She explained that she and Clyde were meeting with Aaron.

Bina turned to Clyde.

"Shoot him for us and do the world a favor," she said.

Aaron interfered on cases; they all felt he was involved when Eve was attacked by her other stepbrothers, and then there was the way Aaron stared at Eve. It all left an impression on Bina. Eve wanted to cheer her on but, as the supervisor, didn't feel she could agree with the sentiment.

"Don't tempt me," Clyde responded without smiling.

"We need a large dinner when you come back," Ray said, breaking the tension somewhat. "I vote for the steak house outside of town."

"It's a good idea," Eve said. She noticed the strain on their faces. She felt like she did with the Tanner murders: no leads and no help. It was a repeated theme. She tried to remember that they had a meeting the following evening and maybe the man who wrote the note would be of help. In the back of her mind, she also knew it could be a setup. It was too much to worry about right now. Meeting Aaron, dinner, and a good night's sleep were priorities.

Clyde followed Eve outside.

She handed Clyde the keys Bina had given her so he could drive.

Another God squad truck pulled behind them as soon as they left the hotel. They were triggering her last nerve.

"I don't think we're going to find the baby," she told him. Her throat closed and she had to work to keep tears from falling. This wasn't the time or place. She would not walk into Aaron's office with red and swollen eyes.

"I'm worried too," Clyde admitted. "Let's see what the worm has to say."

It was almost five when they parked in the empty lot beside the county attorney's office. She didn't see Aaron's vehicle.

"Maybe they closed early and he's gone," she said. "Let's check the front door."

They walked to the door of the lobby. The sky was turning bright orange in the west, but inside the building it was dark. Aaron opened the door. He stared at Clyde for a moment, his mouth set in a hard line. Eve could see he was deciding on whether to let them inside or not. She was too tired to put up with this. The same moment she decided to return to their vehicle, he ushered them inside.

There was an emergency light above the door leading to the offices and it was the first good look she had of Aaron. The best way to describe his appearance was haggard. His hair was sticking up in odd places, his suit wrinkled, and his tie loose. This was very unlike him.

"I didn't expect you to arrive so quickly. I also didn't know you would bring him," he said, refusing to look at Clyde.

There was so much religious dogma tied up in his statement. Clyde was one of the best men Eve had ever known and Aaron the worst.

"*He*"—Eve put emphasis on the word—"is Detective Johnston. You've been introduced before. We've had a long day so if you want to talk, I suggest you use your manners."

Aaron's jaw dropped at her tone. It was the same one she'd used with the two young men on the God squad. If Aaron acted like a child, she would treat him like one. Aaron had never shaken Clyde's hand or acknowledged him. She was tired of all the games. Eve was tired and irritable. If her tone didn't work and he continued with his racism, they would leave.

Eve didn't care that they worked in a polygamist area that believed one drop of so called "Black blood" damned you for eternity. This dogma had been preached to her the entire time she lived in the community.

Her stepbrother's mouth snapped closed.

"Follow me to my office," he said stiffly.

Aaron led them through the door and down the hallway. The overhead lights were off and the blinds were closed. The room was dark except for another emergency light above the door. Aaron took the chair behind his desk and Eve sat in the same one she'd had earlier. Clyde stood in the doorway.

"You've caused an uproar. Where is Sister Danielle?" was Aaron's first demand.

Before Eve could answer, Clyde switched on the overhead light. She had to bite her lip to keep from laughing at Aaron's startled expression. Now that she had a clearer view of him, she could see there were dark circles beneath his bloodshot eyes. He hadn't looked this way during her morning visit.

Clyde filled the doorframe; his shoulders practically touched each side. Aaron glanced at him for a split second and licked his lips nervously. Aaron's insults would not get to Clyde, but he would have no problem making her stepbrother uneasy.

"Ms. Wall is safe," she said, turning the conversation back to the reason they were here, in the hope they could get out sooner. "That's all you need to know about her situation."

He interlocked his fingers and glared. Eve didn't miss his trembling hands. Something was very wrong, but she had no idea what it was.

"I thought we were on the same side," he said.

She didn't know whether to hit her head against the desk or scream. She also needed to add strangling Aaron to that short list.

"If that's a joke," she shot back, "I'm not laughing." She allowed her professional expression to slip away so he could see her contempt.

He ignored her statement, but his eyes slid away from her disdain.

"Removing her from the community will not endear you here," Aaron said.

"If I wanted endearment, I would visit my mother. Ms. Wall asked to be taken from the home."

"Why?"

"It's none of your business. The only reason I'm here is to discover why you lied this morning. Tell me the truth about Linda Wall and her child."

"The high council expects me to bring Sister Danielle back to face consequences for what she has done," he said, disregarding her question.

"What has she done?" Eve asked curiously.

"She has openly disobeyed her husband and she has left the safety of her family."

"She is old enough to go where she wants. There is no law in this country about disobeying a man. Try again."

"You are being difficult." The pompous tone was back in his voice. "The high council wants answers."

Eve leaned forward and placed her hands flat on his desk.

"I don't care what your so-called high council wants. They are, however, a good place for you to start giving me the answers I need. What exactly is this council and who is on it? Include names."

There was so much secrecy within Aaron's religion. As a child she was not privy to the same information the boys were. Aaron would have grown up being told by his father the various levels he could attain within the church. There was no level for Eve that wasn't centered around becoming a wife and mother. To get into heaven, she had to be pulled up by her husband and that only came if you obeyed without fail.

"The council of elders. The names of the men are unimportant."

"If you answer to this council of elders as the duly elected county attorney, their names *are* important. I need them for my report."

"I sit on the council so my name is good enough," he said stubbornly. "Our job is to circumvent problems in the community."

"What types of problems?"

"Eve." It was his turn to lean forward. He also went with another tact to show how important and scary he thought he was. "You removed a woman from her home, basically kidnapped her. Howard Wall is her lawful husband. He is gravely concerned for her well-being."

"First, he is not her lawful husband. Bigamy is still illegal in this state. Second, are you talking about the same Howard Wall who lied about his missing child and said his wife was delusional about giving birth?"

"From what Brother Howard told me, it is Sister Linda who is delusional and has been suffering for quite some time. He has done everything in his power to help her. There was no recourse other than to find her professional help. I told you before, there is no child." Aaron checked his watch.

"We found the baby diapers, Aaron. I know you've seen the booking paperwork. You lied to me earlier and you are still lying." This was getting them nowhere. She couldn't figure out what he was up to. "It shouldn't surprise you that Danielle Wall is worried that what happened to Linda, could also happen to her."

"What are you talking about?"

"Why don't you explain isolation to me?"

Aaron tried to hide his shock, but it was too late. His expression hardened.

"Is that what Danielle Wall told you?" he demanded.

Eve reined in her anger. She'd been in similar situations with Aaron before. He would push every button he could until she lost her cool. Isolation was one of many secrets she as an outsider was never to know about.

"Yes," she said calmly. "Danielle told me about isolation and I'm asking you to explain it to me."

He was incapable of a blank expression. She could almost see his brain scrambling for a way out.

"I didn't order Mark to pull that stunt at the hotel earlier." Deflecting and changing the subject was what he'd decided on.

Eve was done with this farce.

"We're past that. I'm leaving." She stood. "You won't answer my questions and I'm finished playing your stupid games. A newborn baby is in danger, and you are once again hindering my investigation."

"There are things you don't understand," he said. The whine was back in his tone.

"Tell me what's going on." She was so tired. "Aaron?"

He glanced at Clyde then quickly turned his gaze back to hers.

"There is a man in the community who claims he is prophesizing."

"What exactly does that mean?" She didn't bother sitting down.

"He believes God has appointed him the new prophet."

Eve wasn't surprised and wondered why more men didn't claim to be a prophet. The benefits were huge—choosing your own wives, everyone giving you money, and making your own laws. You were also able to talk directly to God. They should have been coming out of the woodwork in droves.

"Will people follow him?" she asked instead of making it into the joke it was.

"The council thinks some community members already have," Aaron said. "We suspect he took Howard's child."

It was a huge slip-up on Aaron's part. He'd just admitted that he'd lied to her earlier and she had it recorded. Surprisingly he didn't seem to understand what he'd said. Something had thoroughly shaken him. From his appearance to his inadequate answers, Aaron was in panic mode.

"You need to ask Howard Wall who stole the baby," she said, and took a small step back. The heat of Clyde's body was there like she knew it would be. She had to delve even further to see if Aaron slipped again. "This so-called prophet should make his announcement public; why doesn't he?" she asked curiously.

Aaron's eyes shifted to Clyde then back and she saw a small twinge of relief in his expression. Maybe he did realize his mistake and was hoping she and Clyde had missed it.

"He doesn't have the resources to take over," Aaron said quickly.

"Who is *he*?" she asked.

He relaxed even more. "We don't know."

Of all the stupid things to say. It felt like he was making things up as he went.

"Why wouldn't you?" she asked, putting mild curiosity in her tone.

He shrugged. Again, this was very un-Aaron-like.

He might not be good at hiding his expressions, but Eve was. Her face went blank.

"You must know something," she said.

"He is building followers," Aaron replied. He looked at his watch again. "He's only approaching those in trouble with the council while trying to stay under the radar."

"Are women and children involved?"

"Possibly." His expression turned calculating. He was feeling comfortable with his lies now. "The high council wants you to investigate. We believe this man is somehow taking funds away from the church and the number is large enough that it's a felony."

It was time to call him out on his BS. The church would never ask for her help.

"Aaron, you are completely full of shit and I'm tired of it spilling from between your lips."

Eve left and didn't look back. The sun had gone down. She and Clyde were halfway back to the hotel when she finally spoke.

"He's always hiding something, but we're close to whatever it is this time and he's afraid. The men on this council of elders would never ask for our help. They would consider it holding Satan's hand."

"He was lying through his teeth," Clyde agreed.

"Now we need to figure out why because it's somehow tied into Linda and her baby."

They were a mile from the hotel when a truck pulled in front of them and slowed down. The God squad behind them moved up on their bumper and another dark lifted truck came in close on the passenger side.

"Unclip your belt and lift your feet up on the seat," Clyde said. "As soon as I pull over, slide into my place, and get out behind me. Stay low."

SEVENTEEN

Eve quickly did as he said. Clyde pulled to the left and slowly came to a stop. He swung the door open and got out. She was directly behind him. Clyde had his gun drawn. She pulled hers out as soon as her feet hit the ground. The trucks had boxed them in on three sides. She and Clyde stood behind the SUV's door, but it wasn't good cover.

"Take my six," Clyde told her. He meant the six o'clock position at his back.

Eve turned around and scanned the area. The God squad truck still had its brights on and she shaded her eyes with her left hand.

She now understood why Aaron had wanted her to come to his office. Even if she'd brought Bina, he thought women were easily intimidated and wouldn't have objected. Whoever controlled him planned this stunt and Aaron had gone along with it. It was why he'd kept checking the time.

"We just want to talk," Eve heard behind her. She didn't look. He was Clyde's worry.

Another man stepped from the back of the SUV. It was hard to see, but she could tell his lifted hands were empty.

"Just talk," the man said to Eve. He moved farther away from behind the SUV so he was in her direct line of sight. His hands remained up. He was the young man she hadn't handcuffed at the Wall home.

She kept her gun pointed at his chest, her finger along the barrel ready to pull the trigger. The young men on the God squad believed they were on a holy mission. They would do what they were told even if that included killing her and Clyde.

The vehicle's brights went off and she could now see a third man close to the driver's side door of the truck she was facing.

"Get your hands up where I can see them," she yelled at him but kept her gun trained on the man closest to her.

"We've been sent to deliver a message." The voice again came from behind her, directed at Clyde.

"Deliver it," he said.

"It's dangerous for you in this town. You need to leave and not return."

Clyde muttered something under his breath. Eve could only guess that it was something insulting.

"Get in your vehicles and drive away or someone will be shot," Clyde told him.

"This is your only warning," the man said, his voice slightly deeper than the one in front of Eve but still young.

"We heard you. Leave, I won't repeat myself." Clyde's voice had grown harder. He was tired of playing their game. Blocking the SUV and restricting her and Clyde's movements were technically kidnapping. The felony degree was even higher because they were police officers.

The two men in front of her moved away. A few moments later, the truck doors slammed. The vehicles roared off.

"Do you know where the county attorney lives?" Clyde asked through his teeth.

"I do, but he isn't worth it. We need to get back to the hotel."

Clyde holstered his gun.

"They used kids to deliver a message. What is wrong with these people?"

"Aaron is involved too," she said, her gun hanging at her side.

"Agreed. It explains the bullshit in his office and the attention he paid to his watch," he grumbled. "We're sitting ducks out here."

"Yeah," Eve agreed. "We need to get back to the hotel."

She walked around the SUV and got in through the passenger door. The young men had pulled their stunt in an area without streetlights. Eve kept an eye on the side mirror as Clyde drove. They didn't receive an escort back to the hotel.

"Aaron hoped I would come alone. He set this up," she said into the quiet car. "He was told what to do and he did it. Someone is pulling his strings and he's desperate. He was a complete failure during Hannah's case. He can't be on solid ground." She took a minute to replay the evening in her head. "Think about it," she told Clyde. "He had one flimsy excuse after another tonight. Did you catch his slip about the baby?"

"Yeah. He doesn't lie well."

"He never has."

"Do you have a problem taking both vehicles to dinner?" Clyde asked. "I don't want all of us trapped inside the van together."

"No problem at all," she replied.

Eve sent a text to the others as they pulled into the lot. Clyde parked in front of their rooms.

Ray and Collin were waiting with Bina in her room. Eve told them what had transpired. Clyde stood by while she spoke. He was upset and until they were inside the room, she hadn't realized how badly. Everyone kept giving him furtive glances.

"Are you still willing to go out for dinner?" she asked them when they finished discussing what had happened. "Clyde recommended taking both vehicles and if we go, I agree."

"We can't let them think we're afraid," said Bina.

It was settled and they quickly loaded into the van and SUV. They still didn't have a God squad escort as they headed out of town.

The restaurant wasn't busy and they requested the booth in the back corner where they could talk with a bit of privacy. She observed her friends. They were in varying stages of sleep deprivation. Even Bina was showing signs. It was a dangerous position for them. The young men had been honest when they said this was a dangerous town.

"We need to discuss the note under our door," Eve said after they ordered their food. She hoped food would help her blurry vision and the headache that was growing.

"Could it be another setup?" asked Collin.

"I think it's a good possibility," said Bina. "I don't like it."

"Me either," Eve agreed. "But he's the only lead we have and frankly, we need something."

"Collin and I could go to the grocery store tomorrow and wander by the deli counter," Ray suggested.

"I'm good with that," Eve told him. "Don't scare him away though. Does anyone have anything else they want to bring up?"

They shook their heads.

"I say we relax, eat a delicious meal, and return to the rooms and sleep. We're not in a good place mentally right now."

"Good idea," said Collin, and the others agreed.

They ate delicious bread with mounds of butter while waiting for their meals. By the time they returned to the hotel, Eve was thoroughly stuffed and even more exhausted, but her headache was better.

Neither Eve nor Bina showered. Eve dropped into bed, pulled up the covers, and closed her eyes. She'd told the guys to call Bina's phone in case of emergency so she could turn the ringer off on hers. She would not allow another harassment call to keep her from sleeping.

As tired as she was, she couldn't stop thinking about the missing baby and the lack of information they had on the case. She also thought about her mother and her possible isolation during the years she'd left Eve alone with her stepfather. Each time she fell asleep a random thought about the case would jerk her awake. She checked the clock after it happened a third time. She had barely slept for three hours. She closed her eyes, relaxed her body, and drifted off again.

> *Heavenly and pure, guide me to thee,*
> *oh Father, please keep me sweet as sweet*
>   *could be.*
> *Sleep, baby, sleep.*

Eve sang softly to Little Charlie while cradling him against her chest in the rocking chair. He had been fussy all day and hadn't smiled even once. His nose was stuffy and there was nothing that helped except walking around with his head on her shoulder. Her back hurt and she was so tired. He finally settled down with her rocking him.

Charlie's birth mother provided breast milk, but she wouldn't hold him or offer comfort. His care was fully on Eve's small shoulders. She didn't usually mind, but it was her turn for laundry duty the following day. She had to wash and fold, plus iron and starch all the dresses to be worn to assembly. She would start in the morning and not finish until late at night. She just wanted to sleep.

Charlie whimpered and she thought he was waking up again. She wanted to cry but couldn't take a chance someone would hear her. Tears were bad because it meant she was unable to contain her suffering. No matter what, she had to keep sweet.

She often did chores while holding Charlie even though he was getting bigger and heavier. Her sisters cooked alongside their mothers while the younger ones did dishes and scrubbed pots and pans. Eve, at ten, was now old enough to cook, but she didn't have a birth mother to teach her. The wives didn't like her. They didn't like Little Charlie either.

Her nose rested against his soft curls and she inhaled. She loved his baby scent, but more than anything, she loved his smile. He was perfect and it didn't matter that he couldn't do the things other babies his age were capable of.

They were outcasts and he was the only one in the entire world who loved her. If her mother had been able to keep sweet, she wouldn't have been reassigned to another man. It made Eve mad when she thought about it. Mad at her mother for leaving her. She could never share her secret thoughts because she was told to forget the woman who'd brought her under father's roof. Most of the time she did but when she was tired, like now, she remembered her mother's face.

Eve consoled herself with thoughts of Charlie. If her mother had stayed, he might not have been placed in her charge. He was better than any mom and he loved her more.

Hush, baby, hush, in God's arms, hush, baby, hush.

She hummed after that, too tired to sing the words aloud.

When she was sure he was sleeping, she stood and placed him in the crib, while continuing to hum. She snuggled the blanket around him because it made him feel safe. He fussed a little and she rubbed his back, her eyes closing as she fought to stay awake. She'd decided to sleep on the floor. She didn't want the others mad at him for waking them up. She lay down without a pillow or blanket of her own. Her undergarments and long gown would keep her warm enough.

"Eve, wake up," whispered inside her head. She startled and glanced around the small room. No one was there. She stood over the crib and looked down at the baby blanket. She pulled it away, so she could place her hand on his back.

A tiny skeleton with Charlie's blue eyes lay in the crib.

She screamed.

EIGHTEEN

Eve sat straight up in bed. The image of the small skeleton was vivid in her mind. She looked around the dark hotel room to get her bearings. If she had screamed aloud, Bina would be awake. Her racing heart slowed and she lay back against the pillows. The clock said 5:30 a.m. Sleep was overrated, and Eve decided to take a shower and then go to the lobby for breakfast. She needed to get out of the room and shake off the nightmare.

Bina didn't stir when she came out of the bathroom. Eve slipped from the room and walked to the front of the hotel where the smell of fresh food filled the air. She had just sat down with her waffle and fruit plus her second cup of coffee when Collin walked in. Two truckers had left when Eve entered the lobby and she and Collin were alone.

"Ray's snoring keeping you awake?" she asked when he sat down at her table with a glass of orange juice.

"He doesn't actually snore, but I like teasing him about it." The corners of his mouth turned up.

Eve smiled back.

"You look tired," he said. "Did you manage any sleep at all?"

"Not really. I feel like I should be going door to door and

asking about the baby. If it would do any good, I would."

"I don't understand these people," Collin said bluntly. This was almost identical to what Bina had said. "I try to be accepting, but it's impossible. I can't talk to anyone at church because they don't understand the indoctrination here. To them, these are simply misguided people who need understanding." He paused and looked down at the table, slowly taking the wrapper off the plastic eating utensils in front of him. "I tried speaking to my bishop once. He told me to pray about it." He looked up. "Pray. That was his advice. Laura knows only half the tragedy we see here. It bothers her and I don't like bringing my work home."

"Has she asked you to transfer?"

"She hasn't yet. It's one of the reasons I don't tell her everything."

Eve gave him a level look. "Reconsider. Laura is tough and we all need someone to talk to."

Collin's lips quirked into a semi-smile. "Yes, boss."

"Honestly, why are you awake so early?" Eve asked him. "Did you sleep?"

"The small diapers made me think of the twins. They were born six weeks early. They wouldn't have survived outside the hospital. We can't even do an Amber Alert and it pisses me off. Children should come first, but this town has it backward." He looked away. "They have everything backward," he muttered.

Eve had often wondered how Collin reconciled the polygamy in his church's religious past. The fundamentalists considered theirs the true way, the way it was in the beginning, and Collin's views wrong. The polygamy sect followed the tenants of the first prophet, Joseph Smith, at least when it came to plural marriage. Eve didn't see a commonality after that except they both thought their prophets spoke directly to God and gave them prophecies to share with their followers.

She wasn't sure what she would have thought if Maggie had

taken her to the non-fundamentalist Mormon church after Eve was rescued. Her mother had stopped believing in religion all together. Eve was somewhere in the middle and had decided it was easier not to dwell on it, but Collin did. His family was tightly wrapped in his church.

"Your waffle looks good. I'm going to make me one," Collin said and stood.

Eve drank her coffee and ate her breakfast. She was still carrying this morning's dream in her head. She also couldn't take her mind off Adella's isolation. Something horrible had happened to Eve's mother and isolation might explain it.

She was halfway through her meal when Clyde came in the door.

"No Bina?" he asked, glancing quickly at Collin and giving him a chin nod. It was not unusual for Ray to sleep in later than the rest of them, but Bina was usually the first up. Eve wouldn't speak about the private conversation she and Bina had had. If Bina wanted to share, she would.

"The energizer bunny hit a wall," Eve told him.

"She must have run out of gummy bears. I'm grabbing coffee since the coffee maker is in with Miss Sleepyhead."

"I'll save you a seat," Eve teased, relieved to see he appeared rested.

He came back to the table with Collin behind him carrying a steaming waffle. Clyde had grabbed a cup of yogurt from the small fridge in the lobby along with an apple from the counter where the beverages were set up.

"Yummy," said Collin before he dug into his meal which was covered in butter and syrup.

Clyde ignored him. They had regular go-arounds about their food choices but not this morning.

Bina walked in holding a large steaming mug.

Clyde gave her an evil look and held up his Styrofoam cup. "Want to trade?"

"I made an entire pot and it's waiting in the room. That stuff you're drinking will kill you."

"I don't know how you can tell good coffee from bad," Collin insisted. "I lost a bet with Ray once and had to drink a full cup. Worst stuff I've ever tasted."

"You should have insisted on Tamm's special blend," Bina told him. "This black deliciousness is pure gold."

"Texas tar," Collin grumbled good-naturedly.

"No, that would be oil," Ray said from behind him, and swatted his head.

"Ouch," Collin replied in mock pain.

"Grab food," Eve told Ray and Bina. "Let's have a small meeting here if no one else comes in to eat."

Five minutes later, Eve had refilled her coffee and they were all sitting around the table.

"Clyde will handle the details for the meeting tonight," she told them. Eve knew he already had a safety protocol planned. "I'm going with Ray and Collin to the market." She didn't tell them she needed to keep moving. The nightmare had done a number on her mentally. Sitting and waiting wouldn't help. "I'm still mulling over what happened last night with the God squad. Does anyone have anything they want to impart?"

"They thought you would be alone or with Bina. It's very possible their plans changed when they discovered me with you," Clyde said.

Collin raised his hand slightly. "I agree."

The men in the community would never expect Bina or Eve to fight back. Eve almost wished she'd had Bina with her.

"You're right," she told them. "We'll never know what their real plan was." She couldn't help thinking about their young age though.

"They're dangerous," Clyde insisted at her expression. "Your youngest stepbrothers aren't much older and they could have killed you."

He was right. The age of the God squad members did not give them a pass.

She had also been weighing Aaron's involvement. She expected to walk into his office one day and see a new county attorney sitting behind the desk. When it came to Eve and the team, Aaron was not getting results.

"What's with this new prophet he mentioned?" Bina questioned.

"I think it's bullshit," said Clyde.

"Not so fast," Eve objected. "Think about it. Their prophet isn't coming back. He stole the prophecies from his father and people suspect he murdered him. Why wouldn't others try to get a jump into the highest position? It holds countless benefits."

"Could they pull it off?" Ray asked.

"They're taught to follow blindly. I don't think it would take much work," Eve said. "It makes sense in a weird kind of way. Prophets should be tripping over each other to gather a following." She paused for a moment. "Even though I think it could be happening, Aaron was lying. Something was in play last night and once more, he failed."

"His downfall helps us," Bina insisted.

"The devil we know," muttered Clyde.

* * *

Eve left with Collin and Ray. A God squad vehicle pulled out behind them. Ray checked on the warrant for Howard's phone and the judge's clerk told him it was signed and needed to be emailed and he would do it in the next fifteen minutes. Bina had software that would open the phone and scan calls and texts. It was locked into evidence and Ray sent her a message that the warrant was a go.

The grocery store was small but well stocked. It carried a

little of everything including a hardware section. There were several groups of women in their prairie dresses, shopping in groups of two or three. Wives did not go out alone. They kept their heads down and turned away from Eve. There were no children and only a handful of men who openly glared at Eve.

She approached the deli counter. An older man stood behind it. His look of contempt was expected. He didn't say anything. His tag said TOBIAS. He was the only person working in the department. Ray and Collin would be checking name tags in other departments too.

Eve ordered lunchmeat, disappointed that Eric wasn't there. The ticking of the clock was loud in her head. Frustration added to her worry.

They were back at the hotel fifteen minutes later with nothing new to report. Eve stowed the extra food in the small room refrigerator.

"I want to try and speak with Danielle's sister," Eve said. "I don't want the God squad following. Any ideas?"

"What direction is the house?" Clyde asked.

"East. Here's the map she drew." Eve handed it to him. He gave it a quick glance and gave it back.

"I'll drive the van; Ray, you handle the SUV," Clyde said. "We need to find a dead-end road a few miles from the target so we don't give away where you're going. They'll follow and go to the end of the road to turn around, Ray, you'll pit maneuver and I'll block them with the van. It will give you a few minutes. Cruise close to the target location before we put the plan in action so you're sure where it is. Let's radio up."

Clyde went outside and grabbed the bag that had the radio equipment.

It was about time they were proactive. Eve was tired of waiting and she was out of options.

They placed their radios on their belts and secured the earpieces. Clyde did a radio check and they went out to the vehicles. Collin grumbled at Ray about driving, but they all knew Clyde oversaw training and he assigned who was best for what they needed. Ray was a speed demon at the police training track and had outdriven them all.

Eve had Bina in the SUV with her.

It took ten minutes to get to the area. They crisscrossed streets with a God squad vehicle behind each of them. Clyde's voice came through in her ear.

"I have the location for the maneuver, did you find your target?"

"10-4," Ray answered.

Clyde gave the name of the street that came to a dead end and the street that connected.

"I'll come in behind you," he said. "Stop two houses from the end of the road on the right and I'll pull in front. The GS truck will go to the end to turn around and park. As soon as you hightail it out, I'll stop them. Homes on both sides have block walls and they'll be unable to get around the van. I haven't seen pole cameras, you?"

"Negative," Ray answered.

They had been keeping an eye out for them. Most of the cameras were on light poles. The area they were in wasn't well lit which meant there weren't many poles. It was within the town limits but not too close to the town's center.

"Are we set?" Clyde asked.

"Heading there now," said Ray.

They found the street and pulled in front of the second home on the right. Clyde pulled around them and parked. Both God squad drivers did exactly as Clyde predicted and went to the end of the road to turn around.

"Go," said Clyde while the two trucks were facing away from them.

NINETEEN

Ray screeched the tires and hit the gas as he came out of the turn. Eve and Bina looked behind the SUV as Clyde steered the van into the center of the road. They heard a horn.

"It will only work once," said Ray, laughing, "but it's worth it."

Adella's home was larger than the houses near the Tanner and Wall residences. There was no high wall and it sat on a slight rise with white, wrought-iron fencing surrounding it. A double ornamental gate with a looped chain stopped them from driving the SUV closer.

Bina and Eve exited the van ready to climb the fence, but there was enough room to squeeze between the gates. They walked quickly up the drive.

"Nice place," Bina said.

There was a large eleven-seat passenger van sitting next to the house with a three-car garage. The house was standard community-white with a tan trim. The landscaping was nothing special, mostly dirt with shrubs and a few small trees about twenty feet from the house. There wasn't a weed in sight.

Eve knocked on the mahogany-stained door. Like many of the homes in town, this one did not have a doorbell.

A teenage girl answered. Eve guessed her age at thirteen or fourteen. She was slender almost to the point of emaciation and wore a peach dress that hung on her. She had blonde hair with a small upsweep in front. Her eyes were light blue and panicked at the sight of Eve and Bina. She glanced nervously over her shoulder just as Danielle had done. Eve saw a long braid down her back reaching almost to her waist.

"We're here to speak with Adella," Eve informed her.

The girl shook her head, her eyes growing even larger. She leaned toward Eve.

"You cannot," she whispered. "You need to leave. She will be in trouble for speaking with you. Please," she implored.

Eve handed her a business card.

"Tell her that Danielle is safe and to call me if she can."

The girl took the card, nodded, and closed the door.

They left quickly, slid back through the gates, and jumped into the SUV.

"Was she a wife or daughter?" Bina asked.

"I don't know," Eve replied. The girl was much too thin and it made Eve think of the days without food she'd suffered as a child. She put it out of her mind. "We got lucky though."

She told Collin about the girl taking the card.

"Do you think she'll give it to Adella?" he asked.

"I hope so. She seemed scared, but she appeared sympathetic. It's the best we can hope for."

Eve radioed Clyde.

"We're clear, meet us back at the hotel."

"You're taking away all our fun, but we'll see you in a few."

That meant they were still blocking the God squad vehicles. Two miles away, another black lifted truck came roaring in their direction. Ray waved at the driver when he passed.

"You should have flipped him off," Bina told him.

"Boss in the car so I couldn't."

Her lips twitched.

* * *

They met in Eve's room once both vehicles were back at the hotel.

"What did they do?" asked Ray.

Clyde smiled and Collin started laughing.

"They threatened us and said they were calling the police." Collin laughed louder. "Clyde held his badge up and said we were already on scene. They started making phone calls then sat in the trucks and pouted."

"You enjoyed it." Bina smiled.

Both men nodded.

Eve told them about the young girl.

"Hopefully we'll hear something," she added. "For now, all we can do is wait."

"We aren't very good at waiting," said Ray.

"Truth," Bina replied.

"We need to write our reports."

All but Clyde groaned. Reports were necessary but not anyone's favorite.

Collin and Ray went back to their room to work, Clyde went to his, and Bina and Eve set their laptops up on the table.

"How are you feeling today?" she asked Bina.

"Better. I needed sleep. I'm sorry I laid all of that on you."

Eve shook her head vehemently.

"No. We'll make a better team if we talk about our fears and feelings. I've never really asked about your family, more than how they are doing. I care. I didn't want to intrude on your privacy and I appreciate your sharing. Other than no running water, it sounds like a wonderful place to grow up."

"It was. My family made it that way," Bina said with a slight smile, then changed the subject. "Do you mind if I work on Howard Wall's phone?" she asked.

"Sure. Make a spreadsheet of phone numbers and let me know if there are any text messages of interest."

Eve began typing her report while Bina hooked the phone up to her laptop.

"No text messages at all," she said. "There was a call to Wall's phone the night before the baby disappeared. That same number was called from Howard Wall's phone early the next morning. The first call was ten minutes long and the second, two. Going back five days, there was one additional phone call. It lasted a minute. I'm not finding that number again in the call history."

"That's interesting. What time was the call the morning she disappeared?"

"Five," Bina replied.

"The baby was gone sometime before seven. Email the number to Tamm and see if she can trace it."

Bina tapped on her keyboard.

"Done," she said a moment later. "I've put his calls in a log which includes Linda's call to you. Howard Wall called the county attorney's office days before the baby went missing. I recognize the number. The call was less than a minute long."

"Are there other calls to Aaron's office?"

Bina's eyes scrolled the screen.

"Two others, both the previous month. The first was six minutes and the other less than a minute like the last one."

"Interesting. It's also possible Howard was calling to speak with another attorney, but if he was trying to reach Aaron, I can't help wondering if he confided in him about the baby. The information would go straight to the high council."

"Why do the men allow this kind of control?" Bina asked.

"From the time they're born, they receive the same amount

of brainwashing as girls but with a different message. Boys grow up thinking they will be Gods over their families after death. They're trained in how to preach to their wives and children and listen to their father do it in twice-daily sessions. Inside their future homes, they will never be told they're wrong, argued with, or reprimanded for anything. It's all about power and control. The more wives they're awarded, the more people they have power over. Outside the home others are in charge and the prophet has absolute power over them."

Eve pondered it for a moment.

"Aaron went to college then stepped into his father's shoes after working two years as one of his attorneys. He should have had ten years or more experience before he was elected. The powers that be wanted a yes man and Aaron is exactly that. I doubt the high council has many men his age. He's young for the power he holds and he doesn't want to lose it. He's, unfortunately for him, not good at manipulation and I doubt anyone has ever told him so. He was spoiled as the oldest son. He could do no wrong."

"That makes him very dangerous." Bina held Eve's gaze until Eve acknowledged what she said.

"You sound like Clyde. My stepbrother has always been dangerous."

Bina nodded, assured Eve understood the threat. Eve knew personally how dangerous a man Aaron could be. She looked down at her hand and bent the finger he'd broken so many years before. It ached when her hands were cold. She couldn't forget what Aaron was capable of.

Her phone chimed. It was a text message from Tamm.

Your car was picked up by body shop. They will have it three days. Traffic report sent to your insurance.

Eve typed back:

You're an angel.

I prefer Nephilim.

Eve smiled. Of course Tamm would choose to be known as the offspring of the sons of God and the daughters of men.

She and Bina worked on their reports and took one break to stretch. Typing on their laptops was the boring part of police work, but when things moved fast, which needed to happen in this case, having the initial reports written would help with any arrests later on.

She kept checking the clock. The meeting had a lot riding on it and time dragged while the missing-child clock sped up.

Eve's phone rang and Tamm's name showed on the caller ID.

"This was too long for a text message. Hammon and Bockstater are out of Texas. I'll email their driver's license info to you. No property listed in Utah but both have multiple assets in Texas. What was interesting was they both showed up in the investigation into the prophet. Neither were arrested or charged. They moved off the Zion Ranch and purchased substantial amounts of property. I can't find job listings for either of them."

"Thank you. Keep digging."

"Will do."

The call ended. Eve's stepfather lived in Texas and that was too much of a coincidence. The prophet spoke to his wives from prison and gave them small revelations to share with his followers. Stricter orders came from men higher up the chain. One such man was their bishop. Eve remained in the dark over who that was. If she took a wild guess, she would lay the title on Bockstater's door with Hammon as his puppet.

She continued typing, but thoughts of her stepfather crept in. Aaron was dangerous, but his father was more so. He didn't have Aaron's weaknesses. Eve knew one day she would come face to face with him and she didn't look forward to it.

Collin and Ray picked up dinner at five thirty. They'd had only light snacks for lunch, but Eve barely ate those. Her skeleton nightmare remained troubling along with what she'd learned about Hammon and Bockstater. If they lived in Texas, who really ran Hildale? It wasn't Aaron. She couldn't shake the feeling that everything was about to go from bad to worse.

She moved her food around on the plate then tossed it, hoping the others didn't notice. When she looked at Clyde, his frown told her he'd seen what she'd done. Eve quickly focused his attention on the upcoming meeting with Eric, knowing he'd mention her lack of food later.

Clyde laid out his plan.

As soon as the sun went down, Clyde and Collin walked to the minimart to scope the area. Clyde had paid attention when they passed the old tire shop earlier but wanted to find a way there that evaded the God squad. The minimart where they filled their gas tanks and the only place in town that was open twenty-four hours sat on the corner a little past the tire shop.

The men were gone for thirty minutes.

"It's small with an old, rusted propane tank toward the back," Clyde said about the tire shop when he and Collin returned.

They'd driven past many times, but nothing stood out to Eve.

"The dumpster blocks the view from the street on the west side," Clyde continued. "Two God squad vehicles were waiting in their usual spot next to the hotel. We were able to get around them by taking an alley behind us where garbage is picked up. There's a small amount of light from the businesses so we're not using flashlights, but watch your step. Two blocks over, the alley comes out about a hundred feet kitty-corner from the minimart.

The tire shop is a quarter block west. We'll get in place ten minutes early. Eve, you'll cross the street with Collin from the north. I'll remain in position so I can see cars coming from the east or west." He drew a rough map. "Ray, you'll go over the alley wall here. There are bushes that will hide you and you'll have the best view of the meeting." He made an X that was on the side street that intersected with the main street in front of the hotel. "Bina, we'll leave you here."

No one argued. This part of the meeting was Clyde's operation. While Eve and Collin spoke to Eric, the others would be hidden but close enough in case they were needed.

"It took us eight minutes to walk from the garage to the hotel using the alley," Clyde said. "It will take a few extra minutes to cross the street and circle behind the minimart to get in place on the north side. There is only one streetlamp on the main road. There's no visibility behind the tire shop at all. Questions?"

"No," Eve said, and the others shook their heads.

Clyde handed out tactical flashlights and the radios.

"No street cameras between here and the minimart," he added. "Only one car passed us so there shouldn't be much traffic."

Women did their shopping during the day and husbands were home in the evening for nightly prayer sessions.

"That works," said Eve. "Does anyone have something to add?"

They shook their heads. Eve placed her flashlight in the side zippered pocket of her dark tactical pants then attached the radio to the back of her belt and brought it beneath her shirt while the others did the same. After the earpiece was adjusted, she looked at the time.

"Radio check," said Clyde.

They moved away from each other.

"Turn them low and turn all phones to silent," he reminded them.

"Radio check, one, two, three."

Hands came up around the room.

"You ready?" Clyde asked them.

"Good to go," Eve said.

TWENTY

They went to the back of the hotel and through a gate into the alley. There was minimal light, but they could see without stumbling too badly. The alley was mostly empty, ten feet across, with six-foot brick walls on either side. They stayed in the middle so they didn't need to dodge garbage cans. There were no barking dogs to worry about because the prophet's rules said no pets. Feeding dogs took money out of his pockets.

Ray stopped about halfway and climbed onto a garbage can after Clyde pointed the location out.

"I'm breaking off here," he said after peering over the wall. "The bushes are about twenty feet away. Stay safe."

They kept moving to the end of the alley where the street connected. They checked traffic in both directions before they headed north to the intersection. Bina stayed put at the waist-high bushes along a short three-foot rickety wooden fence. Eve, Clyde, and Collin crossed the main road and went behind the minimart, came out, crossed the street again, and made it to a driveway directly across from the tire shop without cars passing.

"The God squad is gone," Clyde whispered when they were in place.

They could see the side parking lot of the hotel from their location. Eve looked around to be sure they hadn't moved but didn't see them. The team usually stayed in at night and the habitual schedule was paying off right now. She gave an internal sigh of relief. If Eric was trying to help them, she didn't want him running into problems with the God squad and this made it safer for him.

"The back of the shop is dark and hard to see close to the building," Ray whispered into their earpieces.

"Same here," Bina said just as quietly. "I don't see movement, but someone could be there."

There was a long driveway directly across the street from the tire shop. A large tree was about twelve feet from the road. Eve, Clyde, and Collin stayed close to the tree to help them blend into the shadows. Eve tried to make out shapes across the street, but all she could see was the shop and the large metal dumpster on the west side toward the back.

Minutes after they were situated, car headlights approached from the west heading toward the cross streets. The vehicle came in fast. A slight squeal of brakes was the only signal they had that it was making a turn into the tire-shop parking lot. The black SUV careened around the dumpster. Was it Eric?

Gunshots filled the air.

Before her team had a chance to respond, the SUV continued around the shop, took out the fence where Bina was located, and screeched right.

Clyde was shouting within seconds of the gunfire. "Hold your fire." They couldn't see each other and there was the possibility of crossfire if they discharged their weapons.

Ray yelled, "Man down."

"Bina," Eve yelled into her mic.

"I'm good," she yelled back. "They missed me by ten feet, but I can't see Ray."

"I'm going in," Eve said, and started running across the

street toward where Ray had disappeared. The shots had to have come from the vehicle which was now gone. Clyde and Collin were right behind her.

"Collin, stop at the back corner of the building," she said loud enough for him to hear. "Clyde, we're stopping at the dumpster." As soon as she said the words, Ray called out.

"Clear. Eve, get back here now."

She rounded the corner of the tire shop and could see a body on the ground. Ray was down beside him. The man was saying something to Ray and then she heard her name. She slid to her knees beside them and then froze when Ray's flashlight lit up the man's face.

TWENTY-ONE

"I've got your six," Clyde called out to Ray and Eve. "Bina, are you still good?" he asked over the radio.

"Yes, I'm moving to the opposite side of the building from Collin."

"Copy. Hold your position once you're in place," Clyde told her.

The communications were a buzz of noise that Eve wasn't quite registering. Ray had his flashlight shining on the downed man's face.

"I'm calling for an ambulance," Ray told her.

His voice sounded far away and she barely registered when he took out his cell phone and requested police and an ambulance. Eve was staring into the eyes of one of her stepbrothers. Eric, to be exact. It was a common name and she hadn't made the connection.

He was the baby torn from her arms when Maggie had rescued her from her stepfather. Eve hadn't been sure which of her stepbrothers was missing the day before when they tried to intimidate her and Bina. Now she knew it was Eric.

Blood covered his dark shirt and was pooling beneath him.

His eyes were on hers, but she wasn't sure he knew who she was. Then he said her name.

"Eve?" It was soft. Almost a whisper.

"I'm here," she told him.

"I never wanted to hurt you," he coughed. His chest was rising and falling rapidly while the pool of blood beneath him grew. "I begged them not to. You don't deserve their hate."

Eve would process what he was saying later.

"Who shot you?" she asked kindly, and took his hand. His fingers tightened on hers. They were so cold.

He coughed blood this time and the dark circle beneath him continued growing.

"I didn't want to hurt you," he repeated.

"It's okay, Eric." She smiled softly. "Tell me who shot you."

His head moved back and forth, his eyes opening wider.

"My pocket. Get the note from my pocket. Don't let them see it."

"Don't let who see it?" she begged. He was dying. She wanted to help him, but there was nothing she could do.

His eyes closed and she couldn't tell if he was breathing.

"Eric. Talk to me." She squeezed his fingers even harder.

His eyes opened partially.

"I tried to be a good man. I wanted to leave here," he whispered. "Forgive me." He coughed again. "I remember you telling me stories. They are happy memories."

Telling stories was against the rules, but Maggie had told them to Eve when they were alone in her room and she'd passed them down to the younger kids at night if they were upset about something. They were mostly upset over empty bellies because their father had punished even the little ones by making them go without food. She would have thought Eric was too young to remember her stories, but they were probably the only ones he'd ever been told.

"You were a good sister." He coughed again. "It doesn't hurt anymore." His lips curved up slightly.

His fingers loosened in hers. His body relaxed and his gaze stayed fixed but there was nothing behind it.

"No, Eric, don't go," she said uselessly while checking his pulse. There wasn't one.

"I'm doing CPR," she told Ray.

"Eve." It was Clyde. "Let me in closer, I've got it. Take the flashlight."

Eve knew it was too late for Eric, but she had to try. She did as Clyde said. Her brain wasn't functioning properly. She needed to calm down and focus. Clyde began CPR. Eve moved to Eric's other side and lifted his hand, squeezing his fingers. She heard the ambulance and police in the distance.

"Did you get a look at who did this?" Clyde asked Ray who was standing over them.

"The vehicle was a Lincoln Navigator. It was hard to see inside and I can only be sure of the driver, but there could have been two people or more. The windows were tinted."

Eve looked around the area as she held Eric's hand. They were out in the open. What if the vehicle came back? She must have said it aloud.

"If they return, we've got it covered." Ray assured her.

She gazed at Eric, her thoughts on him as a little boy. He'd been almost three when she was taken by her mother. He had been such a good baby and seldom cried. She'd sing to him on the rare occasions he fussed and of course told him stories of princes on big horses, kissing the princess and waking her up. His sweetness reminded her of Charlie. This was why her step-brothers' assault had hurt so much emotionally. She had loved them. Even the other boys were not mean to her unless Aaron instigated it. All her siblings were afraid of Aaron and they didn't want to be on his bad side. Eve was his bad side and it was easier on them if they didn't give her attention. They were only mean in his presence, otherwise she was mostly ignored.

Clyde didn't stop chest compressions. She held on to a small hope that the ambulance would arrive in time even though she knew it was too late. She thought about what Eric had said and started to reach into his pocket.

"This is a crime scene," Clyde reminded her gently.

She withdrew her hand. She had a job to do. Grief would come later. She quickly organized her thoughts.

"I'm okay," she told Clyde, and released Eric's hand. A siren was drawing closer. "Holster your weapons," she called over the radio. The first police unit pulled into the parking lot. She placed Clyde's flashlight on the ground, stood, and unclipped her badge from her waist lifting it into the air. She stayed between Eric's body and the rolling squad car.

It came to a sudden halt about ten feet from her. The officer turned off his siren, activated his brights, and opened his door.

"I'm Detective Sergeant Eve Bennet," she said into the blinding light, her voice loud, filled with authority, and crystal clear.

"Keep your hands where I can see them," the officer yelled, his gun pointed at her chest.

TWENTY-TWO

Eve did as she was ordered, understanding that it took a moment to register a scene like this. Until he'd had time to adjust to them as cops, everyone was a threat.

"Call dispatch," she told him. "Have them send County Attorney Owens to the scene." The bright lights still made it hard to see.

"You don't tell me what to do," the officer yelled.

Okay, that was petty and made her think he knew exactly who he was dealing with. Another squad car pulled into the parking lot.

The first officer moved closer, his gun still trained on her.

"We are law enforcement, lower your weapon," she demanded.

She heard the second officer's door open, but she wasn't taking her eyes off the guy with the gun.

"Get on the ground," he yelled from no more than six feet away. He could see her badge and he didn't care.

"Whoa. We're on your side," Ray said from her right.

The officer kept his gun on Eve.

"We have our badges in the air," she said levelly. "Radio dispatch and have them call the county attorney."

"I told you to get on the ground."

"No." Her patience was at an end.

His gun wavered as Ray moved closer to her.

"He's ignoring the rest of us. This is personal," Ray said.

"Officer," Eve said loudly. "You know I'm with the state taskforce. Video is being recorded of your actions. Don't lose your badge over something stupid." Clyde said there were no video cameras, but he didn't know if her team was filming or not. The officer hadn't looked at anyone but Eve since he arrived. She had to de-escalate the situation before he shot her.

His attention turned to Clyde and his gun jerked in the same direction. He took a step to her right and walked closer to Eric's body.

"Put your hands where I can see them," he yelled at Clyde, forgetting about Eve. Clyde simply ignored him.

"There are five of us," Eve said. "Four of us have our badges out. Detective Johnston is performing CPR. Keep your weapon in your hand, but lower it."

"Shut the fuck up," the officer said harshly. His gun didn't leave Clyde.

"Get the county attorney here," Eve yelled out to the other officer who remained at his vehicle.

The second officer shouted into his radio requesting Aaron at the scene.

Eve's team didn't move. She knew they were ready to draw their guns because she had the same inclination. If that happened, it wouldn't end well. The second officer approached the first one.

"Brother Jarrod, it's me. Lower your weapon. I recognize them from the Tanner case. They're cops."

"It doesn't matter," was his reply.

"If you want to keep your job, it matters. Lower your weapon." This time it was a command. Jarrod glanced at Eve then returned his attention to the other officer who had given the order.

"He shouldn't be touching him," he said.

Clyde watched while he continued chest compressions.

Eve and Ray slowly walked closer to Eric. Their badges were lowered, but their hands were out slightly so there was no misunderstanding. They moved between Jarrod and Clyde.

Jarrod lowered his weapon but didn't put it back in the holster. The other officer walked closer and placed his hand on Jarrod's shoulder. It was shaken off angrily.

Eve turned her back on them and stepped beside Clyde. She looked down at her stepbrother. He wasn't coming back.

"He's gone. You can stop," she told him.

An ambulance pulled in and the crew jumped out. Clyde stood. He had blood on his hands and shirt. They watched as the crew hooked Eric up to wires and started CPR again. They had no choice until a doctor certified death. The heart monitor displayed straight lines.

"No pulse," said one of the men.

Defibrillator electrodes were placed on his chest.

"Clear."

The emergency medical team used the paddles three times, but his heart didn't restart. Too much blood had pumped from his wounds. One of the EMTs called the hospital and spoke to a doctor while CPR continued. Another shined a light into Eric's eyes and recited vitals to the man on the phone.

"Pronounced dead, 2032 hours." CPR stopped.

All she could see was his toddler smile, not the man who had attacked her and caused so much pain.

"Eve," Clyde said.

She shut down thoughts of her past, determined to discover who killed her stepbrother.

"My detective has blood contamination," Eve told the emergency crew. "Please provide antiseptic so he can clean himself."

"No," said Jarrod. "He has evidence covering him." His rage was visceral. First it had been directed at Eve and now at Clyde. She was fed up with his crap.

"Detective Johnston attempted to save his life," Eve told him, her anger rising. "Follow protocol like you would for any officer. If you refuse, I'll file a complaint with POST and you will lose your badge." POST, Peace Officers Standards and Training, was the police overlord in all states. POST didn't care who ran law enforcement in this town. The officer would face a hearing. Eve stepped closer to him, completely blocking him from Clyde when his stance changed and his hand with the gun lifted slightly. "Holster your weapon. This is my crime scene and my murder investigation. Stand down."

Their eyes clashed. He thought he could stare her into submission just like Aaron attempted to do. They were both wrong.

Another vehicle pulled into the small parking lot blocking the ambulance, but Eve was not paying attention to it.

She stood her ground. Jarrod turned in the direction of the vehicle and put his gun into his holster though he kept his hand on the butt.

"Back away from my crime scene," she said, taking a step in his direction. "Now."

He walked several feet away. It wasn't far enough for her peace of mind after the crap he'd pulled. She turned slightly and saw Aaron. Eve quickly strode closer to him to keep him back. Detective mode, she reminded herself. She needed Aaron's help and she had no idea how he would react to his brother's death.

It was well after eight and he was in a suit and tie. He looked far more professional than he had the evening before. A high council meeting went through her head and flittered away. She had to stay on track.

"The ambulance crew needs to decontaminate Detective Johnston," she told her stepbrother, taking his attention from the body. "He's covered in blood after trying to save the victim's life. That officer"—she pointed at Jarrod—"needs to drive my detectives to the hotel immediately so they can bring back our crime scene van." She held up her hand when Aaron tried to interrupt. "Once those tasks are complete and I've secured the scene, I'll speak to you about what happened." It was insensitive, but she didn't see any other choice.

Aaron turned to Jarrod.

"Officer Keb, do what she says and drive her detectives to the hotel."

"But, sir. I was here first," he said angrily with a hint of whine.

First on scene typically meant the case was yours, but it didn't matter if he'd arrived before Eve's team, which he hadn't. She had judicial rights to take over any felony in the county. He was acting like a child who couldn't have a toy. She wouldn't be surprised if he stomped his feet.

Jarrod Keb. His name rang a bell, but there was too much going on to think about it right then. It would have a starring role in her report and it *would* go to POST along with a formal complaint. She did not want this officer standing at her back and he had no right to wear a badge.

"You've been given an order," Aaron said sharply. "Do not make me repeat myself."

Officer Keb stared for a moment then turned abruptly while saying something under his breath she didn't catch. An ambulance crew member walked up to Clyde.

"Step over here with me, sir, and I'll get you cleaned up."

"Ray, take Bina with you and bring back the van and SUV," she told him.

He waved Bina over. She stood about twenty feet away. They followed Officer Keb to his vehicle. Eve was thankful it was a short ride.

She turned to the remaining officer. "I need crime scene tape if you have some." He nodded. "We'll replace it," she assured him. Eve turned slightly and called after Ray, "Bring Clyde a clean shirt. Get a keycard for his room at the front desk."

Ray waved.

The officer retrieved the tape from his vehicle.

"Stay back for now," she told Aaron.

She walked closer to Eric's body and addressed the ambulance crew.

"Leave everything but your gear and back out," she told the two men from EMS who remained kneeling beside Eric.

They detached their equipment and reluctantly returned to the ambulance. Eric's shirt was torn open and the electric probes still on his chest. She turned away and searched for Clyde.

His shirt was off while someone sprayed him with antiseptic solution and gave him wipes to clean his hands. She walked to Aaron.

"Tie the tape to the tree over there," she told him and handed over the end of the yellow tape and pointed.

With an angry grunt, he marched to the tree while Eve held on to the roll. Once it was tied, she made the area the size she wanted. She would have the cars cleared out shortly. Someone on her team would make the inner barrier once they were all here again and the evidence van was available for processing the scene.

"Tell one of my detectives you need a replacement roll when they return," she told the officer who had walked closer. "Thank you for identifying us after you arrived."

He was unsure what to say with Aaron scowling. He simply nodded.

She addressed Collin who stood approximately twelve feet away. "Keep everyone behind the tape."

She gave her full attention to Aaron. The best thing to do was start at the beginning.

"There was a note inside my hotel room door," she said. "It was given to the hotel's owner and she left it in my room. The note wasn't signed, but she told me a man gave it to her. It was white notebook paper and had handwritten instructions to meet him behind this tire shop at eight tonight. She only knew his first name. We arrived a little early and spread out. I was across the street with Detectives Johnston and Smith. A black SUV came from the west on the main street..." She pointed to the road. "It slowed and turned into the tire shop, drove around the dumpster to the back, out of my line of sight. Multiple shots were fired rapidly. We have not yet examined the scene for evidence, and we will know more after we begin," she continued. "Detective Gonzales had the best view. He was standing at the bushes by the alley wall." She pointed in the general direction. "Detective Blau was on the side street and close to the fence when the vehicle continued and took it out. Detective Gonzales is unsure if there was one or more people in the vehicle. It had tinted windows. After the SUV smashed that section of fence, it turned right onto the side road heading south. I haven't questioned Detective Blau on what she saw. I will as soon as we're secure here."

She took a slow steady breath. "The hotel owner told me the young man who gave her the note was named Eric. She did not know his last name and only knew him from the deli counter at the grocery store."

It didn't sink in right away. Aaron looked at the body then back at Eve as it dawned on him.

"No," he said.

Before she could answer, he ran to Eric and dropped to his knees.

"No, no, no," he whispered.

Eve wasn't sure what to do. She wanted to place her hand on Aaron's shoulder, but something stopped her. She simply stood by him and waited. He sniffed and wiped his eyes. Moments later, he rocked back on his feet, still not standing when he looked up at her.

"You did this," he said with so much hatred, Eve took a step back. "Who shot him?"

Eve shut down the emotions she was feeling.

"We don't know. It was dark. We didn't know he was here until after the shots were fired."

"One of your men shot him," Aaron claimed angrily, his voice rising.

"That is not what happened. Get control of yourself. This is a crime scene."

The second officer to arrive was standing close enough to hear his shout and so were the EMTs. It would be all over town within hours.

Aaron looked at Eric. When he glanced back at Eve there were equal parts sorrow and anger on his face.

"You are not overseeing this case. He's your brother," Aaron said.

"Stepbrother and he was three years old when I left. He was not with his brothers today when they came to the hotel." The earlier incident would be part of the investigation, but she kept that to herself for now.

Eve did not tell him what Eric had said to her. It was something else she would keep private for the time being. Aaron was only hearing what he wanted to and he was not on her side.

"I need you to back away so we can start processing the scene. Move your vehicle behind the tape. I'm sorry it must be this way. Someone killed Eric to keep him from speaking to me.

I'll be interviewing you tomorrow morning. Right now, I have work to do."

Aaron stood with his eyes on his brother. Then he turned to her.

"Yes, Detective Bennet," he practically spit. He spoke the words she'd used when she arrived at the Tanner homicides, changing it slightly. "I'm aware of how you manage your crime scenes."

TWENTY-THREE

Collin untied the tape from the tree so Aaron, the ambulance, and the second officer's patrol car could get out. Ray and Bina arrived and Collin reattached the tape after the van and SUV were through. Ray jumped out and took a shirt to Clyde. Bina walked over to Eve.

"Did you see anything when the suspect vehicle drove past you?"

"The driver's window was sliding upward when the vehicle passed me and the tint made it hard to see inside. There could have been a passenger in the front seat or even someone in the back but I couldn't swear on it. The vehicle barely slowed when the shots were fired. In my opinion, whoever it was had one purpose for going back there and that was to kill Eric."

Eve glanced around the area, trying to get her thoughts straight. She watched Ray speak to the second officer and go to the van to grab a roll of tape for him. When budgets were short, things like crime scene tape were handed out grudgingly to patrol officers. Even at the state level, she had dealt with this early in her career.

Someone had set out to kill Eric. She didn't like where her

thoughts were going and things like crime scene tape were easier to consider.

"I'm going to help Ray," Bina said after a moment when Eve didn't ask further questions.

Ray had grabbed another roll of tape to secure the inner scene. Aaron stood at his vehicle which was now moved back. He stared in the direction of the body. Eve could not clearly see his face.

"How are you holding up?"

Clyde had walked up next to her, but she hadn't noticed. He had the new shirt on and held a plastic bag which she figured contained the bloody shirt. Officer Keb had not been wrong; it was evidence, but blood contamination had to be taken seriously and officer safety was the priority.

Clyde handed the bag to Collin, who had also walked up. He turned and took it to the van. Sadly, it had to dry before being officially packaged. They had cords that attached inside the van to hang wet evidence. She wouldn't be able to avoid the van so geared her brain to ignore the bloody shirt.

"I'm keeping my mind on what needs to be done," she told him. "I'll break down later. Right now, we have a job to do."

"Should we be handling this investigation?" he asked softly.

"Yes. Someone shot and killed him because he was meeting us. His note from earlier ties this into our missing baby case."

"Your stepbrothers are now homicide suspects. Eric wasn't with them earlier." Clyde pointed out the obvious and she figured it was to see where her mind was.

She had trouble believing they would murder him. But then, she hadn't believed they would assault her with the intent to kill. She wouldn't be stupid about their possible involvement.

"I'm very aware my stepbrothers might be responsible for Eric's death. If they were, we'll find out and they will be prosecuted." She thought about their visit to the hotel. "Eric could have been working when they came to harass me and Bina. He told me that he hadn't wanted to hurt me. He was part of it though and now we have corroboration." Something else came to mind. "I'm not happy over the scene with Officer Keb. We have this job because law enforcement here is corrupt. I don't trust him or the others in the police and sheriff's department. We got lucky with the second officer on scene. I didn't get his name." That had been a screw-up on her part. She would focus and it wouldn't happen again.

"Ray has it," Clyde said.

"Okay, good. Eric mentioned a note in his pocket. After I have outer scene photos, we'll find it. Hopefully it contains information that helps us figure this mess out. I don't want to disturb the crime scene any more than we already have. Let's start processing."

She glanced at Eric's body. He was twenty-six years old though he appeared younger. He was nice to Harina. It didn't fit with what she knew of the fundamentalist teachings. It was possible she and Eric could have gotten to know one another and been friends. She fought against her emotions then straightened her shoulders refusing to let tears fall.

"What do you need me to do?" Clyde asked gently.

"Thank you for doing CPR," she told him. "Please stay with me while I take the photos. I need to call Tamm. Have Bina, Collin, and Ray keep the scene secure. I don't want anyone crossing our lines, especially Aaron." Eve was determined to concentrate on the tasks before her. It would be an exceptionally long night and they hadn't really caught up on the sleep they'd missed when they arrived. This was only day two of Linda's case and now they had a homicide that had happened in front of them.

She took her phone out and hit Tamm's cell number.

"Hi, it's getting late," Tamm answered with laughter in her voice.

"I know, can you send a medical examiner body pickup our

way?" She hated to ruin Tamm's good mood but wouldn't want anyone else on the other end of the line.

"I don't like the sound of that. Is everyone okay?"

"The team is good. It will be a long night, get the ME team on the road ASAP." She gave Tamm the names of the cross streets.

"Got it. I'm sorry to ask, but is it the child?"

"No. It's one of my stepbrothers."

Tamm went quiet for a moment.

"I'm sorry. I'll be awake, call if you need anything."

Tamm was not a fan of Eve's childhood family, but she was always professional when working and would stay up all night just as they would. Eve would call her back as soon as she had time to explain more about Eric's death.

Footsteps sounded behind her and she turned.

"Your camera equipment," Clyde said, and handed over her bag. He'd collected it from the back of the SUV.

"Thank you." She needed to concentrate on the investigation. She removed her camera and handed the bag to Clyde before she secured the strap around the back of her neck.

The camera was more than just a piece of equipment to her. It had always been an emotional shield from the horrors she witnessed. Maggie had given Eve a much cheaper version as a gift when she was fourteen. It had helped change Eve's narrow world when she was still battling the clutches of her fundamentalist upbringing and searching for answers. The camera grounded her. She squared her shoulders and cleared her mind of everything but the investigation. Eric was a victim and it was up to her and the team to discover who killed him.

She began walking the scene, moving closer to the body as she worked. She snapped photos of the crumbled concrete that surrounded the tire shop, the building itself, propane tank, and even the minimart, diagonally across from where she stood. The soft clicks as her finger hit the shutter button put her further into detective mode.

The minimart faced west and the garage north. The van and SUV's lights were on, but Clyde added his flashlight. She automatically adjusted the lens as she gazed through the view finder for each shot. The darkness filled with her flash. She moved closer to the body and discovered the first bullet casing cartridge.

"Here's two more," said Clyde after she called it out. "They're 40s."

She photographed the three casings before Clyde laid down three evidence markers. She would retake pictures after this first walk-through.

The evidence aligned with the three shots she'd heard. She stepped closer to Eric's body and began taking close-ups. She lowered the camera and studied his torso while Clyde used his flashlight to help her see. She crouched down. One bullet had entered his shoulder. Another had gone into his chest, inches from his heart. She didn't notice a third bullet hole in his clothing, but there was blood covering most of the shirt and the entry could be hidden. The autopsy would give them more answers.

"Eve," Aaron called out when she stood after taking the close-up images.

"Stay here," she told Clyde.

Her emotions were raw, but he was the county attorney and he'd been quiet while she took the photos. She walked over to him.

"I apologize," he said quietly when she was close enough. "I have no idea why he wanted to speak with you. I haven't heard from him in months." He shook his head. "Not since the attack on you."

The door to Aaron's car was open and there was a small amount of light. It was enough to see the redness in his eyes. Even with the tears he'd shed, she didn't believe him. Right now, she couldn't. They were not on the same side and she felt Aaron was doing damage control. He had four other brothers. They may or may not have pulled the trigger, but they were part of this.

"You need to go home and be with your family. We have things under control. It's your brother who died. Send another attorney from your office if you feel it's needed."

"Okay," he mumbled, and glanced down at the ground. He didn't move for a moment and she thought he might say something else. Without another word, he finally turned and got into his car without looking at her.

She walked back to Clyde who was examining the outer wall of the tire shop.

"There's a bullet wedged in here," he told her. "I'll grab my bag while you take photographs of it. We also need to go back and take photos of the markers and start the photolog."

He was helping her stay on track. Unfortunately, she needed the reminder about the photolog.

She snapped the images quickly. She and Clyde started walking the scene again and she took photos of the three evidence markers with the bullet casings and then the wall again as Clyde filled in the photolog.

"I didn't notice vehicles in the area when we arrived. Did you?" she asked when they moved back to the body. Clyde handed her gloves then laid out a small tarp next to Eric.

"One drove from the side street heading south and turned into the minimart without passing us," he replied.

Eve took a moment to digest what he'd said. She needed the time to gear up for what had to be done next.

"I need to search his pockets."

"Do you want me to do it?" Clyde asked.

"No. I'm okay."

She crouched beside Eric again and simply looked at him. She reached out and closed his eyes so she could concentrate on what had to be done. She began searching. His shirt pocket was first. The material was plaid with two shades of blue with white and black stripes. The area around his chest was saturated in blood.

She pulled a single piece of gum out and laid it on the tarp. She found an all-purpose tool in the front pocket of his jeans. The other pocket had a few coins which she added to her growing collection of personal items. He was like many other young men when it came to what he carried on him.

"Can you roll his body?" she asked Clyde.

He got on the other side and rolled Eric his way so Eve could reach the back pockets. The first was empty. The second contained his wallet. She opened it and a piece of notebook paper was folded where the bills would go. He had no money. She noticed it was two sheets of paper when she placed the notes beside the wallet on the tarp. Clyde gently laid Eric's body back to how it had been. He then added an evidence marker next to what Eve had collected. She took photos then reached for the note and opened it.

TWENTY-FOUR

The paper was the same type left in her hotel room. It was folded to fit inside his wallet and when she unfurled it, there was writing on both sides.

- *Stones*
- *Call*
- *Call*
- *Call*
- *Collision*

Each line had a date beside the word. The first line coincided with the attack on her at the Wall residence during the Tanner case. She would never forget that day. She took her phone from her pocket and checked the call log. Each date after *Call* coincided with the harassment calls. The last, *Collision*, was the night her vehicle was hit.

Eric had wanted her to have this. He was trying to help. She pushed back tears. They wouldn't help her bring justice to whoever did this.

His note implied her stepbrothers had assaulted her and

rear-ended her vehicle. They were also behind the harassment calls. It hurt even though she'd known it was them. She flipped the paper over. It had a list of last names, genders, and dates.

The second-to-last line was dated three days before.

- *Wall – girl*

She didn't recognize the other last names, but she knew Aaron most likely would. Three on the list said girl and two said boy. The first name, Whiting, was dated a year and a half ago.

She would ask Aaron tomorrow. There was still too much that had to be done tonight.

The last line had a three-digit number.

- *910*

She had no idea what it meant.

The second page had a map with highways and what looked like hills or rocks. It was marked at the top with the words *Water Canyon*. The main roads were labeled, but after the entrance to the hiking area, it just showed a curved mark that continued for some time. The canyon was northeast of Hildale and had the sheer rock formations you could see from town. It had to be a service road because Eve doubted there was anything else there. It would be a very remote location. At the end of the road, there was an X. She wasn't sure what it meant, but she couldn't help thinking it had something to do with the isolation Danielle had told her about. They would need to check into it, but there were still a hundred other things they had to do to find out who killed her stepbrother and to find Linda's missing baby.

Eric had tried to help. Eve could have helped him get away and he could have started a new life like she had. She wiped her face, refusing to acknowledge the tears that wanted to fall and angry at herself for giving in to them even if it was only a bit of wetness on her cheeks. She had work to do.

She took a photograph of the pages, front and back, with her camera and her cell phone in case she needed to reference them when her laptop wasn't handy. She placed the notes next to his wallet when she was done.

"Grab your evidence bag," she told Clyde, and took off her gloves.

He was looking at her like she would break and that made her angry. She couldn't right now and he needed to understand that. If he placed his arms around her, she would crumble and it wasn't the time. It didn't matter that it was exactly what she needed. If she allowed her emotions to interfere, she would be better off getting another team up here to handle the homicide and that wasn't happening. She put more force into her next words than she would normally do.

"Remove the bullet from the wall so it can be sent to the lab as soon as possible. I'll text Tamm to have a tech head our way in the morning. We can keep everything in the van evidence safe until then. Maybe we can get the lab work back sooner than the bullet extractions from the body during the autopsy."

The autopsy could take one to seven days. The bullet analysis, the same. If they waited, it could be two weeks before they had results and each day was vital right now.

Clyde walked away and Eve sighed in relief. He had to know she was on edge. He also knew now was not the time to show compassion. Eve sent the message to Tamm. Another vehicle pulled close to the tape. It was an unmarked police SUV with front and rear red-and-blue lights flashing. She knew who it was before he stepped from the vehicle.

"Do not cross the tape," she yelled when Police Chief Jackson placed his hand on it. He ignored her, lifted it, and entered the outer scene. She dug into her pocket and flipped on her recorder as she marched to intercept him from the inner line.

"This is my town," he said angrily.

"It's my crime scene and you will now be writing a report." She took out her recorder and showed him the green light so he knew it was on. "If you step closer, I will inform the judge and the city council." The city council hired the police chief, unlike a sheriff who was voted into office. The local council wouldn't care, but the words slipped out before she could stop them. The chief was leery of the judge and she hoped it was enough. "Don't press me," she threatened. She wasn't winning any points with him, but she didn't care. He'd never liked her and he was a friend of her stepfather's, which caused even more friction. She'd dealt with him during the Tanner case and it hadn't been pleasant. He would run over her if she let him. If he had ever wondered why she was put in charge of the taskforce, she was ready to show him.

His eyes sizzled with contempt. If he had his way, she would be lying on the ground in the last throes of death. He was thinking about defying her order.

Do it, she thought to herself. *Please.*

He was dressed casually. It was the first time she'd seen him without the official stars on his collar. His gut looked larger, but maybe the uniform he usually wore disguised his paunch more than the jeans. His button-up white shirt strained at his midsection and the long sleeves were rolled to his elbows.

His blue eyes pierced hers, challenging, and speaking volumes. He wanted to continue walking. He wanted to examine the body, but he hesitated. Eve won the round.

The only person who disliked her more than him was the sheriff, another friend of her stepfather's. He'd visited the house when she was a child and she didn't have good memories of him. She wouldn't be surprised if he showed up too. She had to be prepared. Could the sheriff and chief be related? They had a level of arrogance that was off the charts. Their light blue eye color was similar too though the sheriff won for the creepier of the pair.

"By tomorrow," Eve told him, "I will need your report and that of the two officers who arrived on the scene earlier." With that said, it was time to show she could be professional if he continued following orders. "There isn't much evidence," she informed him. "The ME van is on its way to collect the body. We will have the scene cleared as soon as the deceased is removed. It's Eric Owens, the county attorney's brother. He's been shot at least twice. You may want to contact the person in charge of charity relief. Someone should see Aaron."

Death was one of the few times wives entered another family's home and interacted. The person in charge of relief would arrange for the women to take food and help until the funeral. Eve remembered going to these homes when she was young. It gave her a day off from endless labor. The children enjoyed the respite more than they should have, which made it a sad memory.

The chief didn't acknowledge what she'd said. He looked down at the recorder again, pivoted, and stormed to the two officers who were still behind the outer tape. If they stayed outside the scene, she didn't care what they did.

She shut off her recorder and walked closer to Collin.

"Radio if anyone crosses the tape again," she told him.

"Got it." Collin gave her a concerned look.

She had to stop this.

"Do your job," she told him. "I'll do mine."

She walked quickly back to Eric's body so she couldn't see his reaction. Clyde approached with two large canvas bags and placed them on the ground beside the tarp. One was her evidence bag which she unzipped before removing a log sheet, clipboard, and several manilla folders.

"I've got this," she said. "Remove the bullet from the wall."

He didn't question her. His detective face was back in place. He took a few items from his bag and placed them in his pockets.

One by one, she packaged the evidence then entered the information on a separate log sheet. When she came to the notes, she took a photo with her camera again. Clyde walked from the wall and placed the spent bullet on the tarp. It was a 40-caliber hollow point. She snapped a picture then entered it in the log with the date and time.

She had another worry now. When she was assaulted by her stepbrothers, they'd stolen her gun. It had never been recovered. It was a 40-caliber and the full magazine had carried hollow point bullets. It was a very real possibility that her duty weapon had been used to kill Eric. The Glock 23 was a common police-issue gun, but this was too much of a coincidence. With Eric's note, she felt she had positive proof her stepbrothers had assaulted her which meant they also took her gun. She didn't like where her thoughts were going but she would do her job. If they killed Eric, Eve would see they faced justice for it.

Her phone chimed. It was Tamm.

ME van three hours out. Ten AM on evidence pickup.

She relayed Tamm's message to Clyde.

"Am I missing anything?" she asked. It was standard practice to look over each other's shoulder.

"No. I'll talk to the others and have them make a list. When I come back, we can do the same. If we need to be awake, we might as well gather ideas."

"Sounds good," Eve agreed.

He didn't leave.

"I'm concerned," he said. "I know you can handle this. I'll back off."

"Thank you," was her reply.

"We need to pull Eric's brothers in for questioning. We may make arrests."

This was a warning to prepare her.

"We have positive proof they assaulted me. The evidence may point to them. They took my gun and I know you're thinking the same thing I am. I don't think Aaron is involved because as you know, he doesn't lie well. He was upset. Chances are good he's thinking exactly what we are. He will help them if he can."

Clyde nodded. "Let me talk to the others. I'll be right back."

Eve looked up at the sky. Stars twinkled. The area around her apartment had too much light pollution but here, there were thousands of stars visible. A tear ran from the corner of her eye and she wiped it away. She wasn't even sure why she was crying. Maybe it was because one of her stepbrothers hadn't wanted to be a bad person.

Clyde came back over and they began making a list and discussing the possibilities of what happened. They agreed that Eric had arrived after Clyde and Collin's walk to scope out the location and before the team left the hotel together. That was a twenty-minute window.

Bina's voice sounded over the radio an hour later.

"I'm taking a bathroom break and I'll pick up coffee. Eve, do you want to go with me?"

Eve pressed her mic. "Yes."

Clyde could hear the communication too.

"I'll take her position while you're gone."

She looked at Eric's body, still exposed. She felt guilty for leaving him. She made herself step away. She and Bina crossed the street and walked to the minimart. It was quicker than taking down the scene tape to let the SUV through. They used the restroom which was slightly cleaner than she expected. On scenes, she'd used much worse.

Eve grabbed Collin a Red Bull then joined Bina at the coffee counter. Her brain was running through scenarios that she and Clyde had discussed. A man was filling a large cup with soda and turned around, almost walking into her.

His ice-blue eyes brought back memories she didn't need to revisit tonight.

Sheriff Murray blocked her path.

TWENTY-FIVE

Slowly, he placed a straw in his cup and took a sip, his gaze not leaving hers. To anyone watching, it would appear to be a casual meeting. It was anything but. His eyes held violence, contempt, and lust rolled into one. He wore his ever-present black cowboy hat. Even with the rim low on his forehead, his crystal-blue eyes were beads of aggression. She'd never seen irises the color of his and she grew up in this dominant blue-eyed town. She had no idea who his family was, just that he held power and had since she was a young girl.

He had been in the minimart waiting for her. She couldn't prove it, but somehow, she knew.

When he used to come to her stepfather's home, he'd looked at her just like this. With her sisters, he practically drooled, but with her it was different. He wanted to hurt her. She felt it deep inside and she avoided him whenever she could. Since her stepfather had been the county attorney, to most it wouldn't be strange that Murray visited their house. But he was the only man who stayed for dinner. She would claim a stomachache to get out of sitting at the table with him. It didn't matter that she went to bed hungry, it was preferable to having him watch her.

He'd once grabbed one of her stepsister's breasts after cornering her. He didn't care that Eve caught him. She was a child, what could she do? Her sister took Eve's hand when he stepped back and pulled her from the room. Lilly was two years older. She was never nice to Eve, but that day, she looked in Eve's eyes with fear.

"Stay away from him," she hissed, and pulled her upstairs.

Eve didn't need Lilly's warning.

Now she knew this man for what he was. A predator of girls and women.

"Sheriff," she said with a small nod, no smile, her eyes remaining on his.

He stayed silent and unmoving.

His jeans were black, his shirt, a cowboy-style gray with a blue design on the chest and shoulders. It was something a country western singer would wear on stage. She'd never seen him dressed in any other style. Even at assembly when the men wore white dress shirts, he wore his cowboy clothes. Her stepfather had treated him differently than other men too. He'd been afraid of the sheriff.

"Here, Eve." Bina handed her one of the coffees.

His eyes zeroed in on the younger detective. His expression changed to a sharper sneer. When he was sure Bina had read the disgust on his face, he turned back to Eve.

Eve placed her hand in her pocket, turning her recorder on. His gaze traveled very slowly down her body before moving up again. He met her eyes when he was finished dissecting her. He didn't care who saw him. Eve refused to back down.

Their standoff seemed to take forever.

The corners of his large lips turned into a grin which showed even more menace. He cocked his hat, took a step to the side, and carried his cup to the counter.

"Doo yá 'áshǫǫ da," Bina whispered.

Eve had no idea what it meant, but she could guess. She

helped Bina with the other coffees. She kept checking behind her because she didn't trust the sheriff at her back.

When they walked outside, he was standing next to his vehicle, a lifted white truck with the sheriff's office logo on the side. There was a larger dark van parked beside the sheriff and it was the reason she hadn't noticed the county vehicle. Murray watched them and didn't bother hiding that he was doing it.

The driver of the van saluted the sheriff and pulled out. Had he purposely kept the sheriff's vehicle hidden from their view across the street?

She walked slowly with Bina back to the scene. You didn't run from a predator. She carried two coffees and Bina had two with Collin's drink in a bag on her arm.

"That man is creepy as hell," Bina said when they were far enough away that he couldn't hear.

"What was the meaning of your phrase, if you don't mind me asking?"

"Evil," Bina replied.

"He was a friend of my stepfather's," Eve confided. "He was exactly like that when I was a child. I worried he would marry me. It was a toss-up between him and Aaron for the worst husband possible."

"I just threw up in my mouth," Bina said. "I doubt coffee will remove the taste of his repugnance."

Bina had a way with words.

"I know the feeling." Eve put the encounter aside so she could focus.

They approached the guys and Eve handed the straight black coffee to Clyde and took a sip of hers. It was hot and wonderful even though it wasn't Tamm's special blend. Clyde drank coffee sparingly, but it was that kind of night. Bina gave Ray a cup that had more cream and sweetener than caffeine. Collin took the bag with his Red Bull.

They stood by the SUV. Twenty feet separated them from the town officers and the chief so they spoke quietly.

"If anyone wants to go back to the hotel and sleep, I can ask Chief Jackson if his officers can lend a hand to watch the scene," Eve told them.

As soon as she said it, the chief marched to his vehicle, revved the engine, and drove away. It was possible he'd heard her.

"We're not leaving," Clyde said. "This is still a dangerous situation. You've been threatened repeatedly and now we have a homicide connected to those threats. We're safer together.

The others nodded.

"Okay. We've had longer nights." With all of them on scene, they could focus on the murder and not worry about each other. None of them were bulletproof and whoever killed Eric was walking around free.

A minute later, Officer Keb climbed into his vehicle. Eve watched as he drove across the street. She figured he was taking a bathroom break and picking up coffee the same as they had. He didn't though. He stopped at the sheriff's truck which was still in the parking lot. They started talking and Eve knew he was telling the sheriff everything that had happened. If Murray had asked, she would have done the same as a courtesy to his department so it didn't matter.

So far, their work in town had only brought them face to face with the sheriff twice. Both experiences had been uncomfortable. The only way Eric's death could be worse was if it had happened in the county and she was dealing with Murray instead of Chief Jackson. Straightening her shoulders, she turned her back to the two men to concentrate on the homicide investigation.

They reviewed their notes and spoke softly about their theories. They all agreed her stepbrothers were suspects. Two additional trips for coffee—once Ray and Collin, and the next Bina and Clyde—kept them alert until the medical examiner's van arrived.

"Will you help them?" Eve asked Clyde.

It was something she normally did, but this time it was too much. She didn't want to see Eric's body zipped into the bag. She was tired and it was getting harder to fight her emotions.

Sheriff Murray and Officer Keb remained across the street, but the other officer had left the scene an hour before. Each time she looked toward the minimart, the ball in her gut tightened. There was a reason they stayed and watched. It could be intimidation or something else. She couldn't shake Keb's reaction when he'd arrived on scene. Now that she had time to think about it, he'd been more than over the top. His hostility almost seemed staged. Every instinct she had made her think Keb and Murray were connected to what happened. Maybe she was trying to shield herself from the overwhelming possibility her stepbrothers were responsible for Eric's death. She couldn't let that happen, but the two men gave her a strange feeling.

She'd learned to listen to her instincts and was always sorry when she didn't.

The ME techs worked quickly. Eve turned in time to see Clyde place his initials on the bag and tape after he secured the tape. He walked over after the ME van drove away. He looked as tired as the rest of them. It was time to leave. They stowed the evidence in the van's small safe and went back to the hotel.

The van had an alarm which Bina, as their tech expert, double-checked before they walked toward the rooms.

"It's late and sleep is the most important thing right now, but each of us need to make notes of exactly what we saw when Eric was shot. Write your report in the morning if you need to, but put the key elements on paper tonight."

They all nodded before they broke off and went to their rooms.

Eve's tiredness was also emotional. She and Bina wrote

their notes once they shut the door. It took about five minutes. She needed to turn off her brain and examine the bigger picture in the morning.

The beds had never looked so good. They were too tired for a shower and simply took turns washing up at the sink before crawling into bed.

It was almost three.

Bina flipped the switch off the light. Eve remembered nothing after the room went dark.

TWENTY-SIX

The sun peeked beneath the thick curtains when she woke up. Bina was in the shower. Eve checked her phone and there were no messages. It was a little after six. She stretched and waited for Bina to come out.

Her phone chimed with a message from Clyde.

Collin and Ray picking up to-go plates from the continental breakfast.

She typed back.

Bina in shower. Meet in guys' room?

Mine. 20 minutes?

Bina walked out of the bathroom.
"Breakfast in Clyde's room in twenty?" Eve asked her.
"Works for me."

See you in 20.

She jumped in the shower and cataloged the things she had to do. Clyde had asked the ME techs to arrange the autopsy and get back to Eve with a date and time.

Tracking down and interviewing her stepbrothers was important. The team also needed to interview the people Eric worked with. Getting to Adella was another priority. They had no new leads and it was time for Eve to insist. These were all things on their lists, but it helped to review them while she showered. She washed her hair and her body quickly. She had to hold the sadness back.

She dressed in black tactical pants with ample pockets and another short-sleeved polo shirt, this one dark green. It had her title and name in gold where the pocket would usually go.

She walked out of the bathroom and quickly combed her hair in the mirror. She added a swipe of clear lip gloss because the weather was so dry.

"Ready?" she asked Bina.

"Yep."

Eve stepped to her suitcase and grabbed her duty belt, put it through the loops of her pants, then clipped on her badge and holster. She dug around in her luggage and found her handcuffs and added them to her belt. Last, she placed her recorder in her front pocket for easy access.

Eve felt better this morning even with only three hours sleep. She was sorry she'd snapped at Collin. The wonderful thing was, she knew he would forgive her. Clyde would too. They understood emotions were hard for her and they listened when she needed them to.

They made it to Clyde's door with two minutes to spare.

The guys were already inside discussing the case. Two plates covered with aluminum foil waited. She and Bina brought Tamm's coffee.

"I'd like Collin and Ray to go to the grocery store and inter-view the people who worked with Eric," she told them. "Ask about friends outside his brothers and find them for interviews if you can." She took a bite of scrambled eggs. Not the best but thankfully she wasn't a fussy eater. "Ask the normal questions. Who would harm Eric, things like that. You know your job and don't need me standing over you." She added a smile for Collin's benefit. "Bina and Clyde will come with me to interview Aaron. We'll likely be back at the hotel before you. We'll meet with the evidence tech at ten. After that it will be all about locating my stepbrothers. Anything I haven't covered?" She took another bite.

"We want to know how you're doing." Bina said. "The others are too afraid to ask."

"Better. I slept as much as the rest of you and it's time to dive in and discover what is going on. Linda and her baby are still missing and now we also have a homicide to investigate. The baby is top priority, but we have no lead other than Eric's list. These two cases are tied together. The autopsy will be scheduled in the next week. I think this one can be handled alone by the pathologist."

They stared at her like she spoke a foreign language. She always went to homicide autopsies.

"We know how he died and chances are there's no evidence on the body except the bullets. Interviews are more important. I'll talk to the pathologist and have him call if he finds anything other than what I expect." Eve took another bite of food. "Tomorrow at the latest, we track down the names on Eric's list." She pulled out her phone and handed it to Bina who was sitting beside her. "This is the map in Eric's wallet. That area is desolate. It's low priority right now but we will drive out there."

Bina handed the phone to Ray. He looked at it then he handed it off to Collin. Clyde took it when Collin was done, but he had seen the actual paper and didn't need to see the map. She placed her phone back in her pocket after he handed it over.

She thought for a moment. "After speaking to Aaron, this plan might change. Be ready. Ray, as soon as we finish eating, pull up the report on my assault. My stepbrothers' addresses will be on it. I'm asking Aaron to have them meet at his office. If they won't come in on their own, we'll go to them."

"I have the addresses," Ray said, and pointed to his notebook on the bed. Bina was sitting next to it. "I called Tamm and she had the report waiting."

"Perfect. Anyone else want to add something?"

"Everyone will carry an extra magazine," said Clyde. "Whoever shot Eric is still out there and we need to be prepared."

"Agreed," Collin replied, and the others nodded.

"Clyde and Bina," Eve said. "I want to see the scene now that we have sunlight. Afterward, I'll call Aaron and let him know to meet us at his office in case he's taken the day off."

"I want to look around the area too," said Ray. "Can Collin and I join you?"

"The more eyes the better."

They decided Ray and Collin would walk and check the area outside the scene. Clyde drove the van with Bina and Eve inside in case they discovered additional evidence.

The abandoned tire shop looked even bleaker in the early morning sunshine. The whitewashed walls were peeling with stucco falling off in large chunks. They had checked the garage door the night before and it was locked. The dirty glass had been easier to see through in the dark with their flashlights shining inside but they could still see. There was no sign anyone had walked through the dust on the floor. There was no counter or desk inside, the place was entirely empty. Eve made the decision that they wouldn't waste time by trying to find a key and go inside.

She followed Clyde to the back of the building while the others walked the outskirts of the scene. They'd removed the crime scene tape before they left the night before. A few cars slowed but continued driving and didn't turn around for another look.

A pool of blood was still on the ground and would be there until the next rain unless the owner sprayed it down. Eve stared at the spot where Eric had died. They'd found no weapon on his body. The murder was planned, but other questions ran through her head.

Did his brothers kill him?

Could it be someone else entirely?

How did they know Eric was meeting with Eve?

The most likely answer to the last question was that Eric told someone.

She had to keep an open mind, but, in a town this small, he was no doubt killed by someone he knew.

She looked across the street at the minimart.

"Ray, Collin, check to see if they have video. If so, we may need a warrant, but tell them to preserve if they won't hand it over easily."

The two men jogged across the street and came back five minutes later.

"The guy working called his manager and he told them he would come in later and pull the tape," Collin said. "The camera doesn't point here, but I told him we wanted it anyway."

When they were satisfied that they could do no more at the scene's location, they went back to the hotel. She called Aaron after Ray and Collin drove away in the SUV.

"Yes?" he answered. His voice cracked slightly.

"This is Eve. Are you going into the office today?"

"I'm already here," he said.

"I'm coming over with Detectives Blau and Johnston."

"I'm waiting," he muttered, and disconnected. He sounded like he hadn't slept.

She was about to make a bad day worse.

TWENTY-SEVEN

It was a quarter to eight when they arrived in the van. Aaron waited in the entry and let them into the building when he saw them outside the glass doors. He was wearing the same suit as the night before though his tie was missing and his shirt was half-untucked. His hair stood up in odd places and Eve wondered if he'd spent the night in his office. The red and puffy eyes definitely conveyed a lack of sleep.

They followed him to the back. He side-stepped into another office and grabbed a chair which he carried with him. He placed it against the left wall facing his desk with just enough room for them to walk inside. Eve figured he didn't want Clyde standing in the doorway again. Aaron took his usual chair.

"Do you have anything I should know?" he asked, looking at Eve and ignoring the other two detectives.

"Eric was shot twice. Once in his shoulder and once in his chest. We found three bullet casings. A bullet that matched the casings was lodged in the wall of the tire shop behind where he was shot. It will be picked up today for forensic analysis."

Aaron didn't ask about the caliber. He looked down at the top of his desk with no response.

She didn't feel he deserved her empathy, but it was slowly creeping in.

"Do you have anything we need to know?" she asked.

He released air from his lungs like he had been holding his breath and brought his gaze to hers.

"I went by Mark, Richard, and Danny's place last night. They were not there. Mark's truck was gone. I then drove to Patrick's apartment. He lived with Eric. He did not answer and the lights were off. His truck was in its parking spot. It is the same model and make as Mark's."

He shouldn't have interfered by going there, but Eve wouldn't berate him. She should have expected it.

"Did you try calling?" she asked.

"All night." Aaron lifted his cell phone then slid it across the desk to her. "The code is 7258," he said.

This was not the Aaron she knew and disliked.

This man was beaten, his world shattered.

"What's going on, Aaron?" she asked softly.

He finally glanced at Bina and Clyde before he turned his attention back to her. He didn't say anything, but she could tell he wanted to.

Clyde, who had taken the chair against the left wall, stood.

"Detective Blau and I will wait in the SUV. Text if you need us," he said.

Eve nodded and waited for them to leave.

Aaron stood, walked around his desk, and closed the door. He went back to his chair.

"After the Tanner case," he said, "I have been walking on thin ice. I expected to be removed from the high council, but it hasn't happened. I now expect to have my wives and children reassigned. I have two children ages six and eight."

Eve took a closer look at the picture on his desk. There was a boy and girl standing in front of Aaron. His hands rested on their shoulders, two wives on each side and one on either side of his children, making six wives total. The children didn't look like him. The Owens' genes dominated their family line and she was positive he'd allowed another man to father them. At least he hadn't lied about being a seed bearer. If he genuinely cared about his family, it didn't fit the image she'd built of him in her mind.

"I love my family." He looked down at his desk again and spoke. "Eric sent me a text directly after they assaulted you. I swear I knew nothing about it beforehand. He was afraid you were dead. That's why I went there." Aaron wiped tears from beneath his eyes. "I confronted Mark the following day."

Eve leaned over and pushed his tissue box closer to him. As a child she'd never seen Aaron show any emotion except anger, which usually preluded violence.

"Mark wouldn't tell me who gave the order. I told him you could have died and asked if that had been the order. He wouldn't answer me. He was angry with Eric for telling me. Patrick moved into Eric's apartment to keep an eye on him. They didn't trust him. My brothers were working for someone with more power than I have." He shrugged. "I have no idea who. Mark, for an unknown reason, turned down an assignment on the God squad. That's almost unheard of but he wouldn't divulge why. I don't believe they killed Eric." He finally looked at her. "But I think they know who did."

Eve couldn't help thinking this was part of a setup. Aaron had never cooperated with her before and she didn't believe he would start now. This could be a way to protect his brothers. If Eve put out an Attempt to Locate and her stepbrothers were picked up with weapons, it could go badly for them.

"The bullet caliber is the same as my duty weapon they took the night of the assault."

He nodded. Tears ran down his face.

Eve took out her phone and brought up one of the pictures she'd taken of the notepaper in Eric's wallet.

"This is a list I took off Eric's body. Before he died, he told me it was important," she said, and showed him the names.

"You spoke with him?" He didn't glance at the photo.

"He said he didn't want to hurt me. He told me to find the note in his pocket and don't let 'them' see it." She made air quotes. "I asked who shot him, but he could no longer speak. He died within minutes of the shooting."

Aaron turned his eyes to the names and dates.

"Wall and the date match the day their baby was taken." It wasn't a slip this time. Aaron was no longer trying to hide the fact Linda had a child. He looked through the list again. "The first name, Whiting. I know a woman from the family who was reassigned around that time. I don't know why."

"What about the others?" she asked.

"I know who they are, but I have no idea why they are on the list."

"Are the cases of children born without a seed bearer something every member of the high council would know about?"

"Before you took over the taskforce, yes. They keep things from me now. I'm blamed each time you do something that hurts the community."

What he meant was each time she solved a case he was punished. She wanted to ask him if he was told to interfere, but it wouldn't help right now. She needed to stick with Linda's missing baby, her disappearance, and Eric's death.

"I need to know about isolation. Is it possible Mrs. Whiting wasn't reassigned?"

He ran his fingers through his hair and stared above her head at the blank wall behind her.

"I don't know," he muttered.

"Is there anyone you can ask?

"No." He met her gaze. "I'm in enough trouble already. Asking questions will seal my fate."

Aaron would always care about himself first. He would never change. Even the death of his brother wouldn't alter his self-protective instincts.

"Do your brothers own any other vehicles besides the two trucks?"

"Yes. It wasn't at either place. I'd forgotten about it."

"Give me a description."

"It's a black Buick. An old thing. Eric drove it and enjoyed working on the engine. It ran well. Was it at the scene last night?"

"No," she said. This was the car used to rear-end her. She wouldn't mention that just yet.

Ray and Collin had walked the surrounding area the night before while they waited for the ME techs. They were specifically looking for unoccupied vehicles in the area but hadn't found one. They had deduced that Eric walked or was dropped off. Aaron thankfully didn't ask why she was interested in another vehicle. She wasn't ready to share.

"Leave a message on Mark's phone," she told him. "Ask them to come to your office for interviews. I don't want to put out an ATL. You're an attorney. Convince them it's in their best interest to voluntarily speak with me. It's what innocent people would do."

He stared at her for a moment.

"What if they aren't innocent?"

TWENTY-EIGHT

Clyde drove them back to the hotel. Eve signed the evidence off to the tech when he arrived. Her cell rang shortly after the tech left. Clyde and Bina were in the room with her. She didn't recognize the number.

"Hello?"

"Detective Bennet?" a soft female voice asked.

"Yes, who am I speaking with?"

"This is Adella, Danielle's sister."

Eve's attention turned fully to the call and a bit of her anxiety decreased. *Give me something*, she thought to herself.

"Your sister is safe," Eve said. "I wanted you to know."

"Thank you."

Eve had to go straight to the point because Adella's call could be cut short.

"Danielle told me about your son and that you were in isolation. Can you add to what she said?"

"My baby is gone. I will never see him again. I can never go back to isolation; I would rather die." She was completely defeated. "Please don't ask me to talk about it."

"Where were you held?" Eve asked.

"Somewhere out past Water Canyon. I wouldn't be able to find it, but I recognized the rocks when I was taken there."

Eve knew where it was. Eric had drawn a map.

"You've helped more than you know. If you need me, call this number again."

"Will my sister return?"

"I'm not sure." Eve wouldn't lie. Too many women returned, unable to manage the outside world.

"I hope she never comes back. At least one of us got out."

The call disconnected.

She held her hand up for Bina and Clyde to wait a moment and called Ray's cell.

"We need you back here as soon as possible," she told him.

"On our way, ETA, ten."

"Adella was held in isolation somewhere in the Water Canyon area," she told Bina and Clyde. "The location matches the map Eric drew. We're taking a drive."

They decided to use both vehicles. The terrain would be challenging. If necessary, they could all switch to the SUV which had four-wheel drive. They had a meeting on speakerphone while they traveled.

"We didn't get much from Eric's work," Collin said. "A few names to track down. Eric was pleasant, but he didn't say much to his co-workers. 'What a nice guy' was the general consensus."

Harina had said the same thing. Being nice might be what killed him. She couldn't help thinking he'd told someone he trusted and that person turned him in. Who they turned him in to was the bigger question. She gave Ray and Collin more details on the call from Adella.

"What do you think we'll find?" asked Ray.

"Answers," she said. "Everything that's happened is connected and we need to find the missing link to prove it. I believe Eric planned on giving me his lists and map. There's a reason he drew it and we're going to find out why."

They began the journey by driving in the opposite direction of their destination. The God squad trucks followed them to the county line. There was a back road turnoff to the state park about twenty minutes later. It took another forty-five minutes to reach the park entrance. Eve and Bina took advantage of the restrooms before they started driving again. Half an hour later, they turned onto a well-maintained dirt road and followed it. Eric's map showed a turnoff about a mile after a steep rock formation on the right. They missed it the first time and had to turn around and backtrack.

The dirt road was narrow, bumpy, and surrounded by wilderness. Navigation was difficult. Twenty minutes later, Eve feared they were lost. The road narrowed again and there was no way to turn around without messing up the undercarriage of the van. She was waiting for the call so they could all get into the SUV. Clyde's voice came over the radio.

"I think we've found it. We're stopping here."

The van halted and Bina pulled in close behind. When Eve got out, the van blocked her view so she stepped around. An old, beat-up travel trailer about twelve feet long sat about fifty feet farther up the road, resting at a slight angle against an outcropping of rocks. The outside, once white, was rusted, and yellowed by time and the elements. It had a faded burgundy stripe around the lower part. The windows had large pieces of plywood covering them. An exhaust pipe poked out a few inches on the right side above the door which was padlocked.

"I'll grab the bolt cutter," Collin said.

They walked up on the trailer with Clyde in the lead.

Eve noticed the smell from six feet away.

Feces, urine, and unwashed body odor filled her lungs. Collin came forward and cut the padlock. Clyde pulled the door outward. The smell was even worse. He poked his head inside then quickly moved down the stairs away from the door. His expression told her something was very wrong.

"You need to go in," he said. "One female, alive."

Eve climbed the two stairs and stuck her head inside. The woman sat crouched on the floor in the back corner against a mattress and the side of the trailer. Eve was as shocked as Clyde.

"Bina with me," she said softly. "Everyone else stay back."

The woman's eyes remained locked on Eve's.

"I'm approaching slowly," Eve told her. "Are you hurt?"

The woman didn't answer.

There was no door attached to the small bathroom and no lid on the almost overflowing toilet. The woman's hand was tightly wrapped around a cell phone, her fingers trembling. Eve crouched down in front of her.

"My name is Eve. I'm here to help."

Tears flowed down the woman's cheeks. She stayed frozen in place.

Dark circles surrounded green eyes that were too big for her gaunt face. Her skin was dry and flaking. A wash of freckles covered her nose and cheeks. Her greasy hair looked brown, but Eve realized it could be auburn. There was no righteous upsweep at the front of her head. Her hair was pulled back in a simple braid. She appeared malnourished. There was another word that Eve had never associated with any woman from Hildale. She looked breakable.

Eve glanced over her shoulder at Bina who stood near the door, not coming closer. She took note of the small counter along the wall of the trailer. A can opener and a spoon lay beside open cans of food. The cabinets had no doors and were empty. Two one-gallon water jugs were the only thing she saw, one empty and the other a quarter full. There was no refrigerator and the two-burner stove looked unusable.

Eve kept a tight grip on her emotions. Her anger would do nothing for this woman. She made eye contact with her again and reached for her left hand, taking it gently. The fingers of the woman's right hand stayed tightly gripped to the cell phone.

"I promise, I'm here to help," she assured her. "What is your name?"

"Miriam Whiting," the woman answered hesitantly.

Her last name was at the top of Eric's list. The date next to her name was a year and a half ago.

Eve gently slipped the phone from Miriam's fingers. Bina moved in behind her and Eve handed it over.

"Bina, grab the medical kit from the van," she said, still watching Miriam closely.

"Can you sit on the bed so we can check you over?" she asked gently after Bina backed out.

Trembling fingers squeezed Eve's hand.

"Get me out," Miriam cried, and looked down at her right hand that was now empty. "If I don't call, he will punish me. Please take me out of here before he returns." She was panicking.

"Can you walk?"

"Yes."

Bina came back with the med kit.

"We'll examine her in the van," Eve told her. "Ask Collin to move it closer to the trailer so she doesn't need to walk as far."

The trailer sat partially on large boulders. There was a clear area surrounding it where they could turn the vehicles around.

"Do you have broken bones, anything I need to be aware of before we move you?" Eve asked.

"No, just get me out of here." Her cracked lips trembled.

Eve heard the van pull in closer.

"Bina, help me," she said when Bina walked back inside.

Miriam had stopped crying, but tears slowly began falling again. She wiped them away angrily. "They took my little angel. He was innocent."

Another child taken. Eve couldn't show her anger over

Miriam's missing baby or the condition Miriam was in, but she was determined they would discover who was behind what was going on and they would pay for their crimes.

"I'll do everything I can to find your child," Eve promised. "Right now, we're going to get you out. We'll help you stand."

Miriam placed her hand on the bed for leverage. Eve gripped her beneath the arm to help her balance. Bina took her other side and stayed slightly behind Miriam due to the confined space. They walked slowly to the door. She leaned heavily on Eve and wobbled, almost going down.

"Let me take her," said Collin, who had replaced Clyde at the bottom of the steps.

Eve didn't know if Miriam could make it down the stairs.

"My friend will carry you to the van," she said, giving Miriam no chance to object.

Miriam didn't answer and seemed unaware when Collin lifted, then cradled her against his chest. He turned sideways to get her out of the small door, then quickly carried her to the open door of the van and placed her carefully on one of the bench seats.

"I need you to collect and document evidence," Eve told Bina and Collin.

"I'll grab an evidence bag from the SUV," Bina said. Collin preceded her outside.

Eve sat down next to Miriam. She was upright, her gaze traveling the interior of the van. Her faded blue dress was threadbare and dirty. Women took pride in their dresses and kept them starched and ironed. It was a tedious and backbreaking chore. What Miriam wore was more of a sack than a carefully tended dress.

Eve stood and went to the cooler for a bottle of water and handed it to Miriam. Her hands were shaking so bad, she couldn't remove the cap and Eve did it for her. She needed IV fluids, but to keep her whereabouts secret, they needed to bypass medical services in Hildale and call in an ambulance from the city. Miriam was in bad shape but didn't appear to be at death's door.

Miriam took only a few sips.

"You need to drink as much as you can," Eve told her.

"Is there more?" Miriam asked.

"Yes, there is plenty."

Miriam started drinking and finished the bottle quickly.

"Do you want another?"

"Yes, please."

She drank that one down and now had a third clasped in her fingers.

Eve removed a towel from one of the overhead compartments and used another bottle of water to wet it. She handed Miriam the wet towel.

"I thought you might want to wash your hands and face. I can ring it out and pour more clean water on it if we need to," she assured her.

Miriam took the offered towel and placed the water bottle beside her. She briskly scrubbed her face and hands. She grabbed the water bottle as soon as she handed the towel back to Eve and took another drink, finishing off most of it.

"I never had enough water," she said, and held the plastic up to her face to examine what remained inside. "Or food."

"I have some energy bars. Would you like one?"

Miriam shook her head.

"You are being kind. I'm sorry I smell so foul." She gave Eve a weak smile.

"No," Eve said. "Do not be sorry for that. I have no clothes for you to change into. It could be several hours, but you will be clean and have something else to wear as soon as we can make it happen."

Suddenly, Miriam's eyes darted around the van in panic.

"The phone," she said. "I must check in."

"I can get the phone, but could you explain? I don't want anyone alerted we're here."

"I must check in every hour. There's an alarm. After I've called, I set it again. If I don't, I will be punished. I must check in twenty-four times a day."

"Who do you call?"

"I think it's him, but nothing is said. He knows if I don't make the call."

Eve would ask about *him* when she was sure Miriam was out of danger.

"Okay," said Eve. "Bina has your phone, I'll get it."

She quickly walked to the trailer when she didn't see Bina or Collin outside. Ray raised his chin in acknowledgment. He stood at the far corner on a boulder allowing him to see down the road they'd driven in on. Clyde was on the other side, his expression locked in anger. Both had rifles slung over their shoulders.

Eve stepped inside the trailer while trying to keep her stomach from rebelling from the smell. Bina and Collin were standing in front of the counter.

"There are seven empty cans of food," Bina said, and held up a spoon with her gloved fingers. "No telling when she ate last."

The waste tank was emptied onto the rocks behind the trailer," Collin told her. "Rain was the only thing that washed it away."

"I will interview her in the van. You drive," she told Bina. "The guys can take the SUV. She needs to feel comfortable talking to me."

"Who would do this to someone?" Collin asked. His eyes were haunted.

"Monsters."

TWENTY-NINE

Bina handed her the phone and Eve went back outside. She used her own cell to call Tamm to request an ambulance meet them. The ambulance crew the night before was a good one, but it was unlikely the same men were working right now or that they would remain quiet about Miriam's rescue. If Miriam went into any form of medical distress, she would change the plan and call for air extraction.

"Send them code three," she told Tamm. "I also need a female officer from the state to accompany them. Call Lieutenant Crosby if you need to. Talk to the women's shelter and have a place arranged for her when she's out of the hospital."

"I'll have them on the road immediately," Tamm promised. "The women's shelter will be prepped and waiting."

"Thank you."

Eve disconnected and walked closer to Clyde.

"As soon as Bina and Collin are finished with evidence, we're leaving. Bina will drive the van. You, Collin, and Ray in the SUV."

"We'll take point," Clyde said. "How is she?"

"She's tough, much tougher than I would be." She told him about the hourly phone calls.

"There are not enough ways to physically assault the county attorney. He knew about this," Clyde said, his clenched jaws showing how furious he was.

"I agree and I have several ways you may not have thought of."

"I doubt it." She'd never seen Clyde this angry. He had a death grip on the rifle and Eve wasn't sure if he wanted to shoot someone or use it as a club. She understood perfectly how he felt and knew all of them were on the edge of a very steep and violent cliff. She went back inside the van and handed the cell phone to Miriam who quickly checked the alarm.

"I have four minutes." She looked at the phone like it was a poisonous snake.

"If you don't want to call, it's okay," Eve told her. There were five of them and they were well armed. Her mind had changed about running into whoever did this. She wanted a confrontation. No, she needed it.

"You mean that? You are going to take me out of here?"

Her physical condition was bad and Eve couldn't guess where she was mentally. She didn't mind Miriam's need for repeated assurance that she was safe.

"We're meeting an ambulance from the city and will bypass town. There will be a female officer with them and no one will harm you. You have my word. I need to ask questions which will help me find your baby."

"Thank you." Tears leaked from her eyes, down her face and dripped onto her dress. Miriam didn't seem to notice.

The phone alarm went off and she stared at the screen. Her fingers began violently shaking.

"I can't do it." She thrust the phone at Eve.

"You will not be going back inside that trailer," Eve promised her again.

Miriam briefly shut her eyes.

"Who are you?" she asked when she opened them.

"I'm Detective Sergeant Eve Bennet. The others with me are also detectives. We are a state taskforce assigned to stop what's happened to you and other women. That includes the disappearance of children. We're trained to keep you safe. Bina, who you saw earlier, will drive the van. The men will be in the SUV."

"Thank you," she said again.

"Two of my detectives are taking pictures and collecting evidence. They should be done shortly and we will leave as soon as they're finished. The other two detectives are standing guard. One was a SWAT commander and I promise he knows what he's doing." Eve had never been more thankful for Clyde, not just for his ability but also his persistence. He made the team attend high-risk situational training and Eve knew they could and would defend Miriam with their lives.

Miriam offered a weak smile.

Eve grinned reassuringly. She wanted to find Aaron and wrap her fingers around his throat. He knew exactly what the list meant and he'd all but shrugged it aside, more worried about himself. She walked over to one of the drawers at the back of the van and placed Miriam's cell phone in a manilla folder marking it with the date and time. They would get a warrant for the phone as soon as they could and attempt to trace the number.

Eve couldn't imagine being trapped in a trailer with so little food and water, but then again, she'd never imagined anything that was happening right now. She walked back over to Miriam and sat beside her.

"I'm going to turn on my recorder," Eve said. "We'll talk a bit before I ask questions. I want to be sure I don't miss anything that could help."

"Okay."

She took out the device and flipped it on. She placed it back in her pocket so Miriam didn't concentrate on it. When at all possible, you tell victims they are being recorded. The last thing Eve wanted was for her to think she had been fooled.

"This is Eve Bennet interviewing Miriam Whiting," she began, and followed up with the date and time.

"You said your child was missing? Could you tell me what happened?"

A spark entered Miriam's green eyes. Her shoulders straightened and she was no longer a victim. She was a mother.

"His name is Dustin. He's my little angel." She took a slow breath. "My husband and I were not to have children. The prophet did not see our faithfulness. I did not want to break his laws, but my husband told me it would be okay. After we discovered I was pregnant, he was upset. One of my sister wives reported the pregnancy. I thought my sisters and I would be reassigned, but nothing was done."

"Ben was angry," she continued. "He thought we would be banned from the community after I gave birth. He received a phone call and told me everything would be okay if we gave my little boy away. I begged him not to and he said it was my fault. I had tempted him with my wickedness and he no longer wanted me. He locked me in my room and the next day my baby was gone. He was only six days old."

This was remarkably similar to Adella and Linda.

"He would be eighteen months now," Miriam said sadly. "I tried to run away and find him, but Ben caught me and locked me in my room again." She hesitated. Her next words were spoken softly. "I thought I was being reassigned husbands. I was told I must pay for my sins and he brought me here."

"Your husband brought you?" Eve asked.

"Brother Jarrod."

Eve's fingers tightened into a fist.

"Do you know Brother Jarrod's full name?" she asked, fighting to keep her tone level.

"Jarrod Keb."

"The police officer?" Eve clarified for the sake of the recording.

Miriam grabbed her arm, her face stricken by fear.

"Please do not send me back. Please," she begged.

"You have my word," Eve said. "You will never go back." It made her even angrier that Miriam feared the police. The damn federal judge should have disbanded every law enforcement officer in the county.

Bina opened the door and sat in the driver's seat. Eve gave her a nod and sent Tamm a text. She needed Officer Keb's information. The database search had to be handled securely from Tamm's end so law enforcement in town wouldn't notify him. If he went to the trailer, he would know someone rescued her and it wouldn't be hard to figure out who. He wasn't the only man responsible. Miriam's husband knew who'd taken her and Eve would bet Aaron did too.

Eve placed her hand on Miriam's and squeezed gently. The woman was so thin, the veins stark against her pale skin. Eve was worried she would break a bone.

"How long have you've been in the trailer?" Eve asked.

"Five hundred and twelve days," she said.

Eve had trouble absorbing the number.

"I balled up small pieces of toilet paper to keep count. I added another one each time the trailed warmed to mark the beginning of a new day. After a month went by, I placed them in piles of ten beneath the mattress. I kept the new ones in my dress pocket." She placed her fingers inside her pocket and brought out a handful of small wads of toilet paper.

Eve hadn't noticed the bumpy outline of the pocket or suspected the horror what was inside represented. She couldn't imagine this level of abuse.

"Who brought you food and water?"

"Brother Jarrod. He told me I was awarded to him by the

prophet, but because of my sin, I wasn't yet worthy of marriage. He brought seven cans of food each week and two gallons of water. If I missed check-in, he would be a day or two late. Sometimes, I slept through the alarm and didn't call. I did that two days ago. He is punishing me for it. If it weren't for my baby, I would have stopped calling. Dustin is the only reason I wanted to live."

Miriam loved her son. It didn't matter that he was referred to as a child of sin by her community or that she had been brainwashed to think of him as God's child and not her own. Eve's heart swelled and she was given hope. Her thoughts turned to seven cans of food each week. Eve had noticed Miriam's bleeding gums. Added to her dry flaking skin, it was clear she had severe vitamin deficiency and who knew what else. She was amazingly strong-willed.

"Brother Jarrod emptied the waste tank monthly, but it filled about a week before he showed up to take care of it," Miriam continued. "It's been three days since I've had food. One time, I screamed my anger into the phone when I called and he missed an entire week. I thought I would die." Her voice was devoid of emotion.

Eve's face remained blank. It was the best she could do. She wanted to place her arms around Miriam and hold her. When interviewing a victim, you had to keep your expression neutral no matter what they said. This was the biggest test in Eve's career.

One thing was clear though. Miriam Whiting was a survivor.

"Water was hooked up when he emptied the tank," she continued. "He brought me a clean dress and sometimes the water was too cold, but I had to take a shower for him."

She looked down at her dress.

"He wanted me clean for his use. I worried there would be another baby, but I couldn't fight him. He made me suffer for my sins. He told me if I were good, he would marry me and take me from the trailer. If he let me out, maybe I could escape. I knew that if he caught me, he would kill me." She looked up at Eve. "Sometimes, I was okay with that."

How could she not be? She'd survived eighteen months. She felt guilty for not fighting him when he raped her. Miriam's instincts had kept her alive. Eve had to remember her recorder was running and keep to the facts, not her own personal observations. She would put some in her report.

"Do you have any idea how many times he had sex with you?"

"Only when I was clean."

"You said you showered once a month?"

"Yes."

Jarrod Keb had sexually assaulted her approximately eighteen times.

"How did you stay warm in the winter?" Eve asked, changing the subject. She would request a sex crimes detective do a full interview after Miriam was safe. A nurse would talk to her at the hospital about a sex assault examination. Now was not the time to mention it and this would be Miriam's decision. She was most likely not pregnant due to starvation. It made Eve that much angrier.

"He gave me extra blankets and I buried myself in them. I was always cold, but I hated the warm weather more. Sometimes it was so hot, it was hard to breathe. I had to conserve water all the time. I thought he would eventually forget about me and I would die of dehydration." She looked down at the new bottle of water in her hand and slowly took a drink. "I was always hungry too. There was never enough food to save." She closed her eyes for a moment and rested her head back against the inside wall of the van. "I hated the phone calls."

"Did you call the same number each time?" Eve asked.

"Yes, it was the only one in the phone." She gave a small

laugh that ended in a hiccup as more tears rolled down her cheeks. "I couldn't call anyone because I didn't know where I was. And I was worried they would tell Brother Jarrod," she said. "I was too afraid."

She stopped talking.

Eve could see Miriam's exhaustion, but she had to ask more questions.

"Did you have a midwife?"

"Yes, it was Brother Jarrod's wife, Bonnie. She only performed the duty for couples who sinned. There's another woman in town who delivered many of the babies, but I was told she would not deliver a child of sin."

Bonnie Keb. Eve had missed the connection at Eric's homicide scene. This was too much like Aunt Bertha, Charlie and Becky's midwife. The pattern was obvious. Eve wondered if Mrs. Keb knew what her husband was doing.

Eve needed a quick break. She stood and walked over to the cooler. She removed an orange and peeled it before sitting down beside Miriam on the bench again. She handed her the slices on a paper towel.

Miriam looked at the oranges like they were gold.

While she ate, Eve couldn't help thinking about Maggie. Miriam had been in the trailer for 512 days. It was unimaginable. Was this the dark secret her mother never spoke of? Eve knew in her heart that it had to be.

Keb would spend the rest of his life in prison. Eve didn't say it aloud, but she would keep the promise.

Once Miriam finished the orange, she took Eve's hand and sat quietly with her head against the sidewall. Eventually she fell asleep and her head dropped onto Eve's shoulder. Eve gave herself a few minutes to feel the emotion gathering like a storm inside her and tears ran down her face. She sat with Miriam, imagining horrible things for the men who were responsible.

After she released the anger, she felt better. She stayed vigilant, checking Miriam's pulse while she slept. They intercepted the ambulance three hours later.

The EMTs immediately placed an IV line and hooked Miriam up to multiple wires. She was strapped in and they were ready to leave. Eve stepped into the back of the ambulance.

"I do not know how to thank you and your people," Miriam said.

"We want you healthy and happy." Miriam reached out and Eve grasped her fingers. "I'm going to find your baby," she promised. "I'll be in touch as soon as I can."

"He has red hair like mine." Miriam's fingers tightened briefly before she let go. The female officer assured Eve Miriam would be safe.

Eve stepped down and the large door closed. She stared at the ambulance with more tears streaming down her face as it drove away. She pictured her mother's haunted eyes whenever Eve tried to talk to her about the years she was missing from her life. Eve's stepfather had known what happened. Eve hated him more now than she ever had before.

THIRTY

They arrived at the hotel as the sun was going down. Eve was worn out physically and emotionally. The team met in her room. There was so much to do and it was scrambling her brain. A slight headache didn't help.

"We need sleep," Clyde told her. "In the morning, our minds will be fresh and we can process better. No one has mentioned food and it's been over eight hours since we've eaten."

"I can't," said Collin. "That horrible smell is in my nostrils. I'm wearing it too."

"You and Ray go take a shower. I'll drop off a snack at your room," Clyde insisted. He was a health nut and officer safety meant more than just watching your six. The guys didn't argue.

The three men left the room.

Eve's stomach was queasy along with the headache.

"I'm putting out an ATL on the truck and Buick," she told Bina. "It will give us more leverage. Aaron hasn't reached out which means they have no intention of meeting for interviews."

She called dispatch and placed the ATL statewide. She made sure to emphasize her stepbrothers' names and that they were people of interest in a homicide investigation. By calling local dispatch, the entire town would quickly know she was looking for them.

After she disconnected, there was a soft knock on the door. It was Clyde. He handed over two of his sawdust protein bars and two apples.

"How are you doing?" he asked.

"As tired as everyone else and not hungry." She looked down at the bar and her stomach rolled.

"You'll feel better once you eat. Try to sleep. Tomorrow will be another long day."

"I know." She told him about the ATL.

"Smart move. What are you feeling about the county attorney right now?"

"Death is too good. I doubt we can charge him with a crime at this point. No matter what he does, he seems to weasel out of any sort of punishment. He knew what Eric's list meant."

"We'll get him."

"His church may beat us to it, but losing his standing in the community isn't enough punishment. He needs to lose everything including his freedom," she said.

"People like him have a way of slithering away and coming back."

She gave him the small grin he was pushing for.

"Take a hot shower and eat your protein bar and apple," he said when Bina stepped out of the bathroom. "It will help."

Eve secured the locks on the door after shutting it behind him.

It was her turn in the bathroom.

She allowed the water to stream down her back after she finished washing. She'd turned it as hot as she could stand, which filled the room with steam. She couldn't stop the tears. She'd cried more in the last twenty-four hours than she had in the past five years. They had three confirmed missing babies and more names on Eric's list. She cried for him, and for the women and children. She also cried for her mother.

The image of the trailer wouldn't leave her. The smell was cemented in her brain. The cult treated women like animals. Adella would rather die than go back into isolation, but she didn't ask Eve to help her get out of her marriage. Eve should have pushed and taken the children.

She went to her knees, her heart breaking for those too indoctrinated into the prophet's evil to see a way out. Somehow, Maggie had found the way and she had rescued Eve. Her mother was so much stronger than Eve had ever given her credit for and that too broke her heart. She'd said horrible things to Maggie when she was a teenager. She'd blamed her for the years Aaron tortured her and the hunger in her gut when she was punished.

With a last hitch in her breath, she turned off the water and stepped out from the shower. Her self-pity was at an end. She opened the door and walked into the room wearing her nightshirt. Bina had finished off her bar and apple.

Eve got into bed and grabbed the protein bar from the side table where she'd left it. She removed the wrapper and chewed slowly, wondering if she would keep it down. Either it wasn't as bad as she remembered or she was finally hungry. After the bar, she was able to eat the apple.

She rubbed her temple where there was still a slight ache. She wanted to call her mother but this wasn't the time. Eve's emotions were too raw. Their conversation needed privacy and they had to be face to face.

"Do you think there are other women in isolation?" Bina asked.

It had occurred to Eve too.

"I plan to ask Aaron tomorrow. If he doesn't tell me, you can hold him down while I beat the truth out of him."

"Deal. I may not be responsible if my hand slips to my gun and there's an accidental discharge."

Eve gave her friend a small grin.

"I've got your back. If I saw him right now, it wouldn't be accidental."

Eve had never felt this much anger or need for violence. Bina was obviously in the same place. She stood from the bed to brush her teeth. It felt good to crawl beneath the covers and close her eyes after turning off the light.

Her dreams were all over the place. In one, she was locked in a dark trailer. In another, she was calling to Eric and begging him not to hit her with rocks. She jerked awake and assured herself it was just a dream. In minutes she was out again but woke up with the odor from the trailer filling her lungs before she realized it was just another nightmare. She needed so badly to talk to her mother. The entire night was a lost opportunity for sleep.

* * *

The following morning, they were all up earlier than usual. Ray and Collin gathered breakfast from the lobby again and brought it to Eve's room. Her entire team appeared as haggard as Eve felt.

"Aaron said his brothers were gone when he checked on them. We need to go to their homes. We can't trust Aaron and we need to see for ourselves. Officer Keb's arrest is also up for discussion. It will be tricky. We need a warrant. We'll run into trouble if we don't have this locked up tight."

Tamm had emailed Keb's personal information and they had a home address. He lived on the outskirts of town in the county.

"We should consider bringing in SWAT for apprehension," Clyde said.

He had a good point. Eve had no faith in surrounding law enforcement and they couldn't ask for help. With Judge Nelson on vacation, they had no one local they could count on to keep Keb in jail. Eve was thinking about calling in the FBI for federal charges. She needed a report to send them. Keb was dangerous and they didn't have time to waste. There was a good possibility there were more women isolated who needed to be rescued.

"We need preliminary reports for what we found at the trailer yesterday," she said wearily. "I was hoping to start typing. I'm calling the FBI in as soon as I have something written to give them."

No one argued. They could all see the huge scope of the investigation and that they had to have help.

"The rest of us can drive by your stepbrothers' homes and at least look to see if there's activity," Collin suggested.

"Until the evidence is back on the bullets, we don't have enough to make an arrest for the murder," Ray said. "Any word from the county attorney?"

"He hasn't called," Eve told them.

"I still say we go together to your stepbrothers' homes," said Clyde. "Safety is a huge issue right now and we can't take chances."

"I'm with Clyde on this," Bina seconded.

Until the FBI arrived, they were spread too thin. She had to discover the addresses of the other names on the list and Eve needed Aaron to help her do it. His cooperation was a long shot.

"After we check out the homes, Clyde and I will come back here," she told them. "I'll type the initial for Miriam." She looked at Clyde. "You take the homicide."

He nodded his agreement. She turned to the others.

"You'll collect the video from the minimart and run down the people mentioned at the grocery store. Watch each other's backs and be aware Keb knows Miriam is gone. He'll know we took her and that she would give us his name. He might have left town by now, but we need to be careful. There are others involved too."

"I know what I want to do, but what should we do if he approaches us?" Ray asked.

"Safety first," she said. "If you need to take him into custody, do it and we'll straighten out the logistics afterward. He's armed and dangerous. Don't take chances."

The three detectives gave her a nod.

They talked very little after that and simply ate their food. The bars and apples had helped the night before, but they were hungry this morning and made up for yesterday's lack of calories. They would each carry memories of the trailer like they did of Hannah Tanner. Eve worried her team was at its breaking point. Bina and Collin had both talked about the strain of this job. Her thoughts brought on a cloud of hopelessness that she was having trouble getting past.

When they finished the meal, she called Aaron. It was difficult to speak to him and keep her tone civil. He sounded as tired and as miserable as he had the previous day. She wouldn't forget that he knew what was happening to women like Miriam and didn't care.

"Have you heard from your brothers?" she asked.

"No. They haven't returned my calls. They didn't show up for work either. Have you found out anything?"

"Nothing. We're waiting for forensics on the bullet. Call and leave them another message," she said. "I have ATLs out. You need to explain how it will look if they refuse to be interviewed. They are people of interest right now. Without forensics on the bullets, I have nothing that ties them to the murder. Their disappearance makes them appear guilty. Stress that."

She didn't mention Miriam. She wanted to look into his eyes when she told him about her. She needed the information on the other names. Helping her would dig his grave deeper and he would lie like he always did. She would allow the FBI to interrogate him if he refused to answer her questions honestly.

"I'll try to convince them," Aaron replied with a pitiful whine.

"Do you have anything I need to know?" she asked.

"The man in charge of the high council came to see me. He insisted I take a leave of absence from my office. I told him I had to finish a few things. He's given me until Monday, but they want to meet me in the next twenty minutes and I don't know how long it will take. I'll be in contact with you again this afternoon."

This meant she wouldn't be going to his office this morning. Maybe she would be calmer by the afternoon, but it was doubtful. Aaron was no longer useful to the people who kept him in power. As an elected official, he could not be legally removed from office unless he stepped down or was criminally prosecuted and found guilty, which would have him disbarred. The only law that mattered in this town was the prophet's and Aaron, even with his *elected by the people power*, would buckle. She was sure he would whine and do everything he could to get out of the mess he was in. Licking their boots wouldn't be off the table.

He was at his most dangerous right now.

"Let me know immediately if you hear back from your brothers," she told him.

He was on his own when it came to his high council.

"I'll call if I hear anything," he said dejectedly.

"Do that."

After she relayed the update to the team, they took the van and drove to the two addresses they had. Mark, Richard, and Danny lived in a duplex, Eric and Patrick in a small apartment complex.

Mark's vehicle was still gone and the other truck sat in front of Eric's door. They knocked at both places and no one answered. The drapes of both locations were tightly drawn and they couldn't see inside the windows. She might not have enough for an arrest, but a warrant was a possibility.

Tamm called Eve as they were pulling away from Eric's apartment.

"Highway patrol has a burned-out vehicle an hour west of town. It matches the description of the vehicle that rear-ended you. It's registered to Eric Owens."

"Do you have a phone number for the officer managing the scene?" Eve asked.

"His name is Daniels. I'll text you his number. He's waiting for your call."

The text came through and Eve hit the number immediately. He was still on scene.

"Have you found a handgun?" she asked after introducing herself.

"No. It's clean. Nothing in the glove box or trunk either. We took the VIN off the engine once the car cooled. They used gasoline to douse it." VIN stood for vehicle identification number.

They'd hit a dead end. Her stepbrothers had left it on the side of the road and were now most likely in the truck. Or, whoever they reported to, had given them another vehicle to use.

"Thank you," Eve said.

"They've ditched the Buick," she told her team. "I doubt they're in town any longer. If we're lucky, law enforcement will match the truck's plate and pull them over."

It was decided that Collin, Bina, and Ray would return to the apartment and duplex and knock on doors to interview the neighbors and then hit up the few names they had from Eric's job. They dropped Clyde and Eve back at the hotel and left again in the van.

When she stepped into her room with Clyde following, her

cell rang again. It was the medical examiner's office. She removed her belt, which was heavy with all her equipment, while she spoke on the phone.

"We're backed up," said the woman in charge of scheduling. "We can't get your body in until Tuesday."

"Okay. Thank you for calling."

"Tuesday for the autopsy," she told Clyde. "I still don't know if we'll be able to go. We're too thin as it is. I want to separate the two cases. I'll take Collin for the missing children and you take Bina for the homicide." She needed her attention on the babies. "Ray can jump between cases. If the FBI arrives quickly, we'll put them on the names on Eric's list to make sure those women are safe."

"Good idea. We need the help."

"I'm taking Collin to Aaron's office later this afternoon. I don't mind if everyone comes, but I want the rest of you waiting in the van. He might be more open to speaking with Collin present."

Clyde nodded. "Do you mind if I write my report in here?" he asked. "I'll need to grab my laptop."

"My camera bag is in the back of the SUV and I want to download the trailer images. I'll run outside while you gather what you need. If you have a spare energy bar, grab me one." She tried not to make a sour face. Her blood sugar was dropping. She needed another full meal, but a snack would do for now. The exhaustion was catching up with her again.

She stood and Clyde moved into her space. His arms came around her and she gave herself a moment to simply breathe against his chest. His scent filled her and the warmth of his arms gave her added strength. She finally took a step back and looked up into his eyes.

"Thank you."

He moved away. She grabbed the keys and headed to the SUV and he walked to his room. She was thinking about Aaron and their coming confrontation and paying no attention to her surroundings. She unlocked the back and it swung upward. A noise from behind made her turn.

Jarrod Keb stood three feet away, pointing a gun at her chest.

THIRTY-ONE

"We're taking a ride," Keb said.

Eve wasn't armed. She had her hand on the strap of her camera bag and swung it up and around with all her strength, stepping into the swing and taking her closer to Keb. A forearm circled her throat, placing pressure on her carotid artery. Her feet left the ground. She knew what would happen before it did. Her hand slipped into her pocket.

"Say goodnight, Eve." Hot breath hit the side of her face. "Keb, pull your car around and open the trunk."

She fought it, but darkness closed in.

* * *

Eve opened her eyes in a cramped space with low light. She tried to move. The cold steel of handcuffs secured her wrists behind her back. It took a moment to gain her bearings and remember Officer Keb and his gun. Her body was jostled suddenly and her shoulders cramped. She was in the trunk of a vehicle and she felt sick to her stomach. Her head was woozy.

Had she been hit?

No, she had the oxygen to her brain cut off. It shouldn't make her feel this way. If he'd kept the pressure on her throat, she would be dead. The voice she'd heard seconds before she passed out registered.

Sheriff Murray.

She'd also seen the brim of his hat when he choked her. Terror clutched her insides. She always feared Murray. She'd known since she saw Keb talking to him at the minimart that the two were connected.

Eve was jostled again. It felt like the car was on a dirt road. Her head spun and she had to fight vomiting. The heat was stifling. She was sweaty and uncomfortable, her shoulders ached and all she could think about was water. It was the most pressing need. How long had she been unconscious? Nausea rose in her throat and she rolled slightly in case she vomited. She didn't want to inhale it. The only thing that made sense was that they must have drugged her with something. She breathed deeply through her nose trying to clear her head so she could think straight.

The car's jerking movements didn't stop. Neither did the nausea. She thought she passed out again. Could they be taking her to a trailer? She knew she should do something, but her head was too fuzzy to think straight.

Her legs cramped and she tried stretching but there was no room. She noticed two canvas bags. She twisted slightly. One had POLICE written on the side. She was in the back of Keb's patrol vehicle. He'd driven her out of town in a police cruiser. Her head cleared slightly and she remembered the cuff key in her right boot. With her hands free, she might have a chance. Getting the cuffs to the front became her goal and she curled her body tightly to slide the handcuffs over her feet. Suddenly, the vehicle stopped and she was thrown back. Her head hit the metal of the wheel well.

The world was readjusting when Sheriff Murray opened

the trunk. Her eyes slowly adjusted to the bright light of the sun. He placed his hands beneath her arms and pulled her out. She fell to her knees.

"Not so high and mighty now, are you?" he said in a low drawl.

Keb stood behind him.

Her chin lifted and she met the sheriff's eyes, her own burning with revulsion. She paid for her defiance. His unexpected fist left her gasping for air and she fell sideways. He'd struck her ribs. Her crouched position had kept the strike from causing any severe damage, but it hurt. With her hands behind her back, she didn't try to gain her feet or sit up. She curled into a ball giving him fewer vital organs to attack.

"Get her in the trailer," he told Keb. "Do not lay a hand on her."

"Yes, sir."

Keb pulled Eve to her unsteady feet. Her legs tried to cooperate, but she felt her knees give.

"Stand up or I'll drag you. I'm not carrying your ass," Keb said.

She stumbled, took shallow breaths, and somehow managed to stay upright. Her ribs hurt. Keb grasped her upper arm painfully and pulled her forward. There were trees around her. She needed as much information on her surroundings as possible. She stumbled slightly but again stayed upright. There was a top of a roof through some trees in the distance. It could be a house or barn. The landscape was different and she was not at the other trailer site.

A solid push between her shoulder blades drove her against the side of a two-horse trailer. The outside color reminded her of the small trailer Miriam was kept in. The stall openings were covered with plywood.

The cool metal was all that kept her upright when Keb

released her. *Run*, she told herself, but her feet wouldn't cooperate with her brain. Vomit burned in her throat.

Keb grabbed her again and pulled her up a metal step. He shoved her through when she tried to avoid the door and throw herself off the side of the step. It was purely self-preservation. She did not want to go inside the trailer. His push was enough to get her inside and with her hands locked behind her back, she couldn't stop herself falling. Her head hit the opposite wall, though not hard, and she landed sideways against it. The trailer was warm inside but cooler than the trunk. It smelled like animals and didn't help the nausea she was fighting.

Keb jerked her up by her arm and dragged her to a mattress then pushed her to her knees beside it.

"I'm taking off your handcuffs. If you fight, I'll beat the shit out of you," he said.

Murray had told him not to touch her, but Eve realized beating her was not what the sheriff meant. She was in no condition to fight and compliance would give her a better shot later when the odds were more in her favor. She didn't say anything, simply relaxed as he uncuffed her right hand and then her left.

He shoved her down on the mattress and she prepared to fight. He walked out, laughing.

"Stupid bitch," he said, and laughed louder.

She ran her tongue across her dry lips. She needed water. There was a makeshift counter made of wood along one wall. Eve could see the top of a gallon water bottle from her position. It was very similar to the setup with Miriam though it didn't have a bathroom. She concentrated on the water and was able to stand using the side of the trailer to keep her upright. The shelf held a single can of food, a can opener, spoon, and that precious gallon of water.

She took note of a five-gallon bucket under the counter.

Eve used the wall to keep herself upright and stumbled her

way to the counter. Her head remained fuzzy. All she wanted was water. Her ribs hurt, but she managed to lift the jug off the counter, letting it swing down to the floor. She used the side of the trailer again to get back to the bed, practically dragging the water with her to the mattress.

She collapsed onto it and rolled sideways, her nose nearer the material. It smelled old and musty, but she didn't care. Eve relaxed to give her aching ribs relief. She tried to stretch, but it hurt too badly. The nausea passed again and her need for water returned. She took one long pull from the jug remembering what Miriam had told her about conserving water. She was light-headed from the drugs and she couldn't hold on to important thoughts. She closed her eyes.

She jerked awake suddenly, having no idea how long she'd slept. It seemed hotter inside the small space. Her throat was dry and sore from thirst. She lifted the water and drank several large gulps. It didn't relieve all the ache, but it helped clear her head.

Eve gazed around again. Her eyes landed on the bucket and it occurred to her it was for waste. There was a roll of toilet paper between the corner of the bucket and the wall. She wasn't looking forward to using it.

She needed to think positive thoughts and not give into the self-pity that was swelling inside her mind. Keb and Murray would not defeat her. She could fight and when she got a chance, she would take it. That meant staying physically intact and mentally sharp. It meant complying.

She lay back and examined the ceiling. It was metal like the rest of the trailer. Wood covered the windows. Bolts secured the plywood to the metal walls. The ends of the bolts were round and flat, which didn't help her. She had nothing to grasp even if she could twist them with her fingers.

She studied the flooring. It was rough wood that had seen better days. It held possibilities.

Isolation was how they made the women obey, but it hadn't worked on her mother and it wouldn't work on Eve. Maggie's face swam before her eyes. Her mother had had no one back then. Eve had a team of friends who would stop at nothing to find her. Maggie had gotten away on her own. If her mother could escape, Eve would do the same, she wouldn't wait for her friends.

She drifted off again and woke with a feeling that she was suffocating. It was a dream. She was hyperventilating. Eve lifted the water and took another drink and then another and placed the cap back when she finished.

She crawled to her hands and knees on the mattress and used the sidewall to stand. When she was upright, she reexamined her surroundings. The door. She hadn't checked it. She used the side of the trailer to help her walk again. There was not even a handle inside. She pushed, but the door didn't budge.

On reflex, she almost screamed for help but stopped herself. It was a waste of energy. No one who would help her would be anywhere near this location.

She made it to the counter. Two legs came up from the floor and held a long piece of twelve-inch-wide plywood. If she could bust it apart, she could use a wooden leg as a weapon. Strong and healthy, she reminded herself. If food and water were scarce, she wouldn't be that way for long. She tried to judge the time but really had no idea. When the sun went down and the trailer cooled off, she would eat a little of the food.

It was a store-brand chili. The can opener was the small camping type, considered old-fashioned now. It was all Eve used as a young girl. It had a bottle opener on the end. Another weapon and this one was readily available.

She examined the wooden floor planks once more, looking for weak spots. Standing became too much and she stumbled back to the mattress. Again, despair tried to rear its ugly head, but she refused to allow it to take hold. Miriam had survived with her sanity intact for 512 days. Eve knew it must have been even longer for her mother.

Sleep was the best medicine for now. She needed time to allow the drug to leave her system. She drank one last sip of water and decided she wouldn't have more until after she ate. She sank into the smelly mattress.

When her eyes opened next, it was pitch black. It took a moment for the memories to come back. Keb had held a gun on her and the sheriff had placed her in a chokehold. She was in a horse trailer. It was cooler. She didn't let the dark stop her from opening the can, it just took a little extra time. She used the wall to find her way to the counter. She brought the can of chili, can opener, and spoon back to the bed. It took three tries but she was finally able to remove the lid.

She took a bite of the cold, congealed chili and gagged. Breathing through her nose and out her mouth, she counted to ten and took another bite, this one smaller. She ate half the can and drank more water.

She had no way to brush her teeth and after a brief time she needed to pee. It was a good sign and she smiled into the dark. Her ribs didn't ache as badly either. Pressing the can's lid back down, she rested it next to the water jug on the floor and placed the spoon on top. The lid of the can was sharp and another weapon.

She used the wall again and found the bucket and toilet paper. It was uncomfortable, but she managed. She estimated she expelled a thimble full of pee. She wiped herself and dropped the paper into the bucket. Within a couple of days, the inside of the trailer would smell like Miriam's. The animal musk would be a thing of the past. She went back to the mattress and lay down. This time she took off her boots and socks.

Boredom might be her biggest problem. She was wide awake and could barely see her hand in front of her face. With nothing else to do, she played the pretend game.

She pretended to beat the crap out of Aaron.

She pretended to shoot Sheriff Murray in both legs.

She pretended to cut off Keb's penis.

That was her favorite. She fell asleep thinking about doing it with the lid from the chili can.

THIRTY-TWO

When Eve woke up, she could see inside the trailer. It wasn't too hot, yet. The bad news was she didn't need to pee which meant she was already dehydrated. Her dry cracked lips and slightly swollen tongue reinforced the theory. She drank a little more water and stared at the jug when she was finished. It was now three-quarters full. It could last a few more days although the heat of the afternoon would make reserving the water excruciating. How long would they leave her with limited water and a single can of food?

She rested the plastic jug in the far corner at the head of the mattress so she could avoid looking at it. Her head wasn't spinning today and she didn't need the wall to stay upright. It was time to do something positive and take her mind off the negative. She put her socks and boots on and reexamined the flooring. She'd found several spots where the wood was slightly rotted the day before. She stomped her boot down on one of them and heard a small crack. On a positive note, the crack wasn't visible. The downside was her boot left a mark in the dust. Gazing around, she decided to wad some toilet tissue to move the dust to disguise what she was doing. The thin single-ply paper shredded quickly and barely kept her fingers from getting splinters. Another course of action was needed and she stomped across the floor and back again, covering every square foot. When she was done, she could no longer see evidence of her escape plan.

She would work on it again after dark. With the cracking she'd heard, eventually it would break through. The flooring was her first plan and the team her backup. They wouldn't stop searching. Sooner or later, they would connect the dots. She counted the steps it took to get to the correct location for the rotted wood. Then she did it again with her eyes closed. When she was sure she could find it, she dropped on the mattress in exhaustion.

She ignored the half can of food. It could be the last she had for a few more days. If no one brought her anything today, she would eat it tonight. She had gone hungry before and it didn't scare her. For now, water was the priority. She would drink enough to stay conscious.

After food and water, her most essential problem was discovering where she was. She had no idea how far she'd traveled in the trunk of Keb's vehicle. She could be fifty miles or more from town. Trusting people from surrounding homes wasn't in her best interest. To leave, she needed an idea of how far she would need to travel. With a full gallon, she could break through the floor and make it to Hildale if she were in the fifty-mile range. There were wilderness plants she could eat if she had to. Thirst would be the biggest obstacle.

The hours crawled by. She peed again and didn't look forward to the other need that would eventually be a problem. The trailer would smell, but she could take it.

The number 512 ran through her head. She had no idea how Miriam did it. Her team would be looking for her when they needed to concentrate on Eric's murder and the missing children. Clyde would call in the FBI, she assured herself.

She thought about him and their relationship. She was an idiot. Their job was dangerous and either one of them could die at any time. She should have stayed nights at his place and let the relationship expand from there. He had the patience of a saint and never pushed. Regret would do her no good, but she was determined to make up for her indecisiveness after she escaped. It was time to step fully into her relationship with Clyde and share it with the world.

She took an afternoon nap when it grew too warm. She woke up before the sun was completely down and finished off the chili. She walked over to the toilet paper and tore off a small piece which she rolled into a ball. She placed it in one of her pant pockets.

It seemed like a lifetime—512 days.

She had only been in the trailer for thirty-six hours.

* * *

The next day she had no food. Even though she conserved, the jug was now only a quarter full.

When the sun went down, she curled into a ball on the mattress. She couldn't stop the tears. She'd been stupid to go to the SUV unarmed. Worse, she hadn't paid attention to her surroundings. Self-pity filled her, crushing her resolve, and bringing more despair.

She finally laughed. Tears wasted water. It was the best reason she'd ever had to gain control of her emotions. Murray and Keb would not win. They would need to kill her to stop her from escaping. They would go to prison for the rest of their lives for kidnapping and torture and she would make sure of it.

* * *

A hand gripped her upper arm and rolled her over, jarring her from sleep. Sheriff Murray sat on the side of the bed, a sixteen-ounce water bottle in his hand. Keb stood behind him with his gun pointed at her.

"Sit up and drink this," Murray said.

She didn't question him and greedily took it from his hand once she scrambled upright.

"I am hoping you are in an agreeable mood today. You are hungry and I know you are thirsty. Drink up," he said when she finished only half the water.

"I am going to give you the rules and I want you to under-stand that if you disobey, punishment will be swift and harsh. Answer 'yes, sir', if you understand."

Eve had finished the water, but she was still thirsty.

"Yes, sir," she answered quickly. It wasn't time to fight. She would save her anger for when she had a better chance of escape. If given the opportunity, she was ready to attack and he wouldn't see it coming. She smiled internally.

Murray studied her without saying anything. She stared back and then remembered she had to appear meek. Her chin lowered, bringing her eyes to his chest in submission.

"Do not think I am unaware of what you are doing," he said suddenly.

He didn't contract words and had the fundamentalist cadence to his voice, but his drawl was not normal. She wondered if it was fake.

"You may have been raised under God's eyes, but Satan has had his hold on you for far too long," he accused. "You think complying will catch me off guard. It will not work. Your food and water are based on your willingness to accept your duty and find God's grace as a woman of the faith. I will gladly beat the apostate out of you or allow Brother Jarrod to do it. Do you understand?"

"Yes, sir." She didn't raise her eyes. The address ground on her nerves. He didn't deserve the slightest bit of respect.

"I wanted you as a wife when you were young. Did you know that?"

She didn't think he wanted an answer and remained silent.

"Your father told me you were going to someone else. God had chosen you for me and I was angry with your father for a long time. I had a plan to make you mine, but you were stolen from God and from me."

He reached over and swept Eve's hair from her face, his malevolent expression stopping her next breath.

"A woman's hair should remain uncut. I may punish you for this atrocity."

Then his lips curved into a smile that caused goose bumps on her skin. The intensity in his strange blue eyes made it worse. He wasn't just a predator, he was insane.

She reminded herself to breathe normally.

"The punishments you deserve could very well kill you. I hope you heed this warning and my dictates. You will show gratitude for the food and water I bring. If I tell you to move, you move. You will not hesitate in performing your duty. If you cannot follow these simple rules, you will be punished. Do you understand?"

"Yes, sir." Her mind was reeling. Could she comply if he raped her? He didn't give her time to think about it. His hand went to her breast and his fingers squeezed.

Escape. It was a driving force.

She swung her legs around and managed to knee Murray in the side. The sheriff leaned out of the way when she used her fist. She connected with his arm. He grabbed one of her legs and jerked her to the floor. Before she could move, his fist landed in her stomach taking the air from her lungs. An open hand connected with her face driving her head sideways. His fingers slid into her hair and he yanked her head back painfully. If her mouth weren't so dry, she would've spit in his face. It felt good to fight even knowing she couldn't win.

He slapped her again. Even without air in her lungs, she made a grab for both his legs around the ankles and tried to pull them out from under him. It was futile. It wasn't an open-handed slap this time. His fist caught her in the corner of her jaw. She tasted blood. Oxygen came back into her lungs. Eve tried to get her feet beneath her, but he grabbed another fistful of hair and pulled her up on the bed. His knee came down on her ribs and he held her there. He placed enough pressure against her chest that she couldn't breathe.

"Are you finished?" he demanded, his smile still in place.

Her plan solidified. When he thought he had punished her to the point of compliance, he would be wrong. He was testing her and eventually he would think he'd won. That was when she would have the best shot at taking him down and escaping.

Keb was breathing hard. He'd enjoyed watching the sheriff beat her. She'd seen his sickness from what he'd done to Miriam. If Keb gave her a chance, she would take him down too. Neither Murray nor Keb were the scariest people in the room. She was.

"I guess we will need to beat Satan out of you after all," the sheriff said. "Brother Jarrod, bring my switch from the house."

"Yes, sir."

Eve heard what sounded like a four-wheeler rev before it pulled away. He was gone for about ten minutes. The sheriff kept his knee on her chest the entire time, leering down at her. His eyes remained glacier-bright, enjoying the thought that he'd bested her.

The four-wheeler came back and Keb walked inside. He held a long thin branch in his hand. Her father had used one similar.

She started fighting again.

"Sit on her legs," Murray yelled.

Keb pulled her legs down and sat on them. The sheriff continued leaning on her ribs. He now had the switch in his hand and reared back striking her face. She used her arms to protect herself and he continued his strikes. She could feel the blood on her arms and still he didn't stop. She screamed while Keb laughed.

THIRTY-THREE

They left her with no additional water or food. Did they mean for her to die? She concentrated on the pain. Her arms had cuts and welts. She couldn't begin to describe the bruising. She would live. It could have been worse.

Murray had given her sixteen ounces of water to drink. She would keep what remained in the gallon jug for the next day. Her stomach growled and she ignored it.

She took stock of her injuries.

Her lip was split. Her jaw and left cheek tender. A few of his swipes with the switch had landed on her face. The skin was sore but not bleeding. She felt her ribs and they were also tender but nothing she couldn't manage. If they were broken, she would know it.

She had an idea. After climbing to her feet, she stared down at the mattress. She bent over and put her fingers under the material and lifted. She strained and got it upright, using her shoulder to hold it in place. Her eyes scanned the flooring. A discolored spot caught her eye. The area was larger than the other she'd worked on before. She stomped down and it cracked. She stomped again. Another crack. She put the mattress back in place. She'd gotten lucky and now she needed that luck to hold.

She would wait for food and water before she escaped. She would comply with everything except sexual contact. That was her line.

There was one area where fighting had worked in her favor. Murray had sent Keb to *the house*. It had to be Keb's or the sheriff's home. She knew where Keb lived, but it wasn't far enough away from civilization. He'd said *my* switch. She had to be somewhere on the grounds at Murray's place. She'd seen the roof between the trees. Eve racked her brain but concluded she'd never known where he lived.

She wasn't at an isolated location like the trailer they'd found Miriam in. She was being held on Murray's property. His wives would be there and would possibly have a phone. She would not count on their help willingly, but she had no problem forcing them to give her what she needed. Murray went to work, but she didn't know if Keb would risk going to town. Eve flip-flopped between escaping at night or escaping during the day. She would decide when she had more information.

Her head turned woozy. She returned the mattress to its proper place, sat down, and laid back to rest. When she felt better, she started walking the floor to redistribute the dust from lifting the mattress. If she couldn't make a hole big enough beneath it, she would work on the first location.

She had options. She had a plan.

Overexertion was out of the question with the water situation. She stretched out on the bed and refused to give in to the bad thoughts that cropped into her mind. She concentrated on her burning arms and her fury.

She killed time by going through state statute in her mind. Kidnapping, assault, false imprisonment. Everything Keb and Murray would go away for. It kept her sane.

She finally dozed off. When she woke, all she could think about was her hunger.

That night, she had a slight case of diarrhea. It wasn't pleasant and she worried more about dehydration. No one came the next day and she had an eighth of the water left. At first, she drank it sparingly but then decided she needed it all. Her body was breaking down, her cracked lips were now bleeding. She had trouble standing. Her head spun when she counted the small balls of toilet paper. She didn't have enough water in her system for tears.

Her stomach cramped and she used the bucket several times during the night. The chili had most likely past its expiration date.

The sound of the four-wheeler woke her the following day. She sat upright facing the door, her body trembling. "Stay calm," she told herself. "You need food and water."

The door opened and Murray walked inside.

"Not so hoity-toity now, are you?" He moved closer. His smile turned her warm skin cold.

She gazed at the side of the trailer so she could keep the sheriff in her peripheral vision and not look at him directly. There was no sign of Keb. If Murray touched her, was she too weak to fight him off? If it happened, she would find out.

A plastic bag was slung over his arm. He also had a gallon of water in his left hand. It hurt her throat to see it. Her mouth might be too dry to beg.

"I'll leave these here," he said. "If you behave the next time I come back, I'll have your bucket emptied." He placed the plastic bag and the water jug on the counter.

Then he was gone.

She stood too fast and sank back down on the mattress. The second time, she used the wall to get to the counter. She drank water first and stopped herself while she was still thirsty. He'd left three cans of food. One beef stew and two soup. She didn't check the dates. It wouldn't matter. She decided her stomach couldn't handle the stew and she took a can of soup back with her to the mattress. She'd left the can opener next to the bed as a weapon. She ate half the soup and saved the rest. She would eat the other half when she was sure she would keep it down.

The small water bottle Murray had given her was on the floor by the bed. When her stomach settled, she took it to the counter and filled it. She had three quarters of the gallon left afterward. She could carry it in her hand when she escaped if she was close enough to town to get there in a few hours. It wouldn't slow her down like a full gallon of water would.

She lifted the mattress and stomped the floor with all the fury she felt. It felt good to take her aggression out on the wood. She didn't make a hole, just weakened a larger area. She estimated it would take her a few more tries before the wood split enough to push it through. She lowered the mattress and tucked the small water bottle in the corner between it and the metal wall of the trailer.

She felt better. Her arms didn't hurt to move and the welts had turned to bruises. She would survive.

* * *

The next time Murray returned; she heard the same engine as before. He came in, and Eve noticed a woman behind him standing in the doorway, blocking the light. She wore a pale green prairie dress. Murray had another gallon of water in his hand.

"Good, you are awake," he said, then looked over his shoulder. "Place the clothes and the bucket on the counter and take the waste bucket with you."

"Yes, sir."

When the woman turned from the counter, she noticed her swollen and bruised face. Eve kept her expression neutral, but anger stiffened her body. She breathed in slowly and made herself relax.

"There is water in the bucket for you to wash with along with a rag. Clean yourself and change into the clothes I have honored you with. The bucket will then be used for your waste."

She stayed silent.

"The proper response is 'thank you, sir.'" He smiled. It didn't go to his eyes. He was testing her.

"Thank you, sir." It hurt mentally, but she managed it.

"You have another gallon of water and more food."

She didn't respond.

He studied her for a moment. She tried her best to keep sweet. The only way to do it was to turn her mind away from thinking about shredding his skin slowly from his face.

"Beating the apostate out of you will be satisfying." He placed the plastic bag he carried on top of the counter along with the gallon of water.

Was he going to beat her again? She mentally prepared herself. She would survive. She could take the pain. Her childhood was all about pain, mental and physical. Surviving to see him face justice was all that mattered.

Eve still had almost half of her other water. He left it behind. He pulled another sixteen-ounce bottle from the bag and handed it to her.

Her hand shook when she took it.

She drank the entire bottle while he watched. When she was done, he walked out of the trailer and locked the door behind him. She heard the four-wheeler a minute later. She was still thirsty and went to the counter and drank from the half-filled jug until she didn't think her stomach could keep more down. She used what remained to fill the small bottle she'd emptied minutes before. Her stomach growled, but she wasn't eating yet.

She took off her clothes and scrubbed herself with the cloth in the cool water. It felt incredible. There was a small amount of soap mixed in. When she finished, she placed her head in the bucket and swished her hair around. She had no comb or brush, but it didn't matter. When she pulled her head out, she rung out her hair then let it fall. It dripped onto her bare shoulders. Her hair had reached her waist before and once more she was glad, she'd cut it.

Eve examined the pale green dress that matched the one the woman wore. There were religious undergarments folded beneath the dress. It was too hot to wear them, but she worried about what Murray would do if she didn't. If she hid them beneath the bed and he noticed, he would see the damage to the boards.

Slowly, she put on the holy garments. Eve had sworn many years before that they would never cover her body again. She had cried only once since her arrival, but she felt tears gathering. These clothes were a symbol of oppression. The lower garment covered her from ankle to waist. The upper piece, from stomach to neckline to wrists.

Eve wiped her eyes. She would cry after she escaped and they would be tears of joy.

She didn't put the dress on. She would hear the four-wheeler if he came back and she would have time to pull it over her head. Women slept in their garments not their dresses, so she didn't worry about him arriving if she were sleeping.

She grabbed the empty gallon water jug and placed it on the floor. Carefully she filled the dirty water into it. She would be able to clean herself with it for a day or two. Disgusting but preferable to having nothing.

The bag Murray had brought also had a toothbrush and a small tube of toothpaste.

Pure heaven. Her teeth might be growing fur. She laughed aloud, sounding unhinged. He was playing psychological games with her. That was okay. She would win and he wouldn't see her attack coming.

For the first time since being locked in the trailer, she dropped to the floor and did pushups until her arms hurt. She rose and moved to the mattress and did dips for her triceps. When she finished, her arms trembled. She combed her fingers through her hair and felt almost normal.

She took a nap and when she woke, she stomped on the boards again, tucked the two smaller water bottles into her hiding spot and ate a full can of food. Her stomach had adjusted and she no longer felt like she was starving even though her body was desperate for calories.

Two days later, there was a knock on the side of the trailer and she froze.

"Are you there?" a soft woman's voice asked.

Eve scrambled to the wall by the door.

"I'm here."

"You are not alone."

"What's your name?"

Silence.

Eve asked the woman to speak to her several times, but she had gone.

Eve smiled. The woman helped her stay mentally strong and she appreciated it.

Her squad would be panicked by now. They would also be methodical. Keb hadn't been with Murray on his last two visits. He could be working or possibly in custody for what he'd done to Miriam.

She counted the small bits of paper, one by one.

Seven.

She was nowhere near 512.

THIRTY-FOUR

On day eight, she knew it took fourteen steps to walk the length of the trailer and seven to walk across it. There were eighteen wood panels along the floor not counting the ones beneath the bed. The box was her small world. It challenged her in ways she'd never imagined. It was meant to defeat her mentally by accomplishing one thing.

Isolation.

She hummed her favorite classical toons. She exercised, she stretched. Her mother was in her thoughts often. Clyde would have notified her before it hit the news. Maggie would be beside herself with worry. Eve didn't like thinking about her mother's suffering.

Her thoughts also centered on Clyde. He could be assertive, but this was a police trait she had too. He sometimes pushed hard, but when she stood up to him, he listened and gave her opinions respect. He valued her knowledge and the skills that got her to the leadership of the taskforce.

She pictured him and the team breaking down the clues to discover where she was. He would force those nasty protein bars on them because they would be spending every moment searching for her. She smiled at the thought of the bars. She would give anything for one of them now.

Analyzing Murray also made the time pass. Along with insanity, he coveted power like most fundamentalist men. For most, that power began and ended beneath their roof. They were the God of their household. Murray controlled her food, water, and clothing. It excited him. She dwelled on his visits to the house when she was a child and broke them down in her head.

Eve's stepfather held a higher legal position than Murray but feared him. Her stepfather craved attention from the prophet and it made him proud when it was given. The sheriff's attention caused anxiety. Eve saw it now.

When she was around ten years old, Murray's visits to their home had become more frequent. Her mothers started finding things for the girls to do upstairs. These visits had always taken place when her stepfather was home until the day Eve answered the door.

Murray had arrived unannounced while her father was at work. Aaron's mother, the senior wife, sent her to the door. It was a strange request because it was not something Eve had ever done. It was Aaron's mother's job and she also coveted power in her small, controlled world. Answering the door was an honor. Eve remembered the excitement she felt at doing something so grownup. She hadn't expected the sheriff.

"You are Sister Eve," Murray said, and stepped inside when she stood frozen.

It was not a title given to girls until they married. She looked down, unsure if she should answer. He lifted her chin, his fingers rough against her skin. He was the only man she'd ever seen wearing a hat, but it was his icy eyes that caught her in their trap. She couldn't look away. It was how a rabbit would respond when facing a coyote.

If you run, he'll chase you down and kill you from behind. If you stand facing him, you'll see death strike. Which was preferable?

He'd run a finger across her cheek. Her knees shook. She'd felt so small and helpless. He held her chin so she couldn't move even if she wanted to. A minute turned into a lifetime. One of her mothers walked up behind them and berated Eve for answering the door.

"Go upstairs to your room," she'd said nervously. "There will be no dinner for you."

He'd released her and she ran, tripping over her feet and banging her shins on the stairs. She hadn't cared that she would go to bed hungry. Her only thought had been to escape the look in his eyes.

Aaron's mother had set her up. She'd already voiced her opinion that Eve would never marry her son. Eve's blood was not pure enough.

When her stepfather was told she'd allowed Murray into their home, he summoned her to his office. It was the room she hated most within the house. Aaron's mother denied sending her to the door. Her father used a ruler on Eve's fingers to make her tell the truth. She refused to lie because Satan frightened her more than her stepfather. She'd had to keep her hands on his desk while the ruler snapped down on her small fingers. Her defiance made him angrier, and he brought out the switch. It didn't make her change her story. Her final punishment was water only, for two days and scrubbing every floor of the house on her knees. Aaron had laughed while she worked and his mother checked on Eve regularly and sneered. Eve's young mind couldn't comprehend her lie. Was she not afraid of damnation?

Eve had buried those memories but sitting in the hot trailer uncovered them. Thoughts of Aaron's tortures, her stepmother's lies and hatred, and Murray tried to fill her waking thoughts. When she realized she was allowing them to dominate the space in her head, she thought of Clyde and Maggie. At night she had less success and nightmares consumed her dreams.

Murray came daily, usually in the morning directly after the sun came up. Eve paid attention to his schedule. He brought food and water every other day. He enjoyed watching her. He knew how much it disturbed her even though she tried to hide it. On the days he brought food, the same woman removed her waste and left a clean bucket for Eve to wash in. Murray was very regimented in his daily routine. On the days her waste was removed, she'd hear a knock on the outside of the trailer. The woman didn't speak again, but she made sure Eve was aware of her. Just the sound gave her hope.

Eve would only have one chance to escape and she needed more information about the location of the trailer. She could follow the road out of the area, but it would be easy for Keb or Murray to find her. Her best chance was to avoid the main access and travel across the high desert terrain.

It was time to go. Murray saw through her meekness act. She didn't have a timid bone in her body and she wasn't a good enough actor.

Doubt filled her. Maybe she needed to escape tonight and take her chances. She had close to a full gallon of water. It would last several days. If she could get far enough away, she would find shade and move again at night. Her tracks would be a problem. Around and around, her thoughts tumbled.

She didn't leave that night and slept fitfully. She opened her eyes to sunlight and the sound of the four-wheeler. She pulled on the dress and quickly fastened the buttons. The vehicle didn't stop. This had happened before. She would hear the engine shut off in the distance.

The air was rancid from her waste, but she no longer cared. She had used the plastic bags Murray left to cover the waste bucket. He smiled when he saw it the first time.

This morning the four-wheeler returned ten minutes after it

drove past. Murray unlocked the door and walked inside. Keb was still not with him. The same woman stood at the door though she was a day early. She placed the clean bucket of water on the counter along with another dress and garments before she removed the waste bucket and took it outside. Murray held another bag. He opened it and Eve smelled food.

"I thought you might enjoy a decent meal." He took a foil-covered paper plate out of the bag and walked closer, placing it on the bed beside her. Eve lowered her gaze. She needed the fuel, but she didn't like the look of satisfaction in his eyes. He usually didn't approach her. Had she convinced him she wasn't dangerous?

He placed his hand back inside the bag and pulled it out holding a red apple. He was using psychological conditioning to gain her cooperation. She didn't care, she wanted the fruit.

He rested the apple beside the plate and backed away.

"Throw your soiled clothes toward the door," he said, the smile still in place.

There were clothes on the floor from the last time she'd changed. They were near the foot of the bed. She did as he said. He stood back while giving the orders. He still knew how dangerous she was. She thought about attacking him. Murray was much older, but as the sheriff, his defensive tactics training would be solid like hers and he was stronger. She would need to put him down quickly and be sure he stayed down. She wasn't desperate enough yet. If he broke a rib or another bone, her chance of escaping through the floor would be zero. A direct fight would only cause pain.

He scooped the clothes from where they landed and threw them outside.

"Eat," he told her. "You will be coming to the house today."

Her heart rate sped up. She forgot her submission and raised her eyes to his. She should have kept them on the floor. Whenever he came to the trailer, his strange blue irises caused an uncomfortable feeling in the pit of her stomach. Today was worse. They were almost maniacal in their intensity and his lips were tilted into a grin that made Eve think he was tearing the wings off butterflies and enjoying it.

She quickly lowered her eyes and uncovered the plate.

Mashed potatoes with gravy, corn, and peas, along with a slice of roast beef. It smelled heavenly and it didn't matter that it was breakfast. She attacked the vegetables first. Her body craved the vitamins her canned food lacked. She saved the apple for last.

The meal made it possible for her to leave after the sun went down. This was the most food she'd eaten since she arrived. Tonight was by far her best opportunity. She stuffed herself and she didn't care that Murray watched. He handed her one of the small water bottles after she'd eaten everything on the plate.

"I will wait outside while you wash and change. He pulled a comb from his pocket and handed it to her. It had a hair tie wrapped around one end. "Control your sinner's hair. God will be watching."

He stepped out and closed the door. Eve stuffed the apple between the mattress and the wall. It was coming with her. She hurriedly scrubbed her body and put on the undergarments before she washed her hair. She wouldn't do it naked with him outside the door. Using the comb and hair tie, she pulled her wet hair back and secured it in a ponytail after she put the dress on. She brushed her teeth and put on her socks and boots. Murray walked in minutes later. He gave her a nod of approval.

"Follow Karen and she will lead you to the house."

No threats not to run, just a stare that said he hoped she would. The grin still played on the corners of his mouth.

Eve stepped into sunlight and fresh air. She covered her eyes partially from the brightness. Murray started the four-wheeler and drove away. There were two other women standing with Karen. They wore older clothing like hers. Karen's dress was ironed, her hair had the front swoop of fundamentalist women and was braided down her back. She was young, too young. Had she been kept in a trailer before? It wouldn't surprise her. From the small tidbits of information Murray fed her, it was his job to discipline sinful women.

The other two women were currently being held like Eve. Their hair was braided without the swoop. She turned in the direction he drove the four-wheeler and saw four small travel trailers in the distance. Added to hers, it made five total. He stopped in front of the one farthest away.

"Come," said Karen. She held two waste buckets and had soiled clothing draped over her shoulder. She started walking in the direction Eve was led in from the first day.

Eve took the opportunity to examine her surroundings. They walked on a packed dirt road. She couldn't see the rock walls of Water Canyon. She could be fifty miles or more from town.

"I can take one of the buckets," she told Karen.

The three women ignored her. They didn't look at her or each other. If it were Karen who'd knocked on her door, she didn't want her in trouble so didn't mention it.

"My name is Eve," she said. "I'm a police officer. I won't be here long and I will bring help."

No reaction.

Eve stumbled over a root but righted herself. No one reached out to help. They walked about a hundred yards. The road split into a smaller one and they stayed to the left. It ended at a large two-story home. Power poles came within a hundred feet and a large cable wire connected the electricity somewhere behind the house.

They were close enough to town to have power. The Hildale electrical grid went only twenty miles outside of town. She was closer than she thought. The power poles veered away from the main road and she could follow them when she escaped. They were tall enough to keep in sight while staying far enough away that it might work. There were most likely other homes in the area. She couldn't trust anyone so would need to avoid them.

Murray's house had a large front porch with four stairs leading up to the door. The outer walls were a pale blue with white trim.

The two women walked inside.

"Follow them," Karen said, and continued walking behind the house.

Eve did as she was told. Dim light and semi-cool air greeted her. The windows were kept shuttered against the sun because air conditioning was not something people paid for even though there were months that it was needed. That luxury would mean less money for the prophet.

Her eyes adjusted quickly. The large room held women and children. The two women who walked with Eve were situated on the floor. The other women sat on two large black vinyl couches. Some had children in their arms. A few older children, around four or five years old, were on the floor at their feet. The two women from the trailers sat with straight backs and their hands folded in front of them, their eyes cast down. They had done this before.

She stayed where she was, studying the women and children on the couch. One little boy, about eighteen months old, had bright red hair.

Eve turned when the front door opened. It was Murray with two other women. One was Linda Wall. She recognized her from the family picture they'd found during the search warrant.

"Take your place," Murray ordered Eve.

The other two women sat down hastily.

Eve had noticed one of the women on the couch holding a

small baby. Linda gave the child a quick glance and Eve could see despair in her expression.

Linda's baby was alive. Tears came to Eve's eyes.

She had so many questions. Why did Murray have Linda and her baby? Why was another woman holding the child? Did he keep Linda in line using her baby against her? That thought had a high probability of being correct.

Eve wiped the tears away. Her resolve to leave that night intensified.

She watched Murray take his place in front of the women. She didn't need to see his self-righteous expression to understand what was about to happen. Twice a day during her childhood, the wives and children gathered for a testimony delivered by her stepfather. It was long and tedious and not something Eve wanted to relive. Even the smallest children were expected to sit still and listen.

"There are sinners among you," Murray told the women, his tone revoltingly soft like her stepfather's had been. "They are unworthy of your voice. Do not speak or look upon them for Satan rides their souls. The Lord has given me his trust to implement retribution to the wicked. It is not something I relish, but the prophet has placed these hard tasks before me to make you worthy of him."

Murray was full of crap. He'd enjoyed beating her and every woman here had likely felt his retribution. The fact he'd been the sheriff for so long was the worst part. How many women had he abused through the years?

Eve was determined she would be the last one. She was leaving tonight. The knowledge gave her the strength to sit still and pretend obedience.

As Murray continued in his reverent voice, it made her think about the prophet when he'd visited her stepfather's home. His tone had been soft and almost whiny. Even so, it was filled with authority. Murray sounded just like him.

The room remained quiet when he paused. No amens or hallelujahs. These women were obedient worshippers, their only purpose was to honor the man in front of them.

When Eve was young, her mothers had fully embraced the prayer sessions and would smile and nod as her stepfather spoke. The women under Murray's thumb simply listened in silence with no expression.

"Beware the false prophets and false teachings," he said. "Many of you have delivered children of sin." He looked at each woman sitting on the floor except Eve and he stared behind her at some of the women on the couches. "God cast down upon your heads the punishment of isolation," he continued. "It is my duty to remove the inherent sins of my wives and my future wives. You turned your back on the teachings of your fathers. You are faithless, detestable cowards. My purpose is to redeem you."

Eve directed covert glances to the side where she could see part of a couch by turning her head slightly when Murray looked away. The toddler with red curly hair fussed. He had to be Miriam's son. The woman holding him did not have red hair and neither did Murray. His entire stable of women could be made up of the cult's rejected mothers. This role was assigned to him by the prophet and many men knew about it. They had to.

Eve controlled her anger and finalized her plan to escape while he spoke. Her stomach was full, but she would eat another can of food before she left and take the two small bottles of water with her. The shorter distance to town meant she wouldn't need a full gallon.

She would wait a few hours after the sun went down and follow the road then branch off and follow the power poles. She would run. She'd stayed in shape for just this reason.

The children grew fussier and still Murray rambled on in his ridiculous low drawl. At one point, Karen walked inside and moved out of Eve's line of sight. She had likely killed as much time as she could before she came inside to listen to this drivel. Murray didn't pause at the interruption and Eve was the only one who seemingly took notice. Most of what Murray said was about the responsibility of women and their subservient role. He recited the same words she'd been told as a child, but now Eve was no longer brainwashed and she could see Murray for what he was.

A complete psychopath.

She didn't think he would ever shut up. At one point the smallest baby started crying uncontrollably. Linda Wall bunched her dress within her fingers and moaned when the baby didn't stop.

"Sister Carmen, you are excused. Feed your child a bottle and remember God's eyes are upon you."

The woman holding the baby hastily stood and walked toward the back of the house. Murray continued to spew his garbage.

"You must please and obey your husband in all things for I am commanded by the prophet and God to instill virtue into your souls."

Eve pictured her team. Not during an investigation but when they were at barbecues at Clyde's house with their families. She heard their laughter, and Collin and Ray's endless jabs at each other. Tamm would be hustling around making sure everyone had what they needed, telling them to stay seated while she got it. Tamm was a priceless gem. Bina would be talking to Ray's date. Ray and Clyde would have a few beers. The food was always superb.

It would happen again and she would be there for it.

She had no idea how long Murray spoke.

"For the prophet reveals holy revelations and his word is the word of God." He stopped speaking. The women stayed where they were.

"My wives are excused." He gave the women a fanatical smile, empowered by his testimony.

The women on the couches stood. They walked to the back of the home without a word, carrying or ushering children in front of them.

"Sister Eliza?"

A young woman turned.

"You will join me tonight."

Eve noticed the panic the woman tried to hide.

"Follow me," Murray said to Eve and the other women from the trailers.

They followed him outside. He drove the four-wheeler slowly as they trailed behind him. Linda glanced at her quickly and turned away. The first trailer was Eve's.

"Go inside and think about your sins," he said. She looked into his eyes again. She hated him with every inch of her soul. He closed and locked the door behind her.

The engine revved and he was gone. Ten minutes later, he returned and unlocked the door. Eve stayed sitting on the bed, her eyes down. *Be meek*, she recited inside her head.

He took her hand and she kept it limp, not pulling away. She had to escape. Cold steel circled her wrist with a familiar click. She instinctively swung out with her free hand while trying to jerk the cuffed one away. His fist landed a stunning blow to the side of her face and pain exploded. Her ears rang. While she was stunned, he attached the other end of the cuff to a metal ring by the bed. Eve had noticed it but hadn't realized what it was used for.

Thoughts of sexual assault were like lightning through her brain and she was prepared to kill him. Murray stepped back and smiled.

"You think to defy me with plans of escape. God has shown me your wickedness. You cannot run from His judgment."

He lifted her boots from the floor, placed the full gallon of water where she could reach it, and walked out.

Her boots held the handcuff key. She also needed footwear to run through the brambles and across rough ground. She gave into the panic eating her alive and screamed until her throat was raw. Then she cried. Anguish settled inside her, eating the determination she'd felt earlier.

That night and the next day were the worst she'd had since arriving. Her hatred built and she didn't think it could climb higher. She was wrong.

Murray returned late the following afternoon. He removed the handcuffs from the wall and then her wrist. Stomach cramps had been her companion since the morning without a way to relieve herself. She had no fight left. He used his fingers beneath her chin and tipped her face up like he'd done when she was a child. Tears slid down her cheeks.

He smiled. He'd beaten her. She had no fight left.

"Your mother cried just like this when she broke. After all the work I put in, the prophet assigned her to another man. If she had stayed as my wife, she would never have left or stolen you from your father."

His finger smoothed over the tears on her cheek.

"You were given to me months ago. My wives raise the children of sin to become the army of the righteous. If you obey my commands, you will be gifted with a child. Think about what I have said. If you try to escape me, I will give you to Keb."

He studied her and his smile hardened.

"The next time you speak to the women out of turn, I will leave you cuffed for a week. You will soil your bedding and sleep in it until you are worthy of my attention. God knows your evil thoughts and so do I. The women do not care that you were a police officer. You are a vile sinner and you will suffer for those sins."

He laughed and walked out.

He did not return her boots.

She wiped her eyes and used the bucket. When finished, she covered it with a plastic bag. She would not think of Maggie under his control. Karen or one of the women from the trailers must have told him what she'd said during their walk to the house. It didn't matter.

He said she was given to him months before. Who had that authority?

She ate half a can of soup and felt better. She lay down on the mattress and stared at the ceiling.

That was when she smiled.

Murray thought he'd won.

THIRTY-FIVE

Eve waited two hours listening for any sound of Murray's presence before she lifted the mattress and stomped on the boards with her sock covered feet. The brittle slats of wood split. She got on her knees and pushed one out. It gave her a six-by-eight-inch hole. She stuck her arm through and grabbed the pieces in case they could be seen from outside. She placed them underneath the mattress toward where her feet rested when she was laying down.

Her escape had only been delayed by one day. Her despair the day before had lasted a few minutes, but she needed to convince Murray he'd conquered her completely. The only way to do that had been to purposely allow hopelessness to consume her. It had worked. She rested on the bed preparing herself for the barefoot run. Her feet would heal.

She heard a noise.

"Sister?" a woman's voice asked breathlessly.

Eve moved closer to the side of the trailer. Did she imagine it?

"Are you there?" The woman asked again.

"Who is this?" It sounded like the whisper from before.

"Karen Beckner. Are you okay?"

"Yes, can you get me out of here?" Eve asked.

"I do not have a key to the door."

"I understand. Can you make a phone call?"

"No. He went to town, but he will return shortly. I wanted you to know it was not me who made trouble for you. You are not alone. I must go."

"Wait," Eve cried but the voice did not return.

Eve planned to leave around midnight, though it would be a guess because she had no way of telling the time. She lay on the floor and was rewarded with the sound of a vehicle's engine, faint, in the distance. Murray was home. She paced the trailer, too anxious to sit or lie on the bed.

A woman cried out. Then she screamed. The screams drew closer.

"No, I am sorry. I just said hello. I will repent."

"I warned you. You will go inside with the apostate. She afflicts you with her evil and you will understand the contamination of her soul. You will belong to Brother Jarrod. I cast you from my family."

"No please," the woman sobbed.

The door opened and Murray pushed Karen inside. Her mouth was bleeding and both eyes were swollen almost shut. He pushed her to the floor and she curled into a ball. Eve stood at the opposite end of the trailer from the bed. Murray rushed her. His fist landed in her abdomen. She went down. He kicked her repeatedly in her ribs and then moved to her head. She used her arms to protect herself.

He finally leaned over her. His hands circled her throat and squeezed. Eve brought her knees up, not feeling pain, and grabbed his shirt. She yanked him down against her legs at the same time she arched her stomach. She rolled to gain leverage, but Murray elbowed her in the temple. Her fist connected with his chin.

"You'll pay for that," he yelled, and punched her in the face. He continued hitting her until she almost lost consciousness.

Blood filled her mouth and ran from her nose. She could hardly see.

"Women don't last long with Keb. He is my executioner." He stomped out. "Brother Jarrod, I have two women for you," Murray said a moment after locking the door behind him. He was talking on his phone. "It's Karen, the young one, and the apostate. I have no further need of them. They are not redeemable." His voice faded as he walked farther away.

Time stopped. Everything hurt. Eve knew what Keb was capable of and she had to escape. She carefully assessed her injuries.

Karen cried harder.

Eve breathed in and out slowly. Nothing felt broken. When she was sure she was okay, she walked to Karen and went to her knees.

"Shh," she said a little harshly. One of Eve's eyes was swollen shut, but she could see out the other. "We're getting out of here."

"Keb will kill me," Karen whispered between sobs.

"We don't have much time," Eve told her.

Karen quieted.

"I have a way out. We can walk along the road and hide if he searches for us."

"No. He knows that is where you will be," Karen said. "He said if I ran away, he will kill my baby. I believe him."

That stopped Eve for a moment.

"Will he kill your child if I run without you?"

"I don't know."

"I must bring help back," Eve told her. "It's the only chance your baby has." The thought of the children suffering almost made Eve change her mind. No, she told herself. She knew what Keb would do. Miriam would have died out there. Eve couldn't take the chance.

"Can you stand? Is anything broken?"

"If I go with you, I will slow you down. I can't get air in my chest without pain."

Eve thought of Linda Wall and the other women. It was dangerous for them too and now she knew it was dangerous for the babies.

"I have an idea."

There was a small hole in the mattress. She tore it wider so she had strips of material. I'm going to tie you so he doesn't think you helped me. I'm taking your shoes too." Eve flipped the mattress over. "Are you following what I'm saying?" she asked Karen.

"Yes, I think so, but he will kill you if he catches you."

"I can fight and I'll be ready this time. You must do exactly as I say. It's our only chance. What size are your shoes?"

"An eight."

Eve wore a size seven.

"I'll need your socks too."

After she doubled the socks on her feet, she put the sturdy boots on. She lifted the mattress again and stomped on the floor-boards until she had a big enough hole to crawl through. She would have splinters. It didn't matter. Eve removed her dress and she was left in only the garments. They were off-white and would be easy to see but so was the dress. The garments allowed more movement.

At the counter, Eve removed everything from on top of it. She kicked the wood brace until it came loose and she could pry it off. She pushed it through the hole in the floor.

"Are you ready?" Eve asked Karen.

"Yes. Please don't get caught."

"I need to tie your hands."

"Okay."

Eve tied them with enough of a gap so her circulation wasn't cut off but tight enough so she couldn't get her hands out. She knotted the material several times. A knife would be necessary to get it off.

"I'm bringing help back with me," Eve promised. "Don't give up hope."

"Thank you," Karen said.

Eve slid through the hole in the floorboards as carefully as she could. She ignored the pain of her injuries and the splintered wood digging into her skin. When she was lying on the ground, she kicked the large piece of wood out from under the trailer and gathered the small pieces of wood from the flooring.

There was a partial moon. She could see a little.

She carried the flooring to a large bush and stuffed the pieces in the branches.

She picked up the solid piece of wood and carried it close to the trailer.

"I'm leaving now," she said through the metal. "Be sure to tell him you wouldn't come with me."

"Thank you. Please be careful."

"I will. I promise I'll come back for you."

"For my baby too," Karen said.

"And for your baby," Eve promised again.

She ran straight for the house, stirring up the dust and leaving tracks. She needed Murray to think she was following the road into town. She'd purposely allowed Karen to believe she was going to use the road, but she had another destination in mind entirely.

She circled around Murray's house and headed back to the trailer but on the opposite side of the road. She was escaping to the north, not the west. There would be other roads that intersected. She would follow one of them.

Eve ran as far as she could and then slowed to a walk. Her ribs hurt, but she would survive. Aaron had taught her as a child that she could handle pain and abuse. They were lessons that helped her now.

There were several large boulders ahead that she could make out in the darkness. When she reached them, she leaned against the cool rock and rested for a moment.

A four-wheeler sounded in the distance. She knew it was either Murray or Keb.

She continued at a slow jog. The sound of the four-wheeler stopped. A minute later, she heard Murray yelling. His rage echoed around her.

"God is coming for you!" he screamed. He was no longer the soft-spoken man who testified to his worshipers. This was the true Sheriff Murray.

Eve's rapidly beating heart accelerated even more when a gun fired in the distance. She started running full out again. She had no idea how much time had passed, and she didn't know where she was. The moon rose higher, giving Eve more visibility.

The four-wheeler sounded in the distance. She stopped and let her breathing slow so she could listen. The sound was drawing closer. She'd dropped the wood from the counter ten minutes before, she could move quicker without it. She tried to stay in the trees where the four-wheeler couldn't traverse and hopefully her footprints weren't as noticeable. It wasn't always possible. She knew her prints were giving her away.

Murray would need to kill her. She wouldn't let him take her back alive. She kept moving.

The engine sounded farther away, and she had hope for a short while. But then the sound came closer again and then closer still. She had to find a place to hide.

There were brambles next to a cropping of dense bushes. She scrambled under them, the thorns digging into her skin. The pain was nothing compared to what it would be if Murray caught her.

The light from the four-wheeler drew closer. Murray circled the area and her hiding spot lit up for a moment then moved on. She could see him now. He had his gun on a holster at his waist. He stopped and turned off the engine. The sudden quiet was terrifying and each breath she took sounded loud in her ears. Murray climbed out of the four-wheeler. He turned on a flashlight pointing it at the ground.

He walked closer. She stayed as still as she could. The flashlight lit up where she hid.

"Come out," he said. "You do not want me coming in after you." There was no longer a drawl in his voice.

THIRTY-SIX

She crawled from beneath the bushes and didn't start rising until she was about five feet from him. He held his gun in his right hand and pointed it at her. There was a tactical light attached. Handcuffs were in his other hand.

"You will be sorry for this," he promised.

Before she was completely upright, she charged him head-first. He stumbled back and she went for his face with the can opener. She made contact and slashed his skin.

Murray screamed.

She grabbed the wrist with the gun and slammed it down on her shoulder so the barrel pointed behind her. It went off and her ears reverberated sharply with the sound. She kicked his knee, feeling the impact through her hip. He went down to a kneeling position and she aimed a punch at his face. He blocked it.

"I'm going to kill you," he roared, but it sounded faint to her ringing ears.

He lunged from his knees and tried to grab her. She moved back and he missed. He was bent at the waist and she attacked again. He was ready this time and straightened. His fist slammed into her jaw. The corners of her vision went black. She fell backward and kicked out. She rolled and tried to stand. At the last second, she turned before his body landed on her back. She struck with the can opener again. She jammed the bottle opener part into his eye and wrenched downward.

His scream was that of an animal.

She heard a wump, wump, wump in the distance and saw a light shining from the sky.

A helicopter.

Murray had dropped the gun. She saw it several feet from where he crouched and held his face. She launched her body toward it and rolled so she was facing upward.

Murray stood over her. Eve didn't hesitate. The gun came up and she fired in rapid succession. He landed on her legs, a dead weight. She rolled and kicked him away.

The area she lay in was lit up and the helicopter blades filled her ears. She closed her eyes, the gun gripped in both hands, looking for another target. If it was Keb, his best chance was to shoot her from above. She would kill him too if he gave her the chance. It was why she hadn't emptied the magazine into Murray.

The helicopter moved away. She crawled to some shrubs that barely covered her. The blades stopped rotating and slowly, quiet returned to the night. She needed to find a better spot to hide but froze when she heard a crunching noise nearby.

"Eve."

She lowered the weapon and her hands started shaking.

"Eve, it's me," Clyde said.

He was dressed in all black tactical gear, a helmet too. A rifle was slung over his shoulder and three other men were fanned out around him.

She started crying, adrenaline dumping from her system.

Her entire body shook. She couldn't speak. If she did, her words would be a blubbering mess.

Clyde squatted beside her and removed the gun from her limp hand. He then wrapped her in his arms. She squeezed as tightly as she could. It hurt her ribs and she didn't care.

He'd found her.

She'd known he would.

"Is anyone else out here with you?" he asked, his voice strong, understanding she didn't have ear protection when she'd fired the gun.

His question took her into detective mode. "I only saw one four-wheeler, but Keb could be anywhere."

"We have Keb in custody," Clyde assured her.

"The children?"

"They're safe. The team is at his house."

"Karen needs an ambulance," she whispered.

"She's been taken care of. You need an ambulance too."

She started crying again and relaxed into him, her arms falling to her sides.

Someone placed a blanket beside her and Clyde gently lay her back.

"Mack is a medic and he's going to look you over before we get you into the chopper."

Eve didn't speak unless she was asked questions. Her mind was in too many places. It was over. She'd survived. It didn't seem real.

"We're moving you to a stretcher," the man said. She thought it was the one named Mack.

"I can walk." Eve tried to stand, but her legs and arms didn't work.

Clyde's hand landed on her shoulder. "Listen to the medic," he ordered.

Her head was spinning. She wouldn't have made it. Clyde

helped lift her to the stretcher. He held her hand while two men carried her to the helicopter.

She closed her eyes against the light inside.

An IV was inserted into one of the veins of her left arm.

Clyde kept hold of her right hand. They strapped her in.

She was safe.

THIRTY-SEVEN

A headset was placed over Eve's ears with a small microphone at her mouth. She was able to talk to Clyde. Her head was acting strange and she knew she had asked these questions before but she needed to be sure.

"Did you find Karen?"

"She told us you were out here. She said you would be following the road into town."

"I was worried what she would tell Murray if he hurt her, so I lied."

Clyde smiled.

"What about Linda Wall and the other woman in the trailers?"

"Safe."

Eve closed her eyes. They'd placed something in the IV for pain. She let herself drift.

"I'm going to clean you up," said the medic. "Your eye is swollen shut and your nose is bleeding. You'll have facial X-rays at the hospital."

"I hate hospitals."

He chuckled and Eve closed her one good eye.

"Ow," she said. The antiseptic stung.

"Tell me what happened at the house," she said to Clyde.

"She needs to relax and let the pain meds do their job."

Again, Eve thought the words came from Mack.

"You don't know her the way I do and the last thing you want to do is get in her way."

The man grumbled but went silent.

"Keb has a gunshot wound to the stomach," Clyde said. "One of the SWAT members got him before we went into the air again. Don't know if he'll survive."

That was good. Keb deserved a wound to the stomach. They were painful and often deadly. It was a slow, gruesome death. She was okay with that.

"The other women. Are they safe?"

She'd asked this before.

"Yes."

"I wish I'd shot Keb."

Chuckles filled her ears. She hadn't realized everyone could hear their conversation.

"Don't worry," said Clyde at her expression. "This is a bloodthirsty bunch."

She closed her eyes again and drifted.

They took her to the city hospital.

When a bit of clarity returned, she became aware she was being lifted from the helicopter. Clyde stood behind them. He couldn't follow when they took her to one of the back rooms.

She wanted him there. He made her feel safe.

The garments were cut off. Good riddance.

She was poked and prodded and asked questions. She had thorns buried in her arms, back, butt, and thighs. They hurt worse coming out than they had going in. She hurt all over even with the painkiller the medic had given her.

A nurse walked up when the doctor was finished.

"Were you sexually assaulted?" she asked gently.

"No."

"Do you want a sexual assault exam?"

"No."

"Okay, if you change your mind, ask."

Eve knew why she was insistent. The nurse had possibly been told about Miriam. Eve's condition also made sexual assault likely. Clyde hadn't asked her about her captivity. He was worried about the same thing and wanted the professionals to deal with it until she was ready to talk to him. She had to let him know she was okay. He would be going crazy.

"I'm cold," she said, her entire body trembling.

"I'll get you a warm blanket," the nurse promised.

A minute later, warmth covered her, but the shaking didn't stop.

A hand took hers and she opened her good eye.

Clyde.

"Hi," he said.

"I can't stop shaking."

"You're in shock. They're sending you for a CT scan to check if you have broken bones. You're covered in cuts and bruises."

"I don't think anything is broken, but I won't argue." Her jaw and eye ached the most.

He smiled gently. "That won't last," he said softly.

"What won't last?"

"The arguing. You'll be doing it again soon."

It hurt to laugh.

"I just want a long shower," she told him.

"Soon," he promised, and lifted her hand to kiss the backs of her fingers.

"You look sexy in your tactical gear," she told him.

He no longer wore the helmet, but his pants were tucked into his boots, he had on knee pads, and a drop holster was attached to his waist and leg. An outer black vest with various tactical implements secured with Velcro covered his chest. His arm and shoulder muscles bulged against the skintight short sleeves of the T-shirt he wore. She should make this the standard uniform for the team.

"They may have overdosed you with drugs." His grin showed his teeth and his dimples.

She patted the empty space on the bed beside her. "Sit."

He threaded his fingers through hers and took the offered seat.

"I wasn't raped," she told him. "I don't want you worrying about that."

She saw his relief, but he also looked at her face and she knew it looked horrible. She had suffered. If it happened to him, she would feel as he did right now. Helpless.

"Tell me what happened and how you found me." She had to take his mind off her injuries and she counted on his police training to kick in when he answered her questions.

"I saw the tail end of the squad car leaving the hotel. I also found your recorder which was still running. We couldn't identify Murray's voice. There was no drawl."

Eve hadn't realized it at the time. She'd learned tonight that it disappeared when he was angry.

"Murray put me in a chokehold, and I wasn't sure if I'd managed to turn my recorder on or drop it."

"You did everything perfectly. We argued over taking Keb into custody. He came back to work on his shift like nothing was up. We think he was waiting for Miriam to die and when she didn't call, he wasn't concerned."

That gave Eve pause. Miriam would have run out of water in the next two days.

"I wanted to beat the truth out of him," Clyde said next. "Bina saved my career." He smiled softly, his other hand covering their joined ones. "She went to Judge Remki about putting a tracker on Keb's vehicle and she got it cleared. We placed one on his squad car and one on his personal vehicle which I'll tell you about later. He didn't leave town until tonight and I was losing my mind. I knew they were keeping you in one of the trailers." Clyde stopped talking for a moment to gain control of himself. "The county attorney was worthless. He's a piece of shit. I'm sure he'll make a complaint against me for harassment."

Tears gathered in her eyes. "Thank you for rescuing me."

He shook his head and pride filled his expression.

"You rescued yourself." He caressed her forehead, the only place on her face that didn't hurt. "I'm sorry you had to kill Murray. I couldn't get a good shot with my rifle. I was worried it would pass through his body and into yours."

"I knew you would come. I never gave up hope."

He kissed her fingers then leaned away.

"Don't ever forget, you saved yourself."

Smiling hurt and with the swelling she doubted he could tell anyway.

"Remember *Shawshank Redemption*?" she said. It was one of their favorite movies. "Always have a backup plan."

He laughed until tears rolled down his cheeks.

"I'm sorry you had to shoot Murray," he repeated after wiping his eyes.

"Why? Because you wanted to do it?"

"Yes. And use more than three bullets."

"I thought Keb was in the helicopter. I was saving bullets for him." She'd been thinking ahead. Clyde taught them during tactical scenarios to keep firing until they stopped the threat.

"My old squad was in that helicopter. They think you're a real stud. That was their word, not mine."

"It hurts to laugh," she said honestly.

His smile disappeared.

"I would have rather killed Murray with my fingers around his throat. Keb too."

"Keb will go away for a long time. If he survives, that will be sweeter."

"Are you really okay with shooting Murray?" he asked.

"I like your idea. Strangulation would have been better."

"It may bother you down the road. The lieutenant will make you see a counselor. Don't fight it."

She groaned. "If I must."

"It was the only choice you had," he said, still worried that she would have trouble with what she'd done.

Taking a life had always been in the back of her head since her badge was pinned on her chest. She hadn't known how she would feel about it and she'd hoped she never found out. She had no mental distress over killing Murray and didn't expect to. The world was a better place without him.

Attendants arrived in the room and wheeled her bed away for the CAT scan.

"Promise you'll wait," she said to him.

"I'll be here."

Yes, Eve was strong, she had escaped on her own and killed Murray too, but she wanted Clyde's solid strength by her side so she could relax. It took about forty-five minutes for the scan and then they took her to a normal room.

Clyde waited in a chair.

They moved her into the new bed. He sat beside her and she locked her fingers with his.

"Excuse me." Lieutenant Crosby stood in the doorway.

Clyde released her hand and stood. The lieutenant walked farther into the room and the two men shook hands.

"Your team is waiting to come in. I pulled rank and they aren't happy," he told Eve.

"I'm sure they aren't. I haven't seen them yet."

"I needed to go over a few things and I wanted to see you with my own eyes. Rank has privileges. I also wanted to remind you about the internal investigation. You'll have an attorney to represent you."

"This is bullshit, Lieutenant," Clyde said.

"You know it's regulation, Detective Johnston. Eve will be cleared, but she also needs time to heal." He turned to Eve. "I have a psychologist lined up. Pending the internal and the medical and psychological releases, you may return to work. Now that the official part is over, how are you?" His smile was comforting. It was hard to be the boss all the time and Eve knew he was worried.

"Better than I look."

"That's the best news you could give me because you're one solid bruise and you need ice for the swelling."

Clyde grumbled.

Lieutenant Crosby looked at him. "Detective Johnston, could you bring the other members of the team in?"

Eve and the lieutenant heard Clyde's muttered response as he walked from the room. Crosby's eyebrows lifted.

"Is there something I should know?" he asked.

The state did not have a policy against dating others within your department, but it was frowned upon to date someone you supervised. There was really nothing he could say, but Eve wasn't sharing her and Clyde's personal relationship until they talked about it.

"My team and I have faced extreme circumstances over the past six months. I don't want a repeat, but it's been good for us. Mess with one and you're messing with us all."

"Hear, hear," said Ray who was never good at keeping things to himself. The others followed him into the room.

"I'll leave you alone to be with your family. Call me if you need anything," Crosby said. "You're on admin leave until you're cleared. Please rest."

Eve tried to smile at her friends then immediately grimaced.

They gathered around the bed and Collin placed flowers on the rolling table.

"When you're back on your feet, we're celebrating," said Bina.

"That sounds good. Thank you for keeping Clyde in line," Eve told her.

"And me," said Ray. "I was fully in Clyde's corner. I had a solid tree branch picked out to string him up and cut off body parts until he talked."

"Laughter hurts. Stop," she begged him. Her smile was huge.

"Thank you, again," she told Bina.

"The flowers are from all of us," Collin said.

Eve couldn't stop the tears that trailed down her face. She'd known her friends would never give up. They saw her cry after her stepbrothers' assault and it had bothered her. This time she didn't care. It wasn't just Clyde she could be vulnerable with.

Tears ran down Collin's face.

She looked at her family. Ray and Bina had tears in their eyes. Clyde was like Collin and a wet trail ran down his cheeks. He didn't wipe them away.

"Thank you," she said.

THIRTY-EIGHT

The doctor kept her overnight to be sure she didn't develop double vision or have other complications from an eye socket fracture. The hardest part about the injury was being warned against sneezing or doing anything that could further damage the socket. She was given antibiotics for possible infection and nasal spray to keep her from sneezing.

It didn't seem like a real injury with nasal spray prescribed, but the pain pills told a different story and she knew she would need them for a while.

They found ketamine injections at Murray's house when they served a warrant. They'd done bloodwork on her, but it was no longer in her system. Eve hated the thought of a drug administered against her will, but it was the least of her worries.

Lieutenant Crosby came to her apartment after she was released from the hospital to discuss the internal. The union had assigned her an attorney and she wanted the legal aspect of shooting Murray behind her. She'd rather have known he was spending the rest of his life in prison, but he'd taken that away. He'd planned to kill her and she'd shot him in self-defense. She would never regret it.

"The attorney will speak with you before you talk to internal affairs and he'll be with you during the interview," Lieutenant Crosby told her. "I can be here if you need someone for support."

She smiled the smallest bit because her face hurt and it was the best she had.

"I'm comfortable with the attorney and with the shooting. Stop worrying."

He looked relieved. "You're a strong person. I'm sorry you can't recuperate in peace."

Eve had to change the subject because she was going insane waiting for her team to finish the investigation. She needed details only they would have.

"Is anyone on my squad in serious trouble?"

He chuckled and shook his head.

"They straddled the line several times, but I understood how they felt. It's funny because when you put them together, they were almost what you would call misfits." He waved his hand when she tried to interrupt. "They were very good at their jobs, but they each had authority issues."

"Isn't that most officers?" she asked.

"Not like your group. They failed to make tight connections with other officers and preferred to work alone. Detectives are not meant to be lone wolves."

He was right. And when he referred to the group, the lieutenant was including her too and she couldn't argue.

"You studied their background reports. Even if you didn't realize you were doing it, you chose them because their backgrounds connected somehow. Detective Johnston was the only one who excelled in a team environment. I thought he would have trouble with your authority and I was wrong. The multiple aspects of this case were hard enough, but they came through because they were united. I'm impressed with the taskforce you've built."

"Is that your way of saying you're proud?"

His face flushed slightly.

"I am proud and especially of you. The taskforce idea was well and good for the judge to hand out. He had no idea what he was doing. You've made inroads I never expected. 'Thank you' isn't said enough in this line of work, but thank you. I don't see how any other team could handle this stressful job within the challenging environment you are assigned to."

She appreciated his honesty and his thanks. It made her wonder if she *had* chosen her team because of their loner mentality. Collin and Ray had never worked together and wanted to. She'd never wondered why, past their long-standing friendship. Each person on the squad had easily walked away from their other departments. Bina was the only one who expressed her inability to fit in. Eve was lucky to have them and had known it from their first case.

The lieutenant left after their conversation. He called an hour later to let her know the internal investigation was arranged for the next day. The attorney would be at her apartment two hours before IA. She wanted it behind her.

She had a million questions about Linda's case and Eric's murder but wanted to wait and hear it from Clyde. The team was in Hildale tying up loose ends and it was killing her to be at home and not in the middle of what they were doing. Clyde had said they'd likely wrap everything up in the next two days.

The lieutenant left and Eve was alone. She didn't like the feeling.

She was deep in thought when her cell phone rang. She walked to the side table next to the couch to grab it.

The word MOM lit up the screen.

"Hello," she answered without her voice cracking. She'd thought about Maggie so much.

"Clyde called me. You should have let me know you were in

the hospital. I would have come to see you. I've been so worried."

"They only held me overnight. I'm home now and going crazy."

"Do you want me to visit?"

"Would you?" she asked.

"I took the next two days off work. I could stay with you if you need me."

Tears fell. She wasn't having mental issues over the shooting, but the isolation had gotten to her and she didn't want to be alone.

"Thank you. Please come over and stay the night."

"I have a casserole cooking." Her mother's voice was gruff. She was crying too. "As soon as it's done, I'll be there. Do you need me to pick up groceries?"

Eve thought about the meager food she had on hand.

"What if you come over first and we make a list? With the casserole, shopping can wait until tomorrow." It would take a heavy load off Eve's shoulders. Her mother was a godsend.

With the swelling and bruising on her face, she would cause a stir in public. Eve's story was all over the news. It would blow over quickly, but for now, she needed to stay inside. If she could leave town, she would. Unfortunately, during an internal, you're on paid leave and must be available.

"I'll be there within two hours."

"Thank you, Mom."

"I'll see you soon."

Daisy, who had disappeared under Eve's bed while Lieutenant Crosby was in the apartment, jumped on her lap and rubbed against her.

"I missed you too," Eve told her. Daisy usually didn't like hugs, but she put up with Eve's squeeze for about thirty seconds. It may have been a record.

Her mother arrived ninety minutes later. She embraced Eve carefully.

"It looks worse than it is," Eve said, relishing her mom's arms around her.

"That's not what Clyde said." Her mother examined her face closely while holding on to Eve's shoulders so she couldn't get away. "Can you see from your right eye?" she finally asked.

"A little. The good news is I don't have double vision. The swelling will go down each day and my eyesight will improve. I should be back to normal in a week or so."

Maggie's graying, light brown hair was cut short around her angular face and accented her cheekbones. Eve looked like her though she got her thicker dark hair from her Italian father. Her mother wore a floral top, which lightened her hazel eyes. Blue linen pants encased her legs. The white nurse's orthotic shoes were sturdy and clunky. She was a receptionist at a dental office.

Maggie smiled, her lips trembling slightly, still focused on the damage to Eve's face.

"The term 'run over by a truck' comes to mind," her mom said with a forced smile.

"You should see the truck," Eve replied. "Now, stop that, it hurts to laugh."

"Oh, honey, I am so sorry."

"I hope we laugh so much I forget," Eve replied, curling just her lips into the smile her mother needed.

Maggie leaned forward and kissed her lightly on the lesser damaged cheek. "I'll go grab the casserole and put it in your refrigerator."

Eve hugged her again needing the connection. "I'm glad you're here."

She returned and the smell of the casserole made Eve hungry for the first time since she'd flown in the helicopter.

"Do you want to eat or rest for a bit?" Maggie asked.

"Eat."

They sat on the couch. The food tasted so good and her mother had brought a large salad to go with it. Eve had seconds of the salad. She had to take small bites and chew carefully, but the food was too good to resist.

Her mother refused help with the few dishes and put the remainder of the casserole in the refrigerator along with the salad. Eve swore Maggie had made enough for ten people, but it was nice to know she could eat more later.

She joined Eve on the couch when she was done.

"Do you want to tell me what happened or would you rather talk about something else?" Maggie asked carefully.

Eve took a deep breath. This conversation had been building for years.

"I want to talk about the isolation trailers and Murray."

It took only a second for Maggie's expression to reflect the pain those words caused.

"I never imagined he would hurt you too," Maggie said. "It's one of the reasons I was upset when you took on your new assignment. I never wanted you to have any contact with that man or to know what had happened to me." She looked away, not meeting Eve's eyes.

She took her mother's hand.

"Why?" Eve's emotions were raw with worry over what her mother must have suffered. She needed to know.

"He was such a terrible man. The only good thing was he wasn't assigned as my new husband. Clyde only told me you were missing. It never occurred to me that Murray was still re-indoctrinating women. After you escaped and I saw his name on the news, I've been worried about what you must think of me."

Eve's fingers tightened on Maggie's.

"Never think about that again. We need this conversation out in the open. It's time for you to talk about what happened."

"I owe you that much," Maggie said.

"No, you don't. You owe yourself a release from baseless guilt."

Maggie's lips trembled.

"The church tried to force us to return after I took you away. I wrote the horrors down and gave them to my attorney. I threatened to go public about what they did to me. The threat gave us protection, but I felt guilty for staying quiet."

"Murray, Keb, and the cult are the guilty parties, not you or any of the women who suffered at their hands. If I'd known, I would have told you that."

Maggie shook her head; remorse hadn't left her expression.

"I deserved your anger and condemnation for not keeping you safe," Maggie said and looked down at their joined hands. "I still feel that way." She smiled just a bit. "My therapist is helping me deal with these issues." The smile disappeared. "I allowed your father to abuse me for years. You don't remember much about him, but he was a horrible man. I put up with his mistreatment for too long. I was afraid of him. He threatened to take you away from me and I lived in terror that he would. It wasn't until he promised to hurt you physically, that I finally left."

"What was his threat?" Eve asked.

"He told me he would break your arms and the police would believe it was me and put me in jail. We had little money and I wanted to find a job. He didn't want me to make friends because he couldn't handle losing control. When he said he would hurt you, I could finally walk away."

She lifted her gaze to Eve's.

"I filed the restraining order, but he found us. He dragged me down the hallway so I couldn't get to a phone. A neighbor heard me screaming and called the police. When they arrived, I ran to the front door. He was holding you and threatened to hurt you if the police didn't back out. Even with that, he only got thirty days in jail."

Eve vaguely remembered her mother covered in blood and screaming. Eve had been four years old at the time. Why couldn't she remember more?

"He would never stop. That young polygamist man approached me. I believed every word he said. I was desperate."

Her mother's hands were shaking.

"You don't need to talk about this, Mom."

"I do. You've needed to know what happened for years now. I didn't have the courage to tell you. You've been through so much and part of that is because I stayed quiet. Clyde was the only person who kept me sane while you were missing. He's a good man."

Maggie took a moment to compose herself.

"When we first arrived in Hildale, I was easily brainwashed even though I knew what they were telling me was wrong. I tried to follow the rules. I lied to myself which was worse. I thought if I had a stronger faith in God, we would be okay." Maggie looked away, her haunted eyes staring across the room with her memories."

"Your stepfather, William, was an evil man, worse than your father. He also threatened to send me away from you. I didn't know how to escape. It wasn't until Aaron broke your finger that I knew I had to get you out. They monitored me in the house, but I was determined to escape and go to the police. They watched you too closely and expected me to try and take you. I left in the middle of the night and walked to the police department. I knew William had not legally adopted you. I had never signed anything. He showed me the court papers, but they were fake. In those first few months, I wanted to believe."

She released one of her hands from Eve's and wiped her eyes.

"I didn't take you with me because I thought it was too

risky. I planned to come back with a police escort. I didn't know the police were as evil as William. Two of them drove me to the trailer that became my home for the next three years. I didn't see Murray often. He intended to marry me and I was afraid of him. He could be brutal, but you know that." More tears cascaded down her cheeks.

Eve could not imagine three years. She'd rescued Miriam after seventeen months though she always thought of it as 512 days. It had been Eve's mantra while she was in the trailer. She leaned in and hugged her mom.

"I am so, so sorry," she told her. "No one deserved that."

Her mother leaned back and smiled softly after wiping away the tears.

"Thank you. Leaving there was my second proudest moment. It took a long time, but I knew the only way I could get out was to convince them that I was broken. They finally thought I would comply with anything and married me to another man. Four months after that, I escaped. The proudest moment of my life was coming back for you. I am sorry it took me so long. I thought about you every day. I worried they would marry you to someone."

"What happened to my biological father?" Eve asked.

"He went to prison for beating up another woman. After that, he disappeared. I never saw or heard from him again."

Eve had run a background check on her father. It showed the prison sentence and then nothing. With his history, he might have abused the wrong woman. Eve refused to feel bad about it. He needed to stay gone and death was the only thing that guaranteed it.

She hugged her mother again. They stayed that way until Daisy jumped on the arm of the couch next to Eve.

She took Daisy in her arms and looked at Maggie.

"Thank you for rescuing me and being so strong. I knew I got it from someone."

THIRTY-NINE

Eve made it through the internal affairs interview. The two men read her Miranda rights which brought the stark reality of shooting and killing someone home. They were professional and she had no doubt she would return to work. The attorney assured her she would and the investigation was a formality only.

Maggie went grocery shopping while they were at Eve's place and called before she came back.

Clyde had called the night before and said he would be another day. It was hard not to ask what was going on, but, like the conversation with her mom, she wanted to hear it face to face and not over the telephone.

The second evening, she told her mother about Aaron and her other stepbrothers and about Eric's death. Then she told her about Charlie and Becky. They both cried. Her mom left the following morning. Clyde was coming over as soon as he was in town.

She managed light cleaning. It felt good to move and stretch her muscles, but she tired easily and had to take frequent breaks.

Daisy jumped off her lap and ran to the back before Eve heard the knock.

Clyde was standing on her doorstep.

She couldn't get the locks open fast enough.

He pulled her gently into his arms. The hug calmed her nerves. They finally separated and sat on the couch. He pulled her against his chest.

"Tell me everything going on with the cases," Eve said. "I need exact details before I bombard you with questions."

"First, your boss may fire me."

She laughed a little. She was still sore, but two days made a difference. She hadn't taken the painkillers that morning. Her face was a myriad of colors, but the fracture was healing. She knew where her team stood with Lieutenant Crosby and she wasn't worried.

"He won't fire you. We've spoken and he's proud of us. But if he did, we would apply somewhere else as a team," she reassured him.

"I like the sound of that." He leaned back and turned her so she rested more fully against him.

"How many people have you shot in the line of duty?" She had never asked him this question.

"Three."

"Are you okay with it?"

"Yes."

"I'm okay with shooting Murray. I wanted you to know that. My nightmares are about the trailer, not his death. I remind myself he's dead when the dreams wake me up and it helps."

He smoothed his hand over her hair.

"I'm glad your mother could stay with you while I finished in town. I worried you would convince her to drive you there."

"I thought about it," she told him honestly. "I didn't want to be in the way."

"When's your appointment with the therapist?"

"Monday. I go back to the doctor Tuesday. I don't think he'll release me for another week after that."

Her phone buzzed. It was resting on the table in front of them. Clyde leaned over and handed it to her so he didn't need to let her go.

It was a text from Tamm.

You're cleared on the internal. Enjoy your time off. Not public knowledge yet so keep it to yourself.

She showed Clyde the message.

"That woman has superpowers we don't even know about."

Discovering the outcome of an internal before Eve was notified by the lieutenant was definitely a superpower.

"You're somewhat of a hero in police circles right now," Clyde said.

"Argh, I don't like the sound of that," was her disgruntled reply.

"My old squad got an eyeful in the helicopter. They want you on the SWAT team."

"I learned all my moves from you," she told him. "One of the things I did while I was inside the trailer was think about everything you taught that would cause the most bodily damage."

"Definitely SWAT material."

"Stop it. I love my job. They can have SWAT. It's you I'm worried about. Do you miss it?" she asked.

"I'm not going anywhere. I never had this much excitement in SWAT."

"Now I know you're pulling my leg."

"Not in the least. The team needs downtime and regular boring cases for a change. Too much excitement is bad for Bina's heart."

"Is she okay?"

"Worried about you, like us all. She's the reason we stayed sane. She's as strong as you are."

"Are there more updates?"

"I have one on Keb," he said.

Eve sat up and faced him.

"He survived his wound. On top of our charges, the feds added more. They located two women's bodies by the trailer Miriam was kept in. They found another trailer four miles away. The woman was alive but barely. Keb had left them both to die. It's very possible he'll receive the death penalty. When the State of Utah is finished with him, he'll be prosecuted on the federal level."

"A life sentence is too good for him," Eve said.

"I agree. I don't think he'll get that lucky. He conveniently blamed Murray for most of it, but Linda, Karen, and Murray's wives are cooperating. Keb delivered them to the sheriff. They were assigned for being unmanageable. They each had similar experiences and were kept in isolation trailers until they complied. I read the interview transcripts and they were terrified of him."

"Do we know who gave the order for the women to go to Murray?"

"That was one area Keb stayed quiet on," Clyde told her. "The women were told their assignment to Murray came from the prophet. I don't believe it. Someone else is pulling those strings."

"I think the same thing," she said. "Blaming everything on a man in prison for life is an easy out for them."

"We'll discover who it is."

They would.

"I need more updates," she insisted. "What about Bonnie Keb, the midwife?"

"She isn't cooperating. From what we gathered she handled only specific births. The babies were taken within a week of delivery. Her husband picked them up and took them to Murray. The sheriff was unable to have children and he gave the babies to his wives as special gifts."

Eve felt bad for his wives but worse for the mothers of the babies.

"What about Aaron?"

"Judge Remki is officially censuring him again." Clyde's expression mirrored how she felt about it.

"The high council told him to vacate his office. Is he still there?"

"Your disappearance changed things and he slipped through the cracks for now. He's still nervous and I think he's on the way out. If he grew a set, he would insist that he's elected and there is nothing they could do about it."

Aaron the weasel.

"Anyone else named in this mess?"

"No, but Chief Jackson is filling in for the sheriff until the next election," Clyde said.

"Oh joy. I wonder who will get the honors for Aaron's position if he does leave?"

"I'm sure whoever it is, they will be someone just as worthless."

She laughed.

"I have news about the bullets," he said.

Her smile disappeared. She inhaled, ready for the worst.

"Go ahead."

"It wasn't your gun. It was Keb's duty weapon. He killed Eric and confessed to it, hoping for a plea deal. That was before the FBI found the other bodies. He used his personal vehicle to do the drive-by. Another interesting fact. Keb's badge number is 910. Eric knew how dangerous he was and tried to warn you."

Eve was still coming to terms with Eric's death.

"Do you know who betrayed him?"

"He'd spent time with Keb so it could have been him. Eric

might have discovered what he was up to, but we may never have all the answers."

She closed her eyes for a moment. Eric's brothers hadn't killed him. The thought had bothered her more than she'd let on.

"Have my stepbrothers been located?"

"We think they're in Mexico. Their license plate was recorded at the border. If they're found, Mexico should extradite for their assault on you, a police officer."

"What about the other babies in Murray's home?" she asked.

"They're all accounted for. Miriam would like to see you when you feel better. Adella and her two children are with her at the shelter. She received an emergency order of protection against her husband for abandoning their baby. You did good."

She needed time to absorb everything that had happened. The rock she'd carried in her gut since the harassment calls started was gone.

"How is the team?" she asked.

"They want to see you. If you feel up to it, we could have a barbecue at my place tomorrow night."

She leaned in closer to him. Her next question was not a hard one and she felt she knew his answer.

"May I spend the night and stay through the weekend?" she asked.

He studied her for a moment and placed his hand in her hair, bringing her closer.

"I thought you would never say those words." He kissed her.

Just like that, Clyde accepted the change in their relationship.

* * *

She arrived at the barbecue with a bowl of potato salad that Maggie had made and brought over. It was a good thing because Eve's cooking skills were not the best. Clyde had put in a full day at the office. She hadn't seen him since that morning. He'd stayed the night. Collin got to her first. He gave her a long hug.

"When are you coming back? Your replacement has been cranky."

"I'll tell him you said so. Ten days tops. You'll wish I was gone again."

"You look like a horse kicked you," said Ray, and moved in for his own hug.

Collin elbowed him and Ray rubbed his ribs.

"Move aside so I can have my turn," said Bina. "You look much better than you did in the hospital so don't listen to a word Ray says."

She hugged Bina, so thankful for her friends. The hospital was still a bit fuzzy.

Clyde placed his arm around her and gave her a side hug. She surprised him by lifting her arm and threading her fingers through the hand he had on her shoulder. No one showed surprise.

Tamm joined them.

"I missed you too. It's taken every trick I had to keep everyone in line. You owe me." She rolled her eyes when Clyde chuckled.

Eve owed each one of them. Thinking of her family when she was alone in the trailer had saved her sanity.

EPILOGUE

On the last Saturday before she returned to work, Eve stood outside her apartment waiting for her mother to arrive. Maggie had called several days before with a tentative suggestion. It was perfect and Eve suggested that they stop and purchase flowers before the long drive.

Babyland was located on the outskirts of town. There were no cameras to alert the God squad to their presence. As they stepped from the vehicle, Maggie looked around, her eyes going to the rocks of Water Canyon in the distance.

"I saw those rocks as a prison," she said softly.

Eve took her hand and squeezed it. They both turned toward the graveyard. She gave Eve a bittersweet smile.

"I had no idea," Maggie said when she looked at row after row of baby graves.

They walked past the small, tended areas of the babies who were obviously loved, to the back where weeds covered the unmarked graves. Eve carried a shovel and Maggie a rake along with the flowers. Eve started by digging up weeds and Maggie raked them away. They paid special attention to the two graves at the end of the row.

"I know these don't belong to Charlie and Becky. They could be buried anywhere," Eve said quietly. "I've given up thinking they somehow survived. In my mind, my precious brother and sister are buried here."

"I understand," her mother said, and hugged her.

When they were finished with the weeds, Eve dug small holes and Maggie placed the flower-filled containers in the ground.

"We'll come back," her mother promised. She looked around and stopped again when her gaze fell on the tall hills of jagged rock. "I swore I would never return, but this was good for me. It feels..." She hesitated. "Right."

Eve felt the same way. Giving these graves respect helped ease her heart a little more. She held her mother's hand on the drive back to the city while they listened to music.

It was the best day Eve remembered spending with her mother. There would be more. Maggie needed to start living too.

A LETTER FROM HOLLY

Thank you for reading *Lost Little Angels*. I love writing and I'm passionate about sharing the criminality of the fundamentalist FLDS lifestyle, the eerie backdrop for Eve and her team. Click below if you would like to join the email list for future updates. Your email address will never be shared and you can unsubscribe at any time.

www.bookouture.com/holly-s-roberts

Lost Little Angels began weaving through my mind as I continued reading headlines and articles about the fundamentalist polygamy faith. The leader of the FLDS cult sits in prison, but his legacy of men illegally marrying underage girls and abusing them lives on. More and more men are claiming prophet status and getting away with atrocities against women and children. Though Eve Bennet is fiction, the problems are real. I hope she opens eyes and someday the horrendous crimes of the polygamy sect in Hildale and Colorado City will vanish, and these crimes are never repeated. If you or someone you know in the FLDS lifestyle needs help, please visit Cherish Families https://cherishfamilies.org/.

Babyland is a hard truth, and I found the accounts of the midwife and her husband, who ran the graveyard, horrifying. I have a crime blog on my website with more information if you are interested. It includes links to some of my research. I was a sex crimes and homicide detective, and though I'm retired, I believe through knowledge, we will overcome the stigma of talking about and prosecuting incest and sexual abuse. I'm a survivor and I will never stop fighting.

I love hearing from my readers – you can get in touch on my Facebook page, through Twitter, or my website.

Sincerely,

Holly S. Roberts

wickedstorytelling.com

 facebook.com/hollysrobertsauthor

 twitter.com/HollySRoberts

 goodreads.com/hollysroberts

ACKNOWLEDGMENTS

I want to thank Lia Padilla whom I've known since 8th grade. Your friendship has been a blessing. I can't wait to meet you in Vegas again and light up the town. Even if we use walkers, we can do it. To my editing team, Helen Jenner and Billi-Dee Jones: You put up with my artistic panic like no one else could and make my books the best they can be. I am the luckiest writer alive to have found a place with the amazing Bookouture family, thank you. Dizzy and Ava, my needy four-legged companions: You keep the nightmares at bay. For the readers and reviewers, I am humbled by your support.